To Harry

'02

regards

[signature]

The Broken Cross

The Broken Cross

A Novel by
Peter Z. Vogler

Danville Creek Publishing
Danville, California 94526

Although the author and publisher have made every effort to ensure the accuracy and completeness of information contained in this book, we assume no responsibility for errors, inaccuracies, omissions, or any inconsistency herein. Any slights of people, places, or organizations are unintentional.

First printing 1997

ISBN 0-9656650-3-8

LCCN 97-66089

Editing, design, typesetting, and printing services provided by About Books, Inc., 425 Cedar Street, POB 1500, Buena Vista, CO 81211, (800) 548-1876.

ATTENTION MUSEUMS, UNIVERSITIES, COLLEGES, AND PRO-FESSIONAL ORGANIZATIONS: Quantity discounts are available on bulk purchases of this book for educational purposes. Special books or book excerpts can also be created to fit specific needs. For information, please contact Danville Creek Publishing, 20 Tea Tree Court, Danville, California 94526, (510) 837-7619.

DEDICATION

In memory of my family who perished in the Holocaust.

✡ CHAPTER ONE

The train arrived at Gdynia, and only a small gate, guarded by two overdressed Polish sentries, separated Zishe and Yosi from the city of Danzig. The two disembarked as quickly as their luggage would allow. Politely they greeted the gate attendants and walked into the Danzig train station. They were two free men, two comrades.

Zishe had known Yosi all his life. They had attended the same school, played together, celebrated together, prayed together, and then planned their escape together. They were born in Przemysl, a small village near the city of Lwow in Poland. Lwow was about four hundred miles south of East Prussia and Danzig. The small-gauge rails rattled and shook and seldom kept a straight course. The farm animals, wandering freely, frequently forced the train to a halt. The main destination of the train was Gdynia, the only port of Poland. A remnant of the treaty of Versailles, it was a reminder of the German's famous defeat in World War I. No German could be heard on the train, only the Polish, Yiddish, and Russian of peasants.

The train station through which Zishe and Yosi entered Danzig was vast and magnificent. Giant marbled columns supported a Gothic roof and steel girders reflected a grid on the stained-glass windows. If not for the rumbling cacophony of trains, it could have been a Christian church. Tracks led into the station from a hundred directions, the names on the trains announcing their origin: Warsaw, Berlin, Potsdam, Hamburg.

1

Yosi had gone to the information center to find the easiest way to get to their destination. Zishe knew they both had a good command of German, but he hadn't seen Yosi for over ten minutes and was beginning to worry. Zishe wanted to search through the crowd, but he was afraid to leave the spot where he had agreed to meet Yosi. Suddenly he saw his friend coming toward him, gesturing that he had been successful.

They had read and studied everything they could about where they were going. News of Hitler, with his band of brownshirts and virulent anti-Semitism, had reached them, but it was 1931 and a democratic government still ruled Germany. Danzig was still a free city. Zishe and Yosi's goals were freedom, prosperity, and happiness; never had life seemed more promising.

Carefully following the instructions, they boarded the bus marked "Langfuhr." The bus moved quietly into the traffic. Giant posts with red, green, and yellow lights blazed at street intersections, directing the movement. Store windows were filled with merchandise of every shape and type. It was all beyond imagination, yet completely within reach. Grocery stores and delicatessens lined the streets. Plentifulness and opulence were everywhere. No more sparse dinners or missed meals, no more inconvenience. It was all here to be had for just a little effort, a little work.

"*Langfuhr, Langfuhr. Alle abstiegehn fur Langfuhr,*" the driver announced.

Startled, Zishe and Yosi grabbed their bags realizing this was their stop. Scurrying along the aisle, with their polite "*Entschuldigen sie mir*" sounding more Yiddish than German, they disembarked as the bus bolted away, leaving them among the many foreign signs and street names. Following their map, they traced out the streets that led to 518 Milschkanngasse, where they were expected.

Their German helped them translate the directions. They were proud they could speak and understand German. No one laughed or cursed at them, reminding them that they were Jews in the derogatory manner of the Polish. Confidence filled them as they approached the door with the large bronze knocker.

Rose Bernstein and her husband Herschel were the official tenants of the flat. And although they had signed the rental agreement and were responsible for the monthly fees, they were not the sole occupants. During the two years they resided here, there had been a steady flow of emigrant Jews from Poland, Rumania, and Ukraine. At times the rooms were so crowded it seemed physically impossible to squeeze another person in, but they could always seem to manage yet one more, maybe even two. If a payment was left by an emigrant, that was well and good. If it wasn't, it was all the same to the Bernsteins. Some time later the Jew could return the favor, if not to them, then to another Jew in another place.

Rose and Herschel were *richtige*, or righteous saints. Their love for others spilled over. They couldn't do enough to help. If someone needed clothes, they had just the right piece. If someone was hungry, *kreplech* and chicken soup, *blintzen* matzo balls, gefilte fish, and fresh bread with thick butter appeared almost instantly. Never had wanderers been so fussed over. Even if an emigrant didn't have a penny, even if he was in debt, everything was given in the same spirit. And if by accident he woke up and found some money in his pockets, which were usually empty, Rose and Herschel would deny the kind act with mischievous smiles.

Both now in their sixties, the couple had come to Danzig many years before. Rose had round dimpled cheeks and seemed to always be smiling, singing, cooking, and cleaning. She was everywhere at once, never tiring. She wore the same simple blue shawl day after day, only occasionally changing her dress. Herschel was a man of strength and kindness. He had a full beard and piercing brown eyes below gray eyebrows. The two had been in love since childhood. They married and gave birth to six children all in the same tiny town in Ukraine not far from Kiev. Each additional birth added to their happiness, as if God was blessing them for each Jewish child they brought to earth.

In her small but successful shop, Rose created a variety of delicacies. Customers came from miles around, ensuring the financial security of the Bernsteins. Life was good, until one Easter day, the surrounding Ukrainian peasant mobs were stirred to a frenzy of religious passion by their local priests. They acted out their old hatred, revenging themselves on the defenseless Jews in the name of their Lord. It was yet another pogrom but unequaled in barbarity. Rose and Herschel's six children were murdered by the mobs that descended on the town. They lost everything that was dear to them. In their tortured hearts, they realized they would never have children of their own again—that portion of life was over. But the Bernsteins could not be held down for long. In the midst of their terror, they lost their fear. "God gave and He took away," they said. "Such is life, it must go on. But not here, not in this godforsaken town." The town lay in ruins; not a family had been spared. The Bernsteins had to sell whatever was left of their possessions to pay for their passage from Ukraine. Government papers required palms be greased—a bribe here, another gold piece there. The times were hard for everyone, so they were doubly hard for Jews.

The move to Danzig was good for them and helped them forget the past. They began to believe that all had not been lost. The Bernsteins felt life was difficult for a purpose, so they opened their home and hearts to the poor and exiled, to every Jew who passed through Danzig. At the news of a new slaughter or massacre, they braced themselves for another wave of refugees.

Word about the Bernsteins had gotten around along the freedom road linking all the towns and villages in the Jewish Pale. Every Jew heard of their kindness and generosity, so it was not by accident that Zishe and Yosi established their first residence with them.

A happier welcome party could not have been imagined. There was hugging, kissing, laughing. All the joy of the world was contained in this richly carpeted flat. Zishe and Yosi could hardly believe their eyes. There was a large grandfather clock, a dinning room with rococo tables, chairs, divans. It was a palace, a museum filled with riches—and they belonged. They were home.

Questions about Przemysl abounded. There was no stopping the bouncing babble of words. It made no difference if they understood each other or not, if the words were Yiddish, Polish, Lithuanian, or Rumanian. They loved and cared—that was what mattered. A hundred dialects were blended in this beautiful lilting language called Yiddish.

A few people here were from Przemysl; most were from towns Zishe and Yosi had seen only on maps: Chemichil, Jelochov, Tihulav, Byelov. Their names sounded Polish, Lithuanian, Latvian, Ukrainian, Byelorussian, Rumanian. They had come here because they were Jews, seeking freedom from anti-Semites, beatings, and pogroms. They were always hoping for a better life, a Jewish life without fear or hate, where the law would protect them instead of punishing them, where they could walk with dignity and respect.

A young man wearing the drab uniform ghetto Jews had adopted over the centuries was arguing with an older man about the conditions in Danzig. "Does the leopard change its spots? The lemming change its course? Does the Christian, even when imbued with the sweetness of his Jesus, ever stop repeating to himself, 'The Jew killed my God—my Jesus'?" he asked passionately.

Zishe listened sadly for the image of Jesus had always affected him deeply. There was something haunting about Jesus's story that reflected the suffering of every Jew. Zishe knew he was not the only Jew who understood this truth. Zishe wanted to prevent his people's suffering. He wanted to save them from harm. He had a premonition he would someday die for them.

He felt a strange compassion for this group, a feeling of having known them forever, long before he was born. He knew them through all their adventures, through the agony of their exiles, through the centuries of their wanderings in Spain, France, Rome, and Palestine. A current ran through them he felt connected to beyond memory or words.

Zishe had always seen peculiar things. Angels would visit him. He could tell what people were thinking, see far into the future, and view translucent spirits hovering around peoples' thoughts. These visions happened when he least expected it. Zishe couldn't control them. He felt that God was behind them, helping to guide him.

He was afraid to talk about them. People might think he was dabbling in sorcery or in league with the devil. Yosi was the only one in whom Zishe would confide.

"It's different here and yet the same. Freedom is guaranteed by law, but getting justice can be another matter," the young man was saying. "Outwardly the German acts without violence. The ritual of politeness, *Gemutlichkeit*, is practiced, but underneath it's the same age-old prejudice, the kind of hatred you can't lay a finger on because it's so buried in pride of nation, race, church, family, and state."

Someone else added to the discussion. "How can you speak this way of a nation that has brought to civilization the finest productions of man's achievements? Think of Beethoven, Mozart, Schubert, Bach, Goethe, Schiller."

People began arguing back and forth. Zishe made himself comfortable. He liked to hear stories and he suspected this would be a long evening.

"There's always been good people in this land, but the roots of hatred go back a long way," an old man said, a scowl on his face. He paused. "During the great plague a few centuries ago, a tragic event occurred in a village nearby. The story was told to me by a Jew whose ancestors knew the people involved." He wiped his forehead before he began.

The terrible event took place in a village with storybook houses and people dressed in long black attire from a time long ago. An old man was carrying wood he'd just cut, but the hump on his back prevented him from carrying a full load.

"Look at the hunchback. Let's throw something at him."

A small procession of people began to pelt him with rocks and pebbles and pushed him off-balance. He walked with a rolling, swaying motion, one arm on the load and the other almost touching the ground.

"Ain't he a beauty? Want a kiss, honey?" A young woman taunted, placing her hands on her hips, swinging them low while exposing her bosom.

"Leave me be. You're too pretty to be making fun of me." He barely looked up as he continued on his way.

"Poor little hunchback, poor little hunchback. You must've done something real bad to be so twisted and ugly." She laughed and everyone joined in.

He walked to a humble cottage and knocked on the door. A woman answered. "Here you are, ma'am." He reached over and released the strap holding the wood on his back. "I'll light it for you. That should keep the house good and warm."

The day was ending. He lit the candle and stoked the coals on the stove.

"Is there anything else I can do for you?" He looked up at the couple. The man was dressed in his best suit with a yarmulke on his head, while his wife seated the children at the table.

"Thank you. You have done enough for us already. *Shalom.*"

"And you have a good *shabbos!*" He mispronounced the word, but he wanted to let them know he respected their Sabbath.

It was freezing cold outside, but he had to stop at a few more houses on this round. The Jews were always kind to him. They treated him with respect and courtesy. He was only too glad to help them celebrate their Sabbath by performing the few small chores their religion prohibited. "They're nice, real nice. I like them," he said aloud. He liked to talk to himself. He stroked the cross in his hand and fingered the rosary. He'd told the priest of all their kindness. "I don't care what other people say. Father, they love God so very much. They talk to him as if He were one of them. He must love them a lot." He could never quite figure out why the priest got so upset whenever he mentioned anything nice about them.

"They're of the devil, my son. They killed Christ," the priest told him.

He must know what's best—he can read and he knows the Bible. I'm not smart enough to get anything right. Christ, God, Holy Ghost—I always mix them up, he thought.

He was lucky to stay alive; there were few jobs in town. The winter was difficult; there was not enough food for all. The few stray cattle had little flesh on their bones and had to fend for themselves. The ground was too dry and hard even for hay to be grown.

Talk of the plague was on everyone's lips and on everyone's minds. The pestilence couldn't be stopped; once it was discovered, it was too late. No one was immune—rich, poor, priest, or thief. Everyone had some special defense: a talisman, an ointment, a prayer—anything to fend off this cruel Black Death. Smoke from the burning corpses filled the air. It was said the Jews were to blame, they were in league with the devil. Somehow they were spreading the disease. It was said the Jews worshiped the devil, poisoned the wells, and drank the blood of innocent babies.

"We should've burnt them all before it struck," some said.

"I hear wherever they got rid of the Jews the plague never got started," others claimed.

"Burning is the only solution!"

The priest said, "The source of disease is the devil."

"I've never seen them do anything," the hunchback said. He was sitting away from the crowd all by himself. No one liked to be near the hunchback.

"Look who's talking. Let's see you dance, little cripple. You're blind as a bat and twice as ugly."

He was used to these taunts. He had no anger or hate.

"Let's get the Jews before it's too late." The shouts came from all about. There was complete agreement, except for the hunchback, who was still trying to be heard. Led by the priest and the mayor, the crowd fanned out in a well-planned maneuver executed with precision.

Captured and bound, the Jews were herded through the town. "You're going to burn. We're going to have a Jew roast," the crowd jeered.

The sound of a flute gave a hint of the mood as they sang and danced and threw rocks. "Tie them up against the railing and lay the hay in bundles at their feet!" The priest was still giving the orders. All the Jews were tied with their hands behind them to the posts surrounding the temple.

"Hear O Israel, the Lord our God is one." The prayers were on every Jew's lips. They were reciting the Kaddish for their own deaths. *"Sh'ma, Yeskadesh, adonai elohenu..."*

"Shut up! Stop that eternal chatter, that devil talk!" The priest was livid with rage. "How dare they mumble their chants to a God who stopped listening to them long ago. Put the torch to the temple. This is the house of Satan. We'll be free of Jews at last. The plague won't strike us."

"Wait, wait, put the torches away!" the hunchback cried. He was trying to hurry, but his legs were too short and his crooked back made walking difficult and slow.

"Look who's talking—if it isn't the hunchback." The crowd broke out laughing.

"Don't," he said, completely out of breath. "Don't."

He still had a few yards to go, but they had no trouble hearing him. "Don't what?"

The priest was distracted by the spectacle.

"Leave them alone! They're good people," he said.

"Good people?" The priest, the torch in his hand, was the only one not laughing.

"Yes, they're very good people. They treat me nice. They don't laugh at me." He was still out of breath, but his speech was coming out strong. "They're God's people. I see them praying all the time, just like Jesus. Yes, Father, they pray like He does. *Our Father who art in heaven."* He started the Lord's Prayer staring up to the sky.

"That's for Christians, not Jews. They don't pray that way. They are pagans. Poor crippled soul. God has punished you so. But if you keep this up, He'll really get mad and send you straight to hell."

The priest lit the torch and ignited the first bundle. A small girl of eight or nine repeated the Kaddish without stopping. The hunchback came at the priest with a terrible rush, clinging to his knees, not allowing him to proceed.

"Get off of me, you ugly ape." The priest was screaming and kicking but the hunchback held on. All the bundles had been lit by the crowd except the one with the rabbi, but the priest couldn't quite reach it.

"Yeskadal, Yeskadesh, sh'ma raba." The prayers were increasing as the flames leapt across the people to the temple's stained-glass windows. The smell of burning flesh filled the air and through the smoke the little hunchback was crawling from pole to pole trying to save at least one person. The crowd and the priest retreated as the walls crumbled.

The synagogue lay smoldering for days. The town was covered with soot and ashes. Three hundred miles away, the plague stopped as suddenly as it started. The dead were buried and the mourning ceased. Life returned back to the way of the past. The plague was forgotten, but in its last gasp, the plague traveled three hundred miles to strike every soul in the town that had burned the little hunchback, the Jews, and the temple. Some said it was God's revenge.

The room was quiet. The old man sat down. He looked tired.

A young man bundled in a heavy coat broke the silence. "So the little hunchback was a saint, a Just Man. He listened to Jesus's words. But the rest acted just like their people today would."

Zishe listened to the sighs. He could hear the fear in their voices. He watched the soul of the little hunchback ascending, his deformed body now transformed into a splendid and magnificent one. A Just Man, Zishe thought, like in Proskurov.

There were the angels showing Zishe the Jewish souls ascending from the ashes, now alive and more beautiful. They looked so happy, surrounding the little hunchback, reviewing all that happened on earth.

An angry defiant voice brought Zishe back to earth.

"It's their religion. It's so anti-Semitic," a woman was saying.

"It's not their religion. It's how they're taught," a broad-shouldered man replied authoritatively. "I've read their Bible. There's nothing anti-Semitic about it. After all, it's about a Jew written by Jews," he said, brushing back the hair from his face. "Their church is the source of our problems. Especially during Easter. Their priests get them all fired up with the usual lies. They distort what's written, falsely accusing us of killing Jesus." He paused and gazed around the room.

Zishe could feel the suspense.

"Like what happened in my village, not long after the Chmielnicki pogroms."

"Another story?" someone said.

"Yes," he said, folding his muscular arms. "It's sad yet very beautiful. I'll tell it exactly as it was told to me by my mother, her mother, and my great-grandmother." He leaned on the chair in front of him and looked around the room.

The town surrounded the city, stopping just short of its massive iron gates. The large cathedral could be seen from every window. High on a hill, it loomed above the countryside. The Jews lived in the town just outside the gates. They could enter the city only with special permission. They were happy to be left to themselves. The town was their own. David was the cantor and violinist in the synagogue. He was just shy of eighteen. He wrote music that defied explanation. It could elevate any occasion to unheard-of heights.

People would ask him how he wrote such music at such a young age.

"It's not me. It's given to me completely done. I just copy it down," he'd say.

"Given to you? By whom?"

"I just let myself become totally empty, like a vessel. Then I see the music."

"You see music?"

"Yes, I see the composition."

"You mean you hear it."

"No, I see it. All at once from every angle, like a statue."

He took no credit for his efforts. When he played, he forgot who wrote it. His teachers were the old masters, cantors, and musicians who were dead.

His poor, uneducated parents couldn't understand his talents. They had no time for music or entertainment. There was too much work and very little money. But they often told the story of how he started playing. When he was three, a man came to their house hungry and his parents fed him. The man offered money in exchange but they wouldn't accept. Instead, the man opened his suitcase and pulled out a violin.

His mother would say, "My son couldn't stop staring at the violin. He picked it up and it was like the music was coming right out of him. I'd never heard anything like it. Even the melodies were from somewhere else."

The violin was too large for him, so he put it between his legs. Since then he never stopped. He played on anything he could get his hands on. There were no musical manuscripts in his house or the town. They were only for the very rich. He played without books, from his own memory. He played because it gave joy to himself and everyone around. He was never paid. He earned his keep by the sweat of his brow just like his parents and the rest of the town.

Rosh Hashanah and Yom Kippur were special occasions, ten days of music and prayer. David loved the whole atmosphere. The aura of God's presence. The forgiving and the love of one's neighbor.

On Rosh Hashanah and Yom Kippur, the town was overrun with people from miles around. They came to hear the music David played. All the windows of the synagogue were open, the crowd was overflowing. They sat in the yard, on the ground, on the nearby roofs, anywhere—just to hear the music. David played from morning until night. From Abraham to David to Isaiah, he covered the whole history. He described every word with a melody that caught the very essence of the message. On those ten glorious days God descended. Some even said they'd seen him, but all agreed they'd heard him.

All who came had their own special vision. Each melody uncovered their hearts, allowing them to expose their sins without the slightest degree of shame. They had no trouble forgiving when they heard the music.

But life was not easy in this town. The Jews owed their existence to the powers that ran the city. The cathedral cast a long shadow there. The archbishop controlled the city, and he hated the Jews. His orders were harsh and capricious.

The archbishop took great pride in his musical abilities. He wrote masses and cantatas for the glorification of God. But he was not drawing the crowd. He wanted to please God, but above all else he wanted to be famous. The archbishop auditioned and auditioned musicians, but he could never find the right talent. All were as mediocre as himself. It was hard to admit he needed help. After all, he was the archbishop, and this cathedral was attended by cardinals and the king. Christmas was near and Easter was just around the corner. He needed something special to impress his guests. He was desperate.

Then one day a servant girl told him about the Jewish boy who played and drew crowds. It hurt the archbishop's pride, but he decided to go to the synagogue and listen.

The rabbi presided and prayed with the congregation, pretending this was no different than any other occasion. The melody came out of nowhere. It was both a voice and a violin. It wailed while it wove its magic, embracing everyone in the congregation. David was sent even more deeply into the space where the music came from, traveling, soaring to heights he'd never explored before. God whispered through him to the archbishop, whose scowl changed to a smile.

The archbishop sent for David a few days later. The messenger was ordered to give no details. The archbishop was used to having his way, and he didn't have to give reasons.

David's parents were very upset, but they had to oblige. They were Jews and at the mercy of the archbishop.

When David arrived, he was brought to the archbishop's room and served cakes and candies.

"Why am I here?" he asked.

"I like your music," the archbishop replied.

"Thank you."

"I can use you."

"I only write music for myself and the temple."

"Well, consider this a temple. After all, we all worship the same God."

"Well, yes. God is God."

"I need a few good melodies for my services. Let's start with this." And the archbishop pulled out a few psalms from the Old Testament.

David's eyes lit up. "Of course, I can do that."

"Well, go to it. They'll have to be ready by Sunday."

David knew he had no choice. He looked at the psalms and he saw the music. It was done in a matter of hours. He met the archbishop in the music room.

"I didn't know you could read Latin," the archbishop said.

"I know these psalms by heart in Hebrew."

Then the archbishop gave David other texts in Latin from the New Testament to set to music.

"I can't read Latin. I have to understand the words if I am to set them to music."

"These are Jesus's words. I'll translate them for you. I want two cantatas for a full orchestra and chorus." As he read, David listened, and he saw the music before the priest had even finished.

"Here is the second manuscript." The archbishop read, "Blessed are the poor in spirit for theirs is the kingdom of heaven. Blessed are those who mourn for they will be comforted. Blessed are the meek for they will inherit the earth. Blessed are those who hunger and thirst for righteousness for they will be fulfilled. Blessed are the merciful for they shall be shown mercy. Blessed are the pure in heart for they will see God. Blessed are the peacemakers for they will be called sons of God. Blessed are those who are persecuted because of righteousness for theirs is the kingdom of heaven."

"Who said these words?" David asked admiringly.

"Jesus." There was anger in the archbishop's voice.

"I'll go to work immediately."

It was ready the next morning.

The archbishop looked at the scores. "I'm delighted," he said, but there was jealousy on his face. "Here is some money. Go along home. But keep this a secret between you and me."

His parents were overjoyed David had come home so soon. "What did he want you to do?"

He gave them the money but said nothing.

"I didn't write it anyway," he reminded himself. "Let him have the credit."

That Sunday came and went. It was rumored the pope had cried and raved about the archbishop's music.

Soon the archbishop sent for David again. "Your music was well received," the archbishop said, "except that it was said to be almost Hebraic! Because, perhaps, it was in God's

15

original language. Some people are saying that Jesus was Jewish. So now I want you to write the music to this."

The boy read the manuscript the archbishop handed him. These were not Jesus's words but something the archbishop wrote. The story was familiar to every Jew. It was about Jesus, but it was filled with hatred toward the Jews.

David knew he would be imprisoned if he didn't write the music. "Dear God," he prayed, "I can't write music to this. It speaks only of hate." He started to cry. "If I bring life to these words I'll be a traitor to my people."

He was still praying to God for help when the door swung open.

"Well?" The archbishop was impatient. "How much longer before you start?"

"I can't do it." David spoke without fear as he stood up.

"What? Listen, you little Jew, too much depends upon this. The cardinals loved what you did and they think I did it, so now you'd better help me out or I won't get my promotion. If not, this Easter, your people will pay."

After the archbishop left, David reread the manuscript. It was trite and poorly written. The Jews were pictured as bloodthirsty and vengeful, while the Romans came off lightly. But even the archbishop couldn't hide Jesus and his disciples' Jewish ancestry. David saw the melody coming from a great distance. It told the entire story.

"I understand," he said, smiling. "Thank God for letting me see past the words."

He was in a frenzy of creation. Each note was part of the story.

David stared at the ceiling, finished at last. He knew this was a masterpiece. He had copied the true passion as it was handed to him by Jesus himself. He had written the story with music, a language that could not be misunderstood. "I have been true to my people and God. I have written down what I was shown." He had seen Jesus as a Just Man who was murdered because he loved God and people. But he hadn't changed a word of the original manuscript. His music conformed to every sentence and word. The archbishop would be happy and get his promotion and now he could go home.

"Here is the finished manuscript," David announced when the archbishop arrived. The archbishop was surprised to find it finished in such a short time. He thumbed through the pages, amazed and jealous at its greatness.

This boy can write. His Holiness will really like this, he thought to himself.

The play far exceeded the expectation of the author, the pope, and especially the peasants.

"The Jews are God's chosen. They love Jesus so. They were his only followers. The Romans did everything to divide them," everyone said.

The archbishop was shocked as he listened to these statements. They came from the king, the pope, the cardinals, and the peasants. His play was terribly misunderstood.

The boy had not altered a word, he had only set the story to music. The music wove a veil through the text, telling the truth and exposing the lies.

The archbishop got all the credit, but he wanted more. He wanted hate along with the fame. "I'll just have to kill that boy. He's ruined my play. He distorted its meaning. I should have known better than to let a Jew write my music."

David died the next day. The archbishop paid a few gold pieces for the execution.

The Jews mourned their musician. Every Jew saw his soul ascending. David had been a Just Man.

The man sat down. His eyes were moist. He wiped the tears from his cheeks.

God keeps sending Just Men, Zishe thought. He wanted to cry but controlled himself. David's life and death were moving. The story of Jesus's crucifixion always made Zishe uneasy. It bothered him. He could feel Jesus' pain as if it was his.

"Tell them Zishe, about that Easter back at school," Yosi said, his face flushed with excitement. "You know, when Krakowski forced us to kneel in front of the cross."

"They wouldn't be interested. It's just more of the same," Zishe said, blinking. He was seeing Yosi's thoughts. They were painful for him to watch. The wounds haven't healed after all these years. Zishe felt the same fear once again.

"Go on. Tell us, we're all ears. You haven't spoken a word all evening," a pretty young girl said, looking flirtatiously at Zishe.

"All right, you've convinced me," Zishe agreed, walking toward the front of the room. He began to speak hesitantly.

Yosi and Zishe were only ten. All of the school's sixty students, both Gentile and Jew, were crowded together one day to meet the new teacher who was to be the supervisor of all activities related to religious and political truths. "My name is Professor Krakowski," he said, immediately. "And I can see from your observant faces that we shall all get along splendidly." He was square-shouldered with small, steely eyes and a grayish goatee. On a wall behind him a crucifix of Jesus had been installed.

"In a few days," he said, "it shall be Good Friday, when we celebrate our Lord's death and resurrection. So let us start this day as we will every day, with deep devotion and prayer." He crossed himself, kneeled, and began the familiar prayers, "Our Father who art in Heaven, hallowed be Thy name, Thy kingdom come..." and "Hail Mary, full of grace, the Lord is with thee..." and "Glory be to the Father, the Son, and the Holy Ghost..."

Professor Krakowski circled the room. He stared hard at those who weren't saying their prayers. "All those who aren't kneeling down and saying the rosary will stand up. The rest of the class may relax and observe these pagans."

Zishe and nine others stood up. He looked around him, frightened. The class began to titter.

"Quiet, this is a serious violation and not a laughing matter." With that statement, Professor Krakowski took three giant steps landing squarely in front of Manny Liebowitz, the smallest of the ten. "Do you believe in God?"

"Yes—yes, professor," stuttered Manny.

"Well, isn't it nice that you can acknowledge the existence of something higher than Manny," the professor said. Again the class laughed. "Do you believe we should pray to our God?"

"Yes," replied Manny.

"Then why did I not see you kneeling and praying to our Father, the Son, and His mother?"

Manny looked around to the other nine for some help. Professor Krakowski tried a different tactic.

"Do you believe in Jesus Christ?"

"Yes, professor, I believe He existed."

"And you don't believe He exists anymore?"

"Didn't He die a long time ago?" Manny said, pleading.

The professor slapped him on the face. "And your people, you little dirty Jew, killed him. You crucified him, our Lord and Savior." He now pointed at all ten.

"Did that little slap hurt you?" Professor Krakowski said, mocking sympathy. "How do you think our Jesus felt when you scourged and killed Him so long ago?"

"Professor Krakowski," Yosi said, "I believe it was the Romans who crucified him."

"And you—you're very smart. How do you know this?"

"Because it says so in your Bible."

"My Bible," the professor said. "And how is it that a little Jew reads our Bible?"

"Well, I have heard it—"

"Heard it from whom? From your old bearded rabbi whose lies you believe? Who writes in what you call the Talmud? Tell me, who do your most respected teachers say Jesus was?"

"They believe he was a Jew."

"A Jew? Jesus a Jew? I want all ten Jews to stand in the front of the room."

They took their places amid whoops of derision.

"You dirty Jews. You killed our Jesus, our God, and you will be punished for it!" he cried.

The professor motioned to the strongest boys in the class to come forward. "Make these Jews kneel below the cross." It wasn't long before the ten boys were forced down on their knees.

"Admit you killed Jesus Christ," Professor Krakowski demanded as the stronger boys yanked their hands behind their backs.

It seemed like quite a while before Morris gave in. "I killed Jesus Christ. I killed him."

"We use Christian blood; we spit on Jesus' image. We stick pins in his body; we are in league with the Devil," the rest soon followed. Professor Krakowski was beaming as he heard them repeat the prayers after him.

But Zishe wouldn't give in.

"Are you too proud to humble yourself before God?" Professor Krakowski said. "You must need more persuasion. Go ahead, give it to him now," he said to the boys holding Zishe down. "Give it to him until he breaks and makes his confession."

Zishe looked around the room. "I remembered the pain. I thought my arm and shoulder blade would crack and break off. My head was swung back with a terrible whack, and I was forced to look up at the cross. Tears came to my eyes and I couldn't help looking directly at the face and the eyes of Jesus. Jesus's face was at just the right angle with the head inclined downward so I noticed the expression of unfathomable pain that matched exactly what I was feeling. Jesus was a fellow Jew. 'Hear, O Israel, the Lord is our God, the Lord is one.' My lips moved and the ancient Hebrew words came from deep inside me.

"Professor Krakowski let me up then. I thought he must have mistaken my prayer for a confession." Zishe remained standing. He had spoken about something very personal and now felt awkward. Maybe I should have left out the part about how I felt looking up at Jesus, he thought.

"That happened to me too," a young boy said, standing up in his chair.

"Me too. I was also forced. I'm still ashamed of how easily I surrendered," a man said, apologetically. "Only I didn't see anything special in that statue they made me kneel to."

"Convert. Became a Christian. That's all they ever think about when they see us," the woman named Fania said, tossing her hair defiantly in the air.

Zishe listened to her words, admiring her courage.

"And you believe it will be better here?" an old woman said, waving her hands. "Not so long ago, Jews lived in ghettos without any legal protection," she paused, removing her scarf. "Right here. In this land, where you have placed your faith, your hope. Kidnaping and murder, stealing our land, our homes, whenever they wished, at the slightest whim." Her voice became an angry mixture of Yiddish and German.

"We believe you. Just tell us the story," a young man said, yawning.

"You win," she said, smiling as she began her story.

His name was Wilhelm. He was tall with a rather dark complexion, and he was wearing lace and satin with a sword swinging at his side. There was no question he belonged to a very rich and noble class.

His father was cold and strange, aloof. He was the lord of the castle and everything within miles around. He even had his own private army. He had the power of life and death over all his subjects, including his wife and son. He was religious when it was to his advantage. Proud of his lineage, he expected his son to follow him—to marry, to have children, and to continue the tradition.

Wilhelm's father forced the Jews to loan him money, but he never repaid them. When the money was due he would accuse the Jews of everything from desecrating the Host, to murder, or stealing, or killing Christ.

The Jews were at his mercy. They had no choice but to forgive the loan. They even added a special gift just so he'd leave them alone.

The Jews were a puzzle to Wilhelm. The only contact he had with them was in walking by or seeing them in the marketplace. He always wondered why they were treated with such disrespect and hatred. They seldom looked him in the eye. They scurried into their walled city as soon as it was dark, afraid of the soldiers who were placed outside their gate. He wondered if there was something terribly wrong with them. They looked the same as the rest of the population, except perhaps for their slightly darker skin and hair.

He'd heard all kinds of rumors. "Beware!" they said. "They capture Christian babies. They poison the wells and they cast spells. And they are on very friendly terms with the devil." Fact or fantasy, he couldn't tell. Maybe his father knew more than he'd tell. But his mother was the greater puzzle. She never spoke a word against the Jews. In fact, she seemed to almost protect them from the verbal and often physical abuse her husband would use against them.

"Leave them alone. Don't go amongst them. They are to be left alone. Don't speak. Don't even display any friendship with any one of them." She always spoke in these words whenever any question about the Jews arose.

"Are they bad, Mother?" he would say.

But she only said, "Leave them alone."

He was old enough to make his own decisions. He would do as he pleased. He would go to the walled city where they kept the Jews separated. He wore his gardener's clothes, picked an old horse, and rode slowly away from the castle. He was in no rush, so it took almost half the day before he got to the large iron gate of the ghetto. He dismounted and left his horse outside.

Jews were passing him by in both directions as he walked through the gate. Every inch of available space was crowded with people and houses. The smells and the words were of a different world, but he had a strange feeling he was home. He looked at the Star of David on the stained-glass window of the building not far from where he was standing.

The services had already started. As he entered the temple, he donned the yarmulke that was offered to him. The music was so different, it was close to a cry, like a pain that was exposed to be touched by their God. This is how they bare their souls, he thought. He was surprised they would be so naked and honest. He could not understand the words, but he felt something familiar.

He looked about for a cross or statue of Mary or Jesus. But the chapel was barren except for the front where they kept the Torah. "Hear O Israel, the Lord our God, the Lord is one," they sang.

He had never heard such devotion. They loved their God with all their heart and soul. This was not what he had been told. For the first time in his life, he felt the living presence of God. The Jews spoke to God as a friend. No priest or intermediary was needed to hear them confess. They had direct access to Him but found it profane to pronounce his name.

He felt at home. They even treated him as their own. Gone was that look of fear that made them avert their eyes. Instead, he felt the warmth of their love. They shared the most intimate moments of their life.

What a strange people, he thought on his way home. They even said a blessing for me. They don't believe in the devil. They don't even hate Christians. He thought about his father and all his stories.

Wilhelm's father had a religious adviser. He was the monk that ran the monastery. He hated Jews and constantly schemed of ways to convert them.

One day Wilhelm overheard a conversation between the monk and his father. His father wanted more money

23

from the Jews, but the monk was up in arms about converting them.

"They shall convert or die," the monk said.

Wilhelm's father consented as long as he would get their money. They arranged the necessary details in the next few days including the delivery of the ultimatum.

Wilhelm's heart was very heavy. The thought of letting the monk do this to the Jews turned his stomach. He would have to talk to his father before anything serious happened. It had always been difficult to speak to his father. He was overbearing and very opinionated. Religion had only become important since he'd come under the influence of that monk.

"Good morning, Father." He sat down to the breakfast table. His father barely nodded in acknowledgment.

"The Jews." Wilhelm didn't touch his food.

"What about them?" His father looked up with an expression that showed his annoyance.

"I heard that you and the monk will be giving them an ultimatum."

"Yes, it's about time they became Christians."

"Why?"

"Ask the monk, he knows all the reasons."

"And if they don't?"

"They'll die and I'll have all their property and money. Anyway, it's too late. The monk and all his emissaries have already delivered the ultimatum." He continued to eat his breakfast as if this were just a simple domestic dispute.

"Sir?" the valet said. "Father Platner is here with an urgent announcement. May I let him in?"

"Yes, by all means."

It was the angry monk. He came in perspiring and excited.

"Sit down. Did all go well?"

"They refuse. Those obstinate devils. They refuse to accept the offer."

"What about the money?"

24

"I'm talking about their immortal souls and not about mere earthly possessions. They're speaking of self-immolation of sanctification of the name."

"What the hell does that garbage mean?" his father said.

"They are prepared to kill themselves. They won't accept Christianity."

"Then let them kill themselves."

"No," the monk said shouting. "That will never do. Don't you understand that their God will reward them if they kill themselves in his name? We must force them to be baptized. But if they die, it must be by our hands. There can be no blood." The monk paused, thoughtful. "We must get them before they carry out their threat. We can do this by a ruse. Tell them that we only wish to speak to them. Gather them all in one place and tell them to convert. If they don't, we'll have them burned to death."

"What's the difference, blood or burning?"

"If they burn we'll have done our duty. There will be no shedding of blood."

Wilhelm listened without saying a word. He couldn't allow this to happen. He couldn't understand why he was reacting so strongly to something that had never concerned him before.

His father and the monk left the room. His mother was still seated, but she had barely touched the plate of food that was set before her. He could see she was on the verge of tears.

"What's wrong?" he said.

"Nothing."

"We can't allow this to happen."

"Leave it be. These things have happened before."

"Before?" He was surprised at her casual remark.

"Yes, it happens regularly all over the country. It's been going on for centuries."

"Then I will warn them."

His mother's mouth dropped open. He had never seen her with such a startled expression.

"Mother, please tell me what's wrong."

She started to stammer so badly the words she repeated had no meaning. Wilhelm waited patiently for her to calm down.

"Wilhelm, I was always afraid this would happen."

"I don't understand."

"Please, Wilhelm, I love you with all my heart. You must listen to my story. It's not easy for me to do this. But I've kept it a secret for too long."

"No matter what you tell me I'll always love you."

"Let me go on. The man you know as your father is not your real father, and I am not your real mother."

"Why does he treat me like his own?"

"He doesn't know. I was scared, I never told him."

"You never told him?"

"He wanted a child very badly. I had trouble conceiving. So I pretended I had become pregnant. He never noticed—he was too busy chasing all the girls in the castle."

"Where did you get me?"

"You were kidnaped. I paid some soldiers to go to the ghetto and take the next baby that was born."

"I'm a Jew?" he said. It was not a question—he'd known it in his heart already.

"Yes, you are a Jew. I hope you can forgive me."

"I love you. What you did was wrong, but you gave me all your love." He kissed her and left without a word.

Wilhelm ran after the monk.

"Dear Jews," the monk said to the Jewish Council. "Things have gone too far. Aren't we all God's children? We mean you no harm. There have been too many threats. Let's put them to rest. We can all live in harmony. What we want is quite simple—we want your people to listen to our priests. We ask that you respectfully attend our presentation in the great hall not far outside your city." He stopped and pointed his finger at the council. "Everyone must be there tomorrow."

With that off his chest, he started walking away then turned and said, "That will be exactly at twelve."

Wilhelm wasted no time. He took a horse and rode with all his might. He had to get there fast. The plot was so ugly and evil. He forced the horse to increase its speed. He must warn them. They will never change their religion. If they refused to convert they would all be burned.

The horse crashed through the gate. He rode up to a girl he had met in the synagogue. Others gathered around them as Wilhelm spoke. They listened intently but sadly to the whole horrible story.

"I am a Jew just like you," Wilhelm concluded.

There was not a moment to lose. Everything was at stake. The council, the temple, and the inhabitants sadly acknowledged that what Wilhelm said was unfortunately true. All agreed there was only one thing to do. "God gave us life. Let us return it to him with our own hands."

Never had Wilhelm seen such resolve. Not a tear was shed. The holy words were rising, ascending toward heaven. Each throat gave its life to the knife while repeating to the last the *Sh'ma,* the sanctification of the name.

Noon came, but the hall was empty. The monk was pacing and waiting. "This must be one of their tricks. They'll be sorry for this."

The monk and Wilhelm's father led the soldiers into the ghetto. It was too late. They heard no noise, no voices, only the wind howling through the empty houses. The monk ordered the soldiers to go first. They stared around them in shock.

"They're dead, all dead," a soldier said.

"What? All dead? They can't do this to me." The monk was visibly upset.

Wilhelm's father looked around. Everyone was dead, with their throats neatly cut. Blood was all around.

"Wilhelm," he shouted in anguish as he saw his son. He was among the dead, his hand still holding a knife. "What have I done? This is my fault."

His only son was gone. "Come here," he said to the monk.

The monk came running.

"They are all dead, including my son. Are you satisfied?"

"My lord, this is not what I planned. The Jews are indeed diabolical. This is all their fault," the monk said.

The monk stood, pleading to Wilhelm's father. The sword cut right through him.

Wilhelm's father picked up his son and carried him away.

"Life is so hard," someone said. A few people were sobbing, some moaning. Zishe felt angry. Why don't they leave us alone? he wondered.

Then the angels appeared and Zishe's heart was filled with joy, as he was shown where all those brave souls had gone.

"Things are not the same anymore. At least not here. Danzig is free," a dapper young man said. He was fashionably dressed and his German was perfect. "They treat me with respect, and the law is my friend. I have found no prejudice. Just the opposite. The German people go out of their way to be friendly and polite. They admire us. They are proud of the achievement of their Jews. Einstein, Heine, Franc, Rathner are just a few of ours who have risen to fame. And the German women," he said, with a lascivious grin, "find Jewish men fascinating." He took a sip from his cup.

"Just be careful Mister Know-It-All," another young man warned. He was tall and handsome and smoked while he talked. "You might learn a lesson from what happened to me. It might prevent you from getting into trouble."

"Some more advice? Another story full of pain and sorrow?" the dapper young man said sarcastically, rolling his eyes.

"It happened in Warsaw, but it could well have been here. I was a student when she introduced herself to me," the tall man said, averting his eyes. "She was petite with a smile that showed off her dimples. 'My name is Katrina Petrowski,' she introduced herself."

"My name is Karl." He was surprised he felt so at ease with her immediately.

"How long have you been a student here? What are you studying? Do you live here?" She was as curious as could be.

"Give me a chance to answer," Karl said, laughing.

"Well, are you going to answer or shall I just guess? Or maybe I'll imagine what best suits me."

"You win!" Karl said in amusement. "I will begin with telling you I am a student of philosophy, and I live not far from here."

"But you haven't told me how long you've been here or where you're from, or whether you have a sweetheart." She inclined her face and laughed in a coquettish, teasing way.

Karl could not help laughing. There was just no way of turning this conversation in any specific direction so he gave up and asked impulsively, "Will you come and have dinner with me?"

"Yes, I'd be delighted."

They arranged to meet at a restaurant that had especially good Polish food. Karl arrived on time, but Katrina was not where they agreed to meet. Since the night was especially frosty, he went to wait inside, and there she was already seated.

"What took you so long?" she said. "I thought you might be lost or some awful thing."

"We were supposed to meet outside. Do you realize you got us the best spot in the whole restaurant?"

"I always get the best," she said, taking his hands, caressing and warming them. They ordered wine and began talking. She wanted to talk, and he listened, fascinated.

"I was born in Lodz to a middle-class family. My father is a doctor and my mother occupies herself with several organizations, all devoted to her strong Catholic religious beliefs. I have three brothers, all who are older than me, two of them who are now studying medicine and the other is thinking of becoming a priest."

"And what are you doing here?" Karl asked. "Studying anything particular?"

"Well, that's my problem. I haven't really made up my mind and I really can't agree with the rest of my family. Especially with their rigid religious and political beliefs." She seemed quite sad. "But that's enough about me. I'm dying to find out all about you."

"Why?" Karl was suddenly afraid he would expose too much. "I am not from here. Where I was born is now part of Poland, but used to be Austria. I was taught the trade of a tailor, so I can always fall back on that. Now I am enrolled here in the University of Warsaw. I would also like to find out more about the world and how and why we came about."

"Tell me, Karl, are your parents religious? Maybe they would rather you became a priest and learned another kind of philosophy in the seminary."

He was taken aback. "No, Katrina, I'm Jewish."

Her face lit up. "Oh, you're Jewish, you're Jewish." She seemed so delighted. "I have always loved Jews. I wish I were one."

"I was brought up in a strictly orthodox Jewish home, keeping all the laws and eating only kosher. My parents felt it was important to remain Jewish and uphold the traditions."

"I so admire Jews. Look at what they have accomplished. Einstein, Freud, Spinoza."

Karl laughed. "Well, you're speaking only of those who have made it to the top. Certainly there are men of great learning in your religion who have made contributions."

"Yes, but look at the shadows our church has cast all over the world. They fight against everything in life. They fought against Copernicus, Galileo, Newton. Church is for the superstitious. How can I have anything to do with it after reading Schopenhauer, Neitzche, Spinoza, and Darwin?" Her eyes focused on him. "What is it like being a Jew, Karl?"

"No different than being a Pole, a Russian, or whatever. Why do you expect us to be different? We're human just like the rest of you, except we don't carry any crosses." He hoped that bit of humor would show her the question was silly and couldn't be answered.

She laughed and they continued talking, sharing experiences. Karl knew no matter how much she admired Jews, she was still a Gentile and he had to be careful. But he was lonely and missed female companionship, and Katrina was not only lovely but intelligent.

He brought her home that night but nothing happened. The next morning he congratulated himself for his self-control.

There was a slight chill in the air that day. The class was not very far, and Karl could get there in twenty minutes if he walked quickly. It was one of his favorites. The teacher, Professor Fineblum, was famous for his lectures on great mystics through the ages.

He was thinking aloud to pass the time when he thought he heard his name being called. He looked around. Again, he heard, "Karl." He looked to the left, all around him, but no one was in sight. He thought he was hearing things. He sat down for a moment, then two cold hands closed on his eyes from behind him.

"Karl, it's only me. What are you so afraid of?" It was Katrina. She turned his head around, uncovering his eyes. "Boo! It's me. I scared you, I scared you!" She was dancing in an odd sort of way, sticking out her tongue.

Was she teasing or just acting playfully? He wondered. He tried to put his arm around her, but she moved out of the way. She circled about and he followed in hot pursuit.

"Karl, Karl." She said his name as if she had discovered its melody.

"Katrina, Katrina." He was panting. He never thought he'd desire anyone like this. If I could only have a little contact, a kiss, he thought desperately. But she was gone.

"Karl." He heard his name but she was far away. Then he remembered the lectures, Professor Fineblum and the time. It was already after noon. She must think I am a fool, he thought, acting so out of control. He was so ashamed. He wondered why she was acting this way. Was this her way of showing affection?

It took Karl a long time to finally arrive at the campus, and when he did Katrina greeted him. "Hello, Karl," she said, as if nothing had happened in the woods. "Let's go have a picnic together." She had sausages, wine, cheeses, bread, everything they would need.

"Why did you tease me this morning?"

"Because you're so serious." She again stuck out her tongue.

"It's hard for me not to be serious when I have so many things to do," he said, getting up to leave.

"Wait a minute, stay with me a while." She took his hand. He felt weak in her presence, and he let her take him to a spot where she spread out her picnic. After they ate, he put his hands gently around her feeling this was the right moment for a kiss. She leaned back just as he leaned forward, and he fell awkwardly with his elbows landing in the thick spread of salad on the picnic floor. Then she was off again, heading for the woods, beckoning him.

All he could do was stumble after her as she danced, swaying this way and that, calling, "Karl, Karl."

"Good-bye, Katrina," he said, angrily, in spite of the rush of desire he felt for this girl who was making a fool of him.

"Karl," she came to him, now a different, more serious person. "Please meet me tonight. I promise I will behave. You won't be sorry." She tweaked his cheek and smiled. "I'll meet you where the oak tree grows at the end of the canyon. We won't need to worry about anybody. We'll be able to have the place to ourselves. Is six o'clock okay?"

Against his better judgment but filled with lust, he agreed.

That evening, he had a hard time finding the oak tree where the forest began. I shouldn't be here, he kept thinking, this is crazy. The sun was setting with the shadows adding to the darkness. The trees looked like witches and he was afraid.

"Karl, Karl."

She was waiting by the large oak tree. She was dressed in a full skirt, bonnet, and lacy blouse that showed off her magnificent bosom. She took his hands, laid her head against his pounding chest, and murmured, "Now everything is as it should be. I'm so happy. I'm yours."

Love or lust, whatever it was, it was all-consuming. Nothing mattered but the present moment. Karl completely forgot his doubts.

"Kiss me, please kiss me," she murmured. Pulling his head down toward her, she pressed her moist lips into his, chewing with small bites, her tongue licking, probing at all the hidden, sensitive crevices. They tasted and swallowed and devoured one other.

She offered her bosom and he buried his head, suckling like a baby. She moaned with pleasure. Her hands roamed all over his body, fingers and lips exploring every hollow and curve as they undressed each other. They wrapped themselves into each other, biting, kissing, totally engrossed in their sensual play.

The young man paused. There was pain in his face. He looked around the room before continuing in a loud and angry voice.

"I'm cold," Katrina said. Her clothes were strewn about and she scrambled to collect them. She seemed ashamed and very angry. "Goddamn the weather! Why does it have to be so cold?"

It was dark and very hard to tell which clothes belonged to which body or which part of the body. "Goddamn, look at the mess. All my clothes are filthy." Her voice was shrill, like an angry old crow.

"Let me help you," Karl said, trying to help her into her blouse.

"Mind your own business. I can dress myself. You're still half-naked—can't you even dress yourself?"

"Let's go, Katrina. I'll clear a path."

"I can take care of myself, thank you," she said, and in a huff Katrina left him behind to fend for himself.

It took less time to find his way home, but the cold chilled him to the bone. Once at home, he gratefully warmed himself with a few extra blankets and a roaring fire and fell asleep.

After he awoke, he couldn't quite remember what had happened, but he knew it had been a disaster. "Women," he said to himself. "Who can figure them out?" He felt the bruises and cuts on his lips, cheeks, and throat. He looked at his arms and saw the deep scratches of sharp fingernails. His chest had more of the same. He looked like he'd been in a wild brawl and gotten the worst of it.

On his way back to school that morning, he heard a chorus of angry voices coming from behind the building where the horses were kept.

"There he is." It was Katrina. She was not alone. Her face was somewhat puffy, her teeth exposed in a vicious snarl. "There's the son of a bitch who beat me and forced himself on me."

"Just look at the brute who raped her. You can tell from the bruises and cuts on his face that she put up a fight," someone said.

"*Jid, Jid,* dirty filthy Jew," Katrina started the chant. She was sobbing and crying hysterically. "It's not enough that he killed our Jesus. I was pure, now I'm dirty. Who will ever have me?" Her voice rose and fell between her sobs. "God has punished me because I have been slack in my observance of His church and my prayers and confession-als. You filthy Jew. Look what you did to me," and she exposed her breasts showing a few cuts and bruises.

"Hang him!" At first the words came from only one, but then they all began shouting.

"Give him a good beating, that'll teach him a lesson."

"Roast him alive."

"It's her word against his."

"Maybe she seduced him."

"We made love yesterday evening," Karl said, defend-ing himself. "But we both wanted it very much. It was by mutual consent. I didn't force myself on her. The cuts and bruises are from passion."

"He's a liar," Katrina bellowed. "All Jews are liars."

"Yesterday you spoke quite differently. Today you feel your honor gone and you want to place all the blame on me. I will accept only that part of the blame that belongs to me, that I foolishly listened to you. Look into my eyes, Katrina, and let God be your witness. Speak the truth."

Katrina stopped the crying long enough to look directly into his eyes. The scowl around her eyes faded. "Let him go, he's innocent." A few tears rolled down her cheeks as she averted her eyes.

She left with her friends, leaving Karl standing alone.

The room became silent again. The young man's smile had disappeared. He walked back to his chair.

Zishe also felt sad. He wanted to do as he pleased. He wouldn't allow fear to stop him from meeting any woman whether Gentile or Jew.

"They'll never change. They'll always find any excuse to blame us," Yosi said, angrily.

"I'll never forget that day back in Przemysl. It was Eas-ter," Yosi said, turning toward Zishe. "You remember?"

"How could I forget," Zishe said sadly.

"Do you mind if I tell it or is it too personal?" Yosi asked hesitantly.

"Go ahead. It never was a secret," Zishe said, putting his hand on Yosi's shoulder.

Yosi stood up and cleared his throat.

It started on a quiet Sabbath day. The peasant Zakoski and his wife, returning from the fields where they'd been working all day, discovered their five-year-old son Alexei was gone. With the help of their neighbors and their other five children, they searched desperately but unsuccessfully throughout the wilderness fields for any sign of their missing son. The whole town, armed with pitchforks and torches, turned out to help, searching throughout the night. Every possible site was investigated, including all the houses and fields within miles of the town.

The sun had just broken across the horizon when someone came running with the terrible news. Alexei's body had been found floating upside down in the river near the Jewish part of town. Someone suggested that since the body had been discovered so close to the Jewish part of town, it seemed only prudent to cast suspicion in that direction. The priest agreed.

Every person, young or old, from the entire village went to the funeral. Zishe and Yosi, along with their families, stood in the outer circle with the other Jews. The small coffin, adorned with crosses and flowers, was ceremoniously carried in a solemn procession to the spot for the burial. Muffled crying and a few sobs accompanied the last rites before they lowered the small coffin into the ground.

All eyes were on this priest who was, without doubt, the most powerful man in town. He began to speak. "Now that this small body has been laid to rest, we can be sure his soul is in the company of Jesus. It is we here on earth that must mourn and carry our crosses until the day that all sin will be gone as we prepare for the second coming of our Lord, Jesus Christ. This pure soul, Alexei Zakoski, did no wrong. But this mishap was unquestionably the result of some maniac. In my prayers I have asked the Lord to please advise me, to allow me to be of some help in finding the murderers. I feel most humble and grateful that the Lord has deemed to favor me with His divine guidance. I am not worthy of His mercy, but He has helped me to protect His church from Satan, who is a murderer and the father of lies."

A shudder went through the people that formed the outer circle. "The father of all liars, Satan"—these were the words of abuse normally used against Jews by their Christian brothers.

"I think the entire Jewish community must find the culprits and bring them to us for justice." The priest was speaking directly to the Jews and to their leader, Rabbi Goldstein. "The Jews are now completing their preparation for Passover which, to our misfortune, coincides this year with our holy Easter celebration. It certainly is suspicious that a Christian child was murdered during this time. Jews use our children's blood for their Passover rituals. I am accusing the entire Jewish community of this crime."

The circle of Jews cried out, "No, no. You must be mistaken. This accusation is false."

"Be quiet, you liars, you Satan worshipers," the priest said, turning back up the hill to his church.

The Jews argued about what could be done. The rabbi suggested, "Maybe this problem is not unsolvable. The priest is a reasonable man. I propose that we both sit down and intelligently investigate what happened to this unfortunate boy. After all, no one has seen any signs of a struggle or any wounds, cuts, or bruises that would've caused his death. From the evidence, intelligent men with honorable intent can only conclude that the boy wandered off into the river, drowned, and was carried by the rushing waters into our part of town."

But a man said, "You've got a lot to learn, rabbi. This priest knows when he's got a noose around our necks. He's not going to let us off that easily."

Then another said, "You think if you volunteer one or two of us to satisfy his vengeance, then he would let the rest of us go free and put the problem to rest?"

"My God, who would do such a thing?"

"This is the craziest thing I have ever heard."

"Please," the rabbi said, extending his hands. "What was said may sound cruel, but is it not better for one or two of us to take the blame than for every Jew to pay?

"Let's be practical. Everyone has his price. This priest looks like a man who likes a good life. A few gold pieces is all he's really after."

Zishe's sister Lonka was the prettiest and most beautiful girl in the town. Her long black hair and snow-white skin magnified her large, almond-shaped eyes. Tall and firm of flesh, she moved gracefully in an innocent but sensual way. "May I speak?" she asked.

"Yes, by all means, go on," the Rabbi replied.

Yosi thought he would never forget the look on Zishe's sister's face, the way she stood tall and proud and addressed the other Jews. "The solutions offered so far have all been clever and well presented but lacking in common sense. Who else but a woman has the intuition to know what a man truly desires? The priest is no exception. I have watched him very carefully. To be blunt, he likes gold and fine clothes, but above all, he likes women."

"What is your point?" The rabbi took off his glasses and squinted at Lonka.

"Are you all blind to what goes on around you? Or haven't you noticed that he selects the prettiest girls to assist him, to perform the necessary chores that his office demands? And soon after, they all become pregnant. Then he marries them off to the first available man in town. And the priest is known to have a special appetite for girls that are not available—Jewish girls. What he hates excites him— whets his jaded appetite."

"I can't believe," the rabbi said, "you are suggesting we offer the priest one of our women. The very thought of a daughter of Israel sharing a bed with that man makes me sick to my stomach."

"Well, if he wants one of our women, how do we know which one, how are we sure this will appease him and not make him become even greedier?" another man asked.

"I'm the one the priest is after," Lonka said simply. "He has followed me around, begged and pleaded, even offered me gold and jewels. Leave it to my discretion, but I will do what is required to spare our people."

Stories of Lonka's bravery circulated around the town. Some said that evening, with the full moon to guide her all alone, she walked up the road into the church yard, and they saw the lascivious smile of the priest as he opened the door and slid behind her. Others told a different story. She didn't walk but was driven by the priest's carriage, with him beside her and his arm around her. But what happened between the priest and Lonka in the privacy of the church that night was a complete mystery. It was as if only God should be privy to this event that saved these people.

Early the next morning the church bells rang loudly and clearly, calling the people to hear the special session. The priest was tired, his face was full of shame. He kept his eyes to himself. His skin had turned quite pale and he walked with a shuffle, barely lifting his legs.

His words were slurred and muffled; he seemed to have difficulty in moving his lips. "My sons, my daughters, I stand before you to announce that Alexei's death was caused by an accidental fall and drowning. No one is to blame. He just wandered off as children do and that is all. Please excuse me." He shuffled away. Some thought he was crying, but no one could be quite sure.

"You must be proud to have such a brave sister," a young man said to Zishe.

"Does she still live in Poland?" someone asked.

"Does her husband know?"

The room had become alive with questions. Zishe waited until the commotion had subsided before he spoke.

"Of course Lonka's husband knows. They still live in Poland, in Przytyk, not far from the German border," Zishe said, softly. "But what are we doing here, crying in our pails? We are Jews. Where there are Jews, there is life, there is hope." Lifting the wine glass in his hand, Zishe said, "*L'chayim!* Here's to life."

It was as if a curtain was lifted. Hands reached to fill glasses with the sweet red wine. *L'chayim* ricocheted around the room and glass after glass was raised to lips. Feet started to shuffle, then gathered in intensity as they broke out in the proud rhythm of the dances: old dances, new dances, Russian dances, Jewish dances. They danced with hope and reverence, each step a prayer to God. The songs expressed the innermost part of their *neshuma.* They blessed each other, themselves, their enemies. Their happiness was contagious and too precious to be contained.

In all the languages of the Pale, songs poured forth. Each was remembered and acknowledged with delight. Then a *balalaika* carried the accompaniment to the wistful strains of a Byelorussian gypsy song that cried for home, family, and love.

Zishe was filled with a longing that dwelled in a secret part of him. He felt his longing was a map to an Eden in the center of his heart. This feeling, this whisper of something larger, had always been with him, an undercurrent in his thoughts and actions. Words, pictures—nothing could really express it. But when he sang, when he truly lost himself in song, he was closer to it. His beloved angels would appear at these special times, allowing him to view unspeakable things.

The party ended as suddenly as it had begun. Sleepy, slightly inebriated guests went to bed. Those who had to leave left reluctantly, loitering in the small hallway. As they left, they wished Zishe and Yosi happiness and luck. If they could only be of help, anything, the smallest favor, "Please, just ask," they said, and they meant it.

The voices trailed off. Zishe was tired. The trip had been exhausting, full of unscheduled stops and discomfort. With as much politeness as he could muster, he thanked his hosts and curled up on his small cot.

The next morning, Zishe arose eagerly. There was a great deal of bustling about, with hushed voices whispering greetings and instructions as each bed, cot, and corner of the room was abandoned.

A lonely figure, not more than thirty or so years old, sat head in hand, dejectedly gazing into emptiness. Zishe, folding his blanket, was distracted by this forlorn figure. Approaching him, he silently placed his hands on the man's shoulders and said, "*Was ist los*—what is the matter?"

The man looked up with sad eyes, trying to hide his feelings. He was alone, he told Zishe. He had left a wife and children in Chusacov. He wished they were with him. He wasn't making enough money to send any back home.

"Yosi and I have also left our families back home," Zishe said. "My mother and sister's unspoken sorrow and Yosi's parents' crying was more than we were prepared for. But they didn't try to dissuade us from leaving. We were given leave to go without argument or resentment, as if what couldn't be deterred must be God's way."

Zishe tried to give the man confidence through his touch, but he couldn't wait to start his own search for work. Apprenticed as a youth to a local tailor, he had perfected his skills. When he fingered fine cloth, he was in his own heaven. He was confident his talent would be appreciated in this city. He knew he could imitate the most elegant design and also sew up inexpensive rags, or *shmattes*.

Herr Weiss's shop was a fashionable establishment. On the front were cherubim, gargoyles, and naked beauties carved in bas-relief. Several pretty sales girls smiled politely at Zishe as he entered and asked if they could be of service. He asked to see the owner.

With a measuring tape draped around his neck and scissors in hand, Herr Weiss came toward Zishe. He was balding and short and broad in stature.

Zishe barely announced his name and gave a short description of his skills before Weiss nodded and said, "I need someone. Can you start tomorrow? Early. Six o'clock." Then he darted off to direct a final alteration.

Zishe's mind reeled with questions he wanted to ask. He was standing there dazed when Weiss came back. "By the way, are you a Jew?" he asked.

Zishe proudly answered affirmatively. A frown formed on Weiss's face, and he whispered, "Just keep it to yourself. Don't mention it to anyone, especially my wife. We'll fit you out with new clothes." And then he was off again, leaving Zishe standing in the middle of the floor.

Back at Rose and Herschel's, Zishe met up with Yosi who had also found a job. He was going to work in the small shop of a man from Poland who catered to the large immigrant population. The two were filled with joy. They had both found jobs on their first day. They went out, walking together on the great central avenue of Langgasse, taking in the sights.

A side street with the enticing name of Chocalade Strasse attracted their attention. Yosi laughingly turned to Zishe and said, "I bet you can't resist this street. I bet you'll eat everything in it."

Zishe smiled, amused by the reference to his fondness for chocolate. "And I bet you won't be far behind me," Zishe replied.

They both began laughing, and it became uncontrollable. Just looking at each other sent them into convulsions. They stumbled down the street, holding their sides, like inebriated celebrants. Momentarily catching their breath, they stopped long enough to look at each other, and then began the whole hilarious process all over again, oblivious to the rest of the world.

"Juden, schutzige Juden," a voice said in staccato cadences. *"Verfluchte Juden, dreckige Juden, scheisskopfe."*

A group of about seven boys, hands on hip, brownshirted with arm bands, were advancing toward them. Before the words penetrated their laughter and before Zishe and Yosi realized the graveness of their predicament, the brownshirts had circled them. With no visible avenue of escape, they stood helpless and frozen. The *Pimpfe* continued their chant, now more uniform. *"Jude, Jude, Jude."* Their feet stomped in cadence, and they burst out in the words of their song, "When Jewish blood from our knives flows..."

Zishe knew that to attempt to escape or to fight would be to play into their hands. The brownshirts wanted their prey to do something, anything, to give them an opportunity to show their strength. They were waiting for some sign of inferiority. The singing died down. A boot caught Yosi square in the behind, sending him into the fists of the awaiting *Pimpfe*. Yosi instinctively lifted his arms, covering his head, but they were coming from all directions, and then they were all over Zishe, their fists pummeling him, their boots stamping and kicking.

Zishe thought he heard the shrill sound of whistles. Abruptly, the fists and boots stopped. He could see the faint outline of Yosi's body curled in a protective heap.

"Boys, my boys," he heard, "I think they have learned their lesson." It was the voice of the police. The laws against violence, against beating, were still enforced. The police asked the brownshirts to leave.

With effort, Zishe and Yosi managed to navigate their way back to the Bernstein's. Aside from their blackened eyes, bloody faces, and torn clothes, their bodies had not suffered as they would have in Przemysl. Not wanting to disturb anyone, they silently disrobed, washing their wounds in the small tin basin that had been provided for them. Ashamed, they could hardly face each other. All of the illusions he'd had about Danzig had been shattered. Never again would he allow himself to be trapped so easily, to walk so forgetfully.

✡ CHAPTER TWO

There were many workers in the large factory-like space, so Zishe did not feel too conspicuous when he arrived at work the next day with his face bruised. A steady hum of sewing machines, steam presses, and cutters drowned out conversations, so he concentrated on sewing. He wanted to be left alone. He could not forget the picture of Yosi being pushed, the look of shocked betrayal in Yosi's eyes. But he no longer felt angry or sad. He fell into the comfortable rhythms of the work, hunched over the machine, guiding the fabrics effortlessly under the rapid-fire movement of the needle.

Hour after hour in the following weeks he created garments—vests, trousers, dresses, skirts, blouses—all with ease and confidence. He was a good craftsman.

It wasn't long before Herr Weiss noticed his work and began paying special attention to him. Weiss told him something of his past, letting things slip out at odd moments. He had been born in Berlin to well-off Jewish parents. He had attended the university, where he had indulged in the *Aufklarung*, the German Enlightenment, attending lectures and spending his time at the feet of the current favorite teachers whose rebellious philosophy reflected the undercurrent of dissent in Germany. He was attracted to the camaraderie and the message of hope they delivered. He'd reveled in their brazen call for the assimilation of Jews.

But he'd also become attracted to Christianity, attending Bible study groups. To Weiss, what remained of Jewish life was just an empty shell of its former glory. Gone were the yarmulke, the dietary laws, the strict adherence to the Sabbath. It had been but a small step to acknowledge Jesus, the Jew, as God. He explained to Zishe confidentially it was without guilt he had joined the church, feeling accepted, German, and proud. He could see nothing wrong with his new situation. He was now no longer an assimilated Jew but a German. His family followed suit and they were eager to forget the past.

He had married well, a Christian girl from a well-known German family. It was a comfort to blend in with the mainstream, to be accepted. Except for matters of profit, he avoided contact with Jews.

Zishe was puzzled by it all. His employer had rejected his past. He wondered if he should do the same. He could easily pass for a Gentile. Tall, blonde, blue-eyed, and fair-skinned, he appeared to be the stereotypical German Aryan. And with his new clothes, he blended in with the rest of the population. He could switch adroitly from Polish to Ukrainian, from Yiddish to German.

But he was filled with guilt at these thoughts. His identification with his Jewish heritage was strong. To deny or betray it was cowardly and against every principle of his faith. And yet it would be so easy. No one at his workplace knew his past.

Yet Yosi's image frequently burned in his mind. He could see those sad brown eyes, the large nose with its suggestive hook, the enthusiastic and loud manner of his speech. By denying Yosi, he denied himself. He felt ashamed of the first line of his defense—the ogre of anti-Semitism.

Zishe needed time to think. He walked outside only to watch a troop of brownshirts approaching, singing with patriotic fervor. He was seized with fear. But the brownshirts passed by him without suspicion, offering him their salute. Zishe forgot his guilt. His relief gave rise to an idea that gave him pride. Why not use my disguise to infiltrate Danzig's elite to help my people?

He decided to avoid Yosi. Zishe moved out of Rosa's flat and began dressing smartly.

46

Weiss quickly promoted him. He was working with the rich and selective customers now. Zishe was not only paid well, but with his good looks and elegant manners, he was soon on familiar terms with the wealthy and the important government officials, none of whom suspected his humble Jewish origins. He began to do the things he'd always dreamt of, attending operas, plays, and lectures. He practiced daily, and his German, which was already accomplished, improved.

Herr Weiss was in love with everything German. His home was a cathedral, a monument to Teutonic pride. Frescoes celebrating the folk tales and historic triumphs of Germans decorated his palatial manor. The walls and corners were lined conspicuously with rows and rows of bookshelves devoted exclusively to German philosophers: Goethe, Schiller, Hegel, Fiche, Kant. No evening was complete without the thunderous bellowing of Wagner's music. And it was this that welcomed Zishe when he was invited for his first evening at the Weiss's home.

Frau Weiss greeted Zishe with cold, questioning eyes. She had a pleasing plumpness that gave her figure a matronly look. She guided Zishe on a tour of the manor, describing the history and rarity of the antiques. There were crucifixes of various sizes located strategically on the walls. She made a show of crossing herself devoutly on passing, as if to emphasize to Zishe that he was now in Christian surroundings.

Herr Weiss was a very rich man. His business acumen, along with a substantial inheritance, had enabled him to accumulate a sizeable fortune. His Jewish background was overlooked because of his wealth, and he moved in the highest circles of Danzig's political and business elite. Because of this, the room soon filled with important people.

Gretchen, Weiss's only daughter, was introduced to Zishe. He noticed the crucifix she wore as he bent forward to take her hand. Their eyes met; her eyelids fluttered as she smiled. As they moved into the main room she asked polite questions, expressing interest in him.

Servants outfitted in black dresses adorned with lacy white frills mingled with the guests, carrying trays of pickled hams, chicken legs, potatoes, and an assortment of wines. The conversation was polite and pleasant. Most of the guests mingled, attempting to make others aware of their presence.

The sounds of a Viennese waltz came from the salon. Sated with food and drink, the guests now retired to the giant salon. Sitting facing each other in a large irregular circle, the atmosphere became solemn. This was the time when serious talk about matters of great importance took place. Here the crucial decisions affecting Danzig were discussed.

Gretchen seated herself next to Zishe. He watched her hands, so delicate and expressive, stroking her long blonde hair distractedly. She looked lost, a bewildered, innocent expression on her face, as if she too felt out of place.

The talk in Danzig and in all of Germany was about the emerging political crisis. In the national election on July 31, 1932, the Nazi Party led by Hitler had garnered 230 seats. Although not a majority, his opponents, lacking sufficient unity, had been forced to establish a coalition government. They'd agreed to accept Hitler as chancellor on January 30, 1933. Danzig, being a free city, was not affected directly, but was still impacted by the election.

Herr Dr. Kunzler, a physician and proud official of the National Socialist German's Worker's local party, broke the ice, saying, "Germany is going back to her roots. A pure, Aryan Germany is rising again. Germany has been undermined, her nose rubbed in the dirt too long. And by whom?" He angrily answered his own question. "By the Bolsheviks, masterminded by international Jewry."

Heads nodded. Herr Weiss was also agreeing. Dr. Kunzler continued. "Germany's defeat in nineteen-eighteen could have been prevented if it weren't for the Jewish traitors inside the German Reich. German culture must be pure, unadulterated by Jews."

As if he had totally forgotten his origin, Herr Weiss said, "Very insightful Herr Doctor."

Dr. Kunzler went on to give a discourse on how various scientific works could be used to conclude the superiority of the Aryan race and the inferiority of the Jews. When he was

48

finally finished, someone stood up and began applauding; others joined.

Zishe could understand the poor Ukrainian and Polish peasants, uneducated, illiterate, and superstitious, goaded on by priests and governments, believing this. But these were doctors, lawyers, university professors, products of the German *Aufklarung,* acting out their anti-Semitism.

Out of the corner of his eye he could see Gretchen. She was still seated as he was. Her hands hung listlessly in her lap, her gaze distant and her face contorted. Zishe thought she looked like she was ashamed of what she was hearing.

Everyone sat back down and the glasses were filled with French liqueur poured from crystal decanters. Zishe smiled and Gretchen, surprised by the strange look in his eyes, leaned over to him and whispered something about the weather. There was too much noise to be heard, so Zishe moved his chair even closer. They soon were conversing enthusiastically, oblivious of their surroundings.

"The weather here is different than in Vienna," he said, whispering in her ear. He could smell her perfume and see her smooth, beautiful skin.

"Colder or warmer?" she said, her lips close to his.

"Colder, especially when the winds from the Baltic blow," he said, "but it's refreshing just the same." He felt like kissing her. "You must read a lot with so many books around." Zishe gestured toward the large library in the adjoining room.

"Yes, I love to read. Do you?" she said, pausing to brush the hair from her eyes.

Zishe noticed how blue her eyes appeared, as though they were reflecting the light from the chandelier.

"Heinrich Heine. His poems stir me so. Shakespeare, Tolstoy, Dostoevsky, Dickens, London—" she continued without waiting for his answer. Her voice was breathless and excited. "And you?" she asked.

"Balzac, Stendhal, Twain, and everyone you mentioned," he said. "Philosophy, religion—do they interest you?"

"Not always. They are too much like politics. So argumentative. Words cannot prove anything about God or the universe," she said, laughing.

Gretchen's hand was touching his. Zishe was delighted she didn't try to move away. He could tell she was drawn to him. He knew he could fall in love with her.

"I like to read the Bible," she said, her fingers rubbing against his. "The stories affect me so. I find that book very satisfying."

"All of it?" he said, puzzled.

"Everything, from Adam to Jesus. After all, it's God's word. I believe what is written in it. To me it speaks the truth," she said, her eyes radiating joy.

The voice of Pastor Gluck interrupted their reverie, and everyone in the room again became attentive. His white collar, black clothes, and gray hair gave him a look of piety.

"Being a churchman," he said, "I can only speak with expertise on theological matters. But since religion encompasses man's body as well as his soul, I can't help but agree wholeheartedly with Herr Doctor Kunzler's conclusions. The Jews are and have always been our enemy." He paused. "Chancellor Hitler has wisely stated, 'In standing against the Jew, I am defending the handiwork of the Lord.' And as he so valiantly fights for our Germany wearing, as he states, 'a sword rather than a crown of thorns so that I can drive the Jewish capitalists from the temple of the Lord.' We must join him in the battle. Our Fuhrer's devotion to our Lord is evident. He has said, 'The task Christ began, but did not finish, I will complete.'"

He then quoted from the book of Acts. Stephen's speech to the Jews. "'You stiff-necked people with uncircumcised hearts and ears, you are just like your fathers. You always resist the Holy Spirit. Was there ever a prophet your fathers did not persecute? They even killed those who predicted the coming of the Righteous One, and now you have murdered and betrayed him.' Need I say more?"

Pastor Gluck gazed curiously at the group as if to remember if he had forgotten anything important. "Not having been content to kill our God, they have dared to insinuate, to fabricate, that he was a Jew." He sighed. "How stupid. Do not the scriptures tell us simply, plainly that Jesus said, 'Before Abraham was born I am.' And if Abraham was the first Jew, and Jesus who is God came before Abraham, then God certainly is no Jew. Why, may I ask, did God send from heaven Jesus Christ among the Jews? Because," he said, answering his own question, "knowing their true nature as the incarnation of evil, He chose them above all others to accomplish His great plan of atonement and redemption so we would be saved by His sacrifice."

Pastor Gluck beamed proudly. "But who is a Jew?" Without waiting for an answer, he said, "A Jew is one who has Jewish blood. But as a leopard cannot change his spots, no Jew can accept Christ. His father, the devil, whose blood runs in him, will never allow him to declare the beautiful and lovely words, 'Christ, I love you. I believe in you with all my heart.' The only time he utters Christ's name is to profane him, to blaspheme him, to utter his name in vain."

Pastor Gluck continued. "If someone is taught he is a Jew, but bravely converts and accepts the living Christ, then truly he never was a Jew and could not have even a trace of Jewish blood, but by deception was abducted as many of our precious children were, and made to think that he was born that way. But Christ said, 'You did not choose me but I chose you.... No one can come to me unless the Father who sent me draws it.... For I have come down from heaven...to do the will of Him who sent me and I shall name all that He has given me.'

"So you see, dear beloved, someone who accepts the living Christ was never a Jew. As Paul says in Ephesians, 'For He chose us in Him before the creation of the world.'" Pastor Gluck sat down.

The guests were moved by Pastor Gluck's reverence. Zishe glanced over to see a look of relief on Herr Weiss's face. Zishe was accustomed to the ugliness of the speaker's philosophy. He'd grown up hearing a variety of this talk. At public schools he'd had to listen to the story of the Christ killers—how villainous they were and how Jesus had suffered so because of them. The teachers' fingers would always point accusingly at the few Jewish students, indicting them for the terrible crime of their ancestors. On those days, the taunts and blows would be particularly vicious and brutal.

Zishe listened for a while longer as the rhetoric continued then politely left. But he couldn't forget the evening. The speeches were pompous, terrible, and dull, but Gretchen was alive, vivacious. She filled his thoughts, frozen in that moment they'd first looked at each other. It was only a instant, but her pretty innocence had captivated him. He knew he could never see her socially—her mother would put a stop to that. Zishe was her husband's employee and a Jew. Even if her mother didn't know, Weiss did and that would never do. And yet, the way she looked at him, the way their eyes kept meeting it was as if they were renewing some solemn vow made in another time.... He shook his head to bring himself back to reality.

Gretchen began to make trips to her father's business, ostensibly to see the latest fashions. Although brief, these visits kept the flame alive. On one such occasion, Zishe asked her in the most casual of manner if she would like to take a walk with him on Sunday. He was as surprised by his sudden invitation as she herself seemed to be. They agreed to meet in a park near the Mariakirsche, where she attended church every Sunday.

Still somewhat unfamiliar with the winding Danzig streets, Zishe miscalculated and arrived at the park late. She was already there, seated in an alcove under a tree, dressed in a long, navy blue dress.

She hadn't seen Zishe coming. Startled, she said, "Goodness, you frightened me. I must have been looking in the wrong direction."

Zishe stood motionless, staring at her as if she was unreal.

"Does the cat have your tongue?" she said, laughing. It broke the silence.

"No, nothing like that," he said, sitting down beside her. "I don't have much time. I have to be at mass soon."

Zishe raised his hand and gently stroked her cheek. She showed no surprise, touching his caressing hand.

"Do you have a religion?" Gretched said.

"I once did," he replied, "but that was long ago." He was glad when she asked no more because he didn't want to lie.

"Are you going to church alone?"

"Yes," she replied. Sensing his desire she said, "Would you like to come with me?"

He hesitated, then nodded. They walked, each wrapped in thought, oblivious to the light sprinkle of snow. Zishe felt at peace with her, feeling no need to break the silence.

They followed the pavement leading into the Mariakirsche Plaza. Zishe had forgotten how high and mighty the steeple was. It had been a long time since, as a tourist, he had visited a cathedral. He had forgotten how the stained-glass windows set into the masonry and inlaid with religious figures always affected him. He entered the church with Gretchen at his side. Up the winding column of steps, through the massive doorway, the vaulted, cavernous ceiling accentuated the cross on the altar.

Bach's cantata, *Sweet Jesus,* sung by the boy's choir filled the building. Zishe followed Gretchen's lead, crossing himself, genuflecting with one knee and holding his palms together. She bowed her head, repeating the "Our Father," "Hail Mary," and "Glory Be" prayers. Her fingers followed the beads of her rosary.

Zishe's lips didn't move, his head remained unbowed. He had done as much as he could. He remembered the synagogue in Warsaw, the menorah, the gilded Holy Arc, and the Torah inside. He could imagine the balcony with the women overhead, the arch-shaped, stained-glass windows with their Magen Davids casting a colored shadow on the yarmulkes below. The cantor's sad, pleading voice and the response of the people.

Except for the crosses of Jesus, the stone figures of the Madonna and saints, and the Latin chants, the splendor was the same. Despite the differences, despite the centuries of fight and strife, he felt the same intense longing here for the invisible presence of God.

He watched Gretchen's face as she rose and joined the procession to the altar to receive communion. She looked back and smiled at him. She was an angel. He smiled back. Zishe wondered how she could have such an otherworldly appearance and still be fully aware of everything around her.

Zishe stood up and walked toward the rear of the cathedral. He knew the communion would be long and he was restless. He looked at the oil canvases on the walls that depicted Jesus, the Madonna, and the apostles. They were predictable and overdone, frozen figures showing off the painter's skillful palette but lacking in life and realism. Situated near the rear were small statues of religious figures in various poses. He walked distractedly among them.

Almost hidden in a dark, sheltered alcove, one statue caught his eye. It was a very simple carving of dark, knotted oak, gnarled and roughly polished. The eyes stared at Zishe. It was gaunt, sinewy, its ribs clearly outlined though covered with a tattered coat. Outstretched arms with upward palms and the proud head with its long straight hair pointed straight ahead.

Tears rolled from Zishe's eyes. He had seen this man before. The name Petlura arose from his past. The paralyzing fear came alive all over again.

His mother Miriam's calming words repeated, "Quiet, stay still, my babies, they'll be gone soon." Zishe huddled with Lonka in the storage room deep in the basement. They heard screaming, horrible cries, hooves beating, vicious laughter, and the sound of whips. "*Jid, Jid,* take this in memory, take this, you bloodsuckers, you filthy swine." His hands, covering his ears, blocked out the deafening madness.

Then the screaming stopped, the hoof beats grew dimmer. They arose, helping each other stumble up the stairs together. The rooms were in shambles. The soldiers had taken all the valuables, destroying the rest. The silver candlesticks handed down for generations were gone. The Tenach, the holy scriptures, the commentaries, the Talmud, all were burned. The bonfire still smoldered in the middle of the room. Proskurov was finished. The Petlurists had done their job well. The dead were everywhere, mutilated. Heads without bodies, abdomens, genitals, breasts, arms, and legs were scattered about, adorning the landscape outside. A few souls wandered aimlessly, searching the ruins.

The synagogue was still burning when Zishe and his sister went to look at it. A man with a mad idiot's grin stood outside holding the Torah heroically, his clothes smoldering. He stood straight and tall. Blood streamed from the cuts the whips had made, and his arms stretched outward, palms up, begging God to remember the dead, crying out the words of the Kaddish. No one knew his name for he was not of their village, but he was not forgotten. As the story was remembered and retold, he was always there when the massacre was the worst, where the blows and lashes were the fiercest. He had come to help. He was said to be a *Lamed-vov*, a Just Man, bearing the griefs and pains.

The sculptor who carved this figure touched on the essence of the person he was trying to portray. How could he know about the Proskurov, about the Just Man? What was this carving doing in a church?

Zishe was too absorbed to notice Gretchen at his side until she reached up and touched her kerchief to a tear in the corner of his eye. He took her hand and brought it to his lips to kiss. He put his arms around her and she kissed his cheek. They stood still, embracing.

"Who is this?" Zishe said, nodding at the figure.

"Jesus," she replied.

Now accustomed to the shadows, Zishe read the carefully carved inscription on the base. "'I tell you the truth. Whatever you did for one of the least of these brothers of mine you did for me.'" Further down, the inscription continued, "'For I was hungry and you gave me something to eat, I was thirsty and you gave me something to drink, I was a stranger and you invited me in, I needed clothes and you clothed me, I was sick and you looked after me, I was imprisoned and you came to visit me.'"

Zishe knew the words "brother of mine" were for his fellow Jews. "Whatever you did for the least of these you did for me" could only be the words of a *Lamed-vov.*

"I didn't recognize him," Zishe said. "He is not like the rest." He motioned with his head toward the many crosses with the hanging Jesuses. He couldn't explain to her what was going on inside him. The figure revealed to him that, deep inside, he would always remain a Jew.

They stood staring at the figure in silence for some time.

"Zishe," Gretchen said, finally breaking the silence, "I have to go."

"Ah, yes," he said. "Your mother will worry."

She started walking away, and, turning as if to say goodbye, she said instead, "I love you, Zishe. I just wanted you to know."

He watched her walk away through the entrance door, down the steps, onto the plaza, where she turned onto the path that lead away from the church and disappeared from his view.

He couldn't move, he couldn't call after her. He wanted to reply, to tell her that he loved her too, but he was afraid. She didn't know he was a Jew. He fought the urge to follow her, to tell her everything. He stood there, staring at the *Lamed-vov.* It rekindled his desire to see Yosi again. They had not seen each other since the incident with the brownshirts, and Zishe, now feeling guilty for avoiding Yosi, wanted to make amends. It was hard pretending not to be a Jew. He was constantly on guard. His dreams were troubled with images of exposure, ridicule, and betrayal. He wondered now if Yosi was angry at him for abandoning him. Has Yosi disowned me? Does he consider me a disgrace to our people? he wondered.

This was absurd. I'm still a Jew, he told himself. I may be a Jew in hiding, but I'm not a convert.

✡ CHAPTER THREE

Zishe was disappointed and surprised he couldn't find Yosi among the local Jewish emigrants. Yosi had moved several times, going from job to job, burning his bridges behind him. Every clue to his whereabouts led nowhere, every hunch just another faulty guess.

Life returned to the pleasant comfort of work, parties, and an ever-growing circle of friends and contacts. Zishe stopped thinking of Yosi or his past. He was accepted and honored as an Austrian and treated as a rising star in Danzig's inner circles because of his association with Weiss. His skills were rewarded with increased responsibilities. Being the instigator and chief architect of the business' recent successful expansion to the suburbs of Langfuhr, Suppot, and Oliva, Weiss seriously contemplated taking Zishe into the business as a partner.

It was a hot day and the usual Baltic breeze that cooled the city refused to appear. Summer had indeed come early, with the tourists adding to the already overcrowded conditions. There were heated debates everywhere about Hitler and the Third Reich. Slogans were plastered on every wall calling for a defense of hereditary rights.

Zishe had the day off and decided to go to a particularly beautiful park, Vald, on the outskirts of the city where it would be cooler. He wanted to be alone with his thoughts. Walking quickly, his mind was preoccupied with business.

He thought he heard voices singing to the beat of a band. The sound, which was coming from a street over the hill, grew louder. He could not yet recognize the tune, but it was definitely purposeful and political. He disliked these exhibitions. They were meaningless, accomplishing nothing. He dismissed them as children's games for adults. He changed his course to avoid the parade.

It was too late. A red flag broke the horizon, holstered to the belt of the leader. The rest of the marchers followed straight behind, rows and rows of people blocking any attempt at escape. He had to wait and watch them pass by. They were singing *The International,* the Communist anthem. "Arise you prisoners of starvation /Arise you wretched of the earth /A bright new dawn is awakening." Such a beautiful song. Haven't I heard enough of it in Ukraine and Poland? Zishe wondered.

They held banners, posters with pictures of Marx, Lenin, Stalin, Toegler, engraved with slogans, "Workers of the World Unite," "Down with Hitler," "Down with Capitalism," and "Long Live Socialism." He was trapped. He had to waste his time watching this garish display of spectacular nothingness.

Marching on the far left, wearing dark trousers, a white short-sleeved shirt, and a red sash across his chest, shouting and singing, was Yosi.

Zishe could not believe his eyes. Yosi looked younger, leaner. He no longer had the long, dark curly hair with the side locks. He had a proud, determined look instead of his former innocence. He waved, but Yosi didn't recognize him; he, too, had changed.

The singing climbed steadily to a climax that announced the coming emancipation of the world. Then confusion disrupted the ranks. A few voices sang out-of-sync. The band faded out as the singers self-consciously dropped out one by one.

The marchers turned in the direction of another parade, the sound of another song, the words still inaudible but growing steadily in force. It was the Horst Wessel song of the Sturmabteilung, the SA, the brownshirts. The red communist flag stopped waving. It was held rigidly in anticipation of the signal to continue.

A loudspeaker boomed above the confusion. "Comrades, hold your heads high, show the fascists that the workers of the world are united and can fight."

A whistle blew. The drums rolled and the marching began again. They were now in full swing, a thundering chorus, inspired, refreshed, launching into their repertoire of songs and rushing onward to meet their challenge.

The Communists were good at talk and intellectual debates, but when battles came they were always unprepared. Zishe's mind drifted back to Poland. He'd seen these flag-waving demonstrations all too often. His father was what they called a *Verbrente Rote*, a burning red. He never could resist a red-bannered communist parade. He was full of talk about worker's paradises and worker's rights, and he was always drawn into someone else's fight.

The day was May 1, 1920. The call for revolution was everywhere. Poland was aflame with red banners, soapbox orators, and parades. His father had taken to them as a moth to a flame, always coming back bruised and burned.

He took Zishe aside and said, "I promise you with all my heart this day you will always remember. It will be the start of a new era." He'd put his hands tenderly around Zishe's face. "This is the day the workers of Poland will arise. Say nothing, just watch. I know it from the highest authority." His tone had been hushed and very secretive.

He'd smiled. There was excitement in his eyes as he'd tried to describe the paradise on earth that was full of love— united, classless. It would be free of wars, anti-Semitism, and starvation. Zishe could still hear his father's words ringing in his ears as he prepared to march off to his brigade. "Zishela, you will be proud of your father. You will see the workers of Poland arise, joined by their comrades in Germany, Rumania, Hungary, and the whole world." And his father finished by kissing him good-bye and saying, "Today the revolution begins."

Zishe would always remember his mother crying when she heard how the Polish Army had massacred the Communists. He himself had cried when his father came home one year later, tortured beyond recognition, insane. He'd come home to die.

And now it was happening again. In unison, the stormtroopers stepped around the corner and the brownshirts chanted their oath of blood and death. They came onto the avenue, a sea of swastika-emblazoned arms with whips, batons, knives, and guns, ready for battle. Shouts of "Jewish blood will pour" were hurled sarcastically at the Communists.

Zishe was caught between the two groups. The avenue was blocked by the oncoming Nazis, leaving him no escape. Police on either side waited. Spectators eager for the fight crowded into windows and doorways. Zishe kept looking for Yosi.

A shot rang out and the red flag went down, blood oozing from the leader's head. The Reds, in confusion, scattered. Sharply executing orders, the brownshirts fell in, forming phalanxes. Batons and whips spearheaded the assault. Like lions, the brownshirts singled out their prey, one by one.

The spectators cheered and egged them on. "Kill the bloody Bolsheviks. Crucify them." They laughed at the jumping, dancing feet frantically dodging the whips.

Just as Zishe had expected, the police stepped in when it was over. There were several dead and many were injured, some severely. Blood was everywhere.

The stormtroopers, hands outstretched in the Nazi salute, held their heads high. "*Heil* Hitler" on their lips, they marched away with new vigor.

Then Zishe spotted him. Yosi was leaning against a doorway, his eyes half closed, a pretty comrade sobbing in his arms. He was injured, but not badly so, with just a few bruises on his face and arms.

"Yosi," Zishe barely could say the word. "Yosi, Yosi, it's me, Zishe."

Yosi's bloodshot eyes looked up at Zishe suspiciously.

"Zishe," he said, barely audible. "Zishe," he repeated, distorting his lips to exaggerate that familiar name, as if to remember its feeling.

Zishe knew he had to get Yosi out of there. He placed his arm behind Yosi's back, supporting his body and gently helping him stand up straight. Yosi's pretty comrade was still clinging to him so desperately Zishe had to carry the weight of both of them.

"Where do you live?" Zishe asked.

Ambulances were picking up the dead and wounded, while the street sweepers were busy cleaning up the battle's debris. The police were asking questions, ready to take Reds under any pretext. Zishe struggled under the weight and maneuvered slowly, trying to keep a low profile.

Yosi was still weak, but becoming more coherent. "Turn left when you come to the next doorway where it leads down into the cellar."

They moved down the steps, past an open iron gate, leading to an oak door hidden behind stacks of empty barrels. "It's open," the girl murmured.

The door barely budged, creaking and groaning as it finally gave in to a shove. Except for the light shining through the iron grating above, the room was in total darkness. The girl skillfully guided them across the room up to a paneled wall.

"Stand right here." She motioned to a spot a little further down. "Be very still."

She tapped on the wall in code. A hushed voice came from the wall. "Yes?"

"It's Marcia," she replied. "From the Gorky Unit." The wall panel opened just wide enough to let the three in.

Once in the room, Marcia addressed everyone, gesticulating with animation. "What bad luck. We weren't properly prepared. They knew exactly where we'd be. It was an ambush. With no guns, no batons—we were defenseless, stupid clowns!" Her voice had become shrill.

"Shush, quiet. They will hear us," several admonished in quiet tones.

Zishe led Yosi to an empty cot and helped him sit down.

"So let them. What're you so afraid of?" Her voice boomed. Zishe could see the fire in her eyes reflected in the faint light. "You're spineless bourgeois, intellectual weaklings. The revolution won't be won with the likes of you."

She was obviously the leader and no one dared oppose her. Zishe could see at least a dozen people in the room, on cots and on the floor. They were a sorry lot, taking the scolding like meek naughty tots.

Yosi, raising himself from his cot, turned to Zishe. "This is my dear friend Zishe," he introduced. "Zishe, we need guns, knives, clubs; without these we will never succeed." He said it as if Zishe could get those for them. "As Karl Marx said, 'Socialism cannot be brought into existence without revolution...then Socialism can toss aside all the political veils.... Only by dissolving class and classes, will the Proletariat emancipate itself, without which there cannot be the total redemption of society.'"

Zishe thought about how often he'd seen Yosi before with that ecstasy in his eyes. Their villages in the Pale were often ravaged by armed bands, rampaging hordes bent on revenge, leaving Jewish villages devastated in their wake.

And then rumors would start that the Holy One, Blessed Be His Name, was alive and waiting for the right moment when He would bring about the redemption of the world. Some said He was in seclusion, meditating on the special combinations of the sacred Hebrew letters and their numbers. Others said He was with the Ten Lost Tribes, living in splendor with the angels on the other side of the Great Samhatyon River.

One such rumor had taken hold of their little village when a woman came with news that the Messiah was in Israel. It was said that by further piety, by observing the laws with devotion, his coming could be accelerated. She said that Jews in Frankfurt, Prague, and Berlin were fasting, praying, lying naked in the snow, preparing themselves for passage to the Holy Land to greet the Messiah. Zishe and Yosi had believed and celebrated. The lame danced, the dumb sang, the blind saw. Sorrows, miseries, regrets were forgotten. Yosi's eyes filled with ecstasy as he prepared for the Holy One.

Now Yosi said, "We must stop acting like Jews who never defend themselves, who cower timidly and hide. We must work hard to expunge any *petit* bourgeois tendencies that have clung to us in the past. We must adopt the worker's values if we are to lead the proletariat. There is to be only one class. Religion is the product of the capitalists, a tool to keep the worker's nose to the grindstone."

Zishe knew Yosi was quoting Marx. He wished Yosi well, but he knew they'd chosen different paths. At least I have nothing to be sorry for, Zishe thought. Yosi is denying his Jewishness by merging into a homogeneous Proletariat. I'm still a Jew, even if I'm hiding it.

He had no regrets when he left Yosi.

Zishe had enough of heroics and politics and too much seriousness. a good part of the day was already wasted, but he would not let that get in his way. He was determined now to lose himself in something frivolous, and he thought of the casino at Soppot. Nothing could distract and amuse him as much as gambling. He inspected the money neatly stashed away in his wallet to see if there was enough to spare. All he needed now was someone silly to join him in some harmless fun. He immediately thought of Heinrich.

Heinrich was Gretchen's brother. He was a good sport and he liked Zishe. And he always seemed to have money burning a hole in his pocket. Zishe headed straight to Heinrich's.

"Hello, Zishe." Heinrich was beaming, standing at the door. "What a pleasant surprise. Boy, am I glad you dropped in. Take a look at me." Heinrich twirled around, showing off the uniform he'd acquired.

"You look fierce." Zishe suppressed a laugh, trying to appreciate Heinrich's new look.

"I've joined the Sturmabteilung. I'm a stormtrooper." Standing at attention, his pudgy waist encircled by a thick black belt, he looked like a cocky goon.

"How about going to Soppot to have some fun with me?" Zishe didn't want to waste time on formalities.

"Great. I'll be able to wear my uniform." He laughed. "That will scare all of the little Jews."

Zishe found himself laughing along with Heinrich. He really couldn't help it, Heinrich looked so ridiculous.

The taxi driver smiled when they got in his cab—probably expecting a large tip, Zishe thought. Soppot was quite far from Langfuhr. The driver's face was full of pride as he glanced at his passengers. "Heinrich, Herr Holtz," he said, his voice filled with excitement. "What an honor to be of service to such distinguished gentlemen." He stood at attention. a quick salute "*Heil* Hitler" established the effect that Heinrich's new clothes had on the driver. If they only knew, Zishe thought. A Jew, a cab driver, and a half-Jewish stormtrooper. He burst out laughing at the thought. Then the other two started to laugh. The taxi was weaving, just missing the doors of the cars at its side. They laughed so hard at the sight of each other that they could not stop, even when they were stopped by the *Danziger Polizei.*

Pulling over to the curb, the policeman looked in and shouted, "What the hell is the matter?"

"Nothing, nothing," stuttered the driver. Zishe thought he'd better stop thinking about this joke to avoid impending disaster.

But Heinrich was having too much fun, paying no attention to the desperate signals from Zishe and the cab driver. "*Heil* Hitler," he said.

The police noticed Heinrich at last. "*Heil* Hitler, *Heil* Hitler," came the reply.

Heinrich, hearing his dear Fuhrer's name in such a forceful and frightening tone, stopped suddenly, shocked and delighted at the respect now given to him. "*Heil* Hitler," he repeated, the police clearing a path for them all the way to the casino.

Happy they were not in trouble, Zishe let out a sigh of relief as the valet rushed to greet these distinguished patrons and release them from the confines of the small cab. The driver refused the tip, saying, "I have already been honored." He bowed, clicked his heels, returned the money and said, "For the Fatherland, long live Hitler."

Zishe jumped out. Heinrich followed, now in his glory. Zishe noticed his friend's resemblance to the Fuhrer. Heinrich came out strutting like the hero he was supporting.

What a palace, thought Zishe, inspecting the grounds and the magnificent edifice. Hedges were trimmed to suggest animals and trees.

"This is my lucky day," Heinrich said. "I can always tell when I'm going to have a winning streak."

They walked together on the plush red carpet winding gracefully around Greek and Roman statues.

Zishe overheard the sharp remarks of an argument taking place at the entrance gate. "But we have been patrons here for so many years," a woman pleaded to a guard. She wore a fur-lined hat with matching coat, diamond earrings, and gold bracelets. "There must be some misunderstanding, some mistake." The man beside her wore a stylish hamburg hat; his distinguished gray hair gave him the look of a man used to power.

"I am sorry, Herr Klein, but I am only following orders." The guard was now quite irritated, "And if you will look at the sign, it says you aren't welcome here." The guard turned his back to Klein.

"What sign? What sort of ridiculous rules are you supposed to be enforcing? I came here to play and to dine."

Klein sounded angry and puzzled. He turned to his wife. "These impossible swine with their orders." He swung around, screaming, "orders, orders, orders," in ever-louder tones until he reached the huge gilded entrance, opening the door himself. "I'll show them who they are dealing with—everyone knows my power and my reputation. I'll have the job of that fool in uniform, who displays such an absolute ignorance of proper etiquette," he said angrily as he stormed into the game room.

The guests, distracted by chatting and betting at their games, did not notice the madman in their midst at first. "Concierge, concierge," he shouted, pacing like a lion in a zoo. It took but a moment, but suddenly a ring of guards surrounded him, the concierge directing the guards without saying a word. Upward he was hoisted, hands securely fastened to his shoulders, head and feet poised and balanced. He was quickly thrown right out of the room.

His wife rushed over. "You murderers, you murderers," she said as she tried to raise him, but he defiantly refused. He was not hurt, but he seemed unwilling to give up his dignity.

The guard who tried to stop him earlier now told him, "If you should ever show your face around here again, I will personally with great satisfaction blacken it." He pushed Klein's face right into the sign. "Read this sign so there can be no chance I am misunderstood."

Her husband still in a state of confusion, Frau Klein was the first to see the sign. It was on a post with a swastika.

"It says 'Jews are not wanted here,'" she said in surprise.

"Garbage," Klein replied. "This is all a great big misunderstanding." His face was lifting into a smile. "We are Germans, an old and proud family. We fought in all the great wars." Addressing both his wife and the guard, he said, "This sign is for the *ost Juden*—the east Jews. The eastern Jews are our misfortune."

Zishe knew this could only mean the start of a new wave of hatred. Too bad these two don't understand that none of us is immune to this old hatred, he thought. Instead, they blame it on the poor eastern Jew.

"*Funf gulden* on black," Zishe said, placing the chips on the map. "First spin to win means good luck," he joked. He watched the ball bounce, teeter, and roll into the right spot.

"Twenty-three black," called out the croupier, repeating the same in French, English, Italian, and Hindi.

"Well done," remarked Heinrich as he sat down beside him. Heinrich placed ten *gulden* on number ten.

Zishe was amazed at the risk his friend took. *"Haus,"* the croupier called. Everyone lost except the one man who bet with the house, but he had hedged his position by scattering his bets all over the board.

"This is my game," bragged Zishe, and he upped the ante doubling his chips on the black. "Ten on black."

Again luck was with him. Time after time, whether the numbers were odd or even, black or red, his money always happened to be on the right spot.

Heinrich now followed Zishe's lead. They had to ask for additional trays to hold their winnings. Zishe forgot everything—his work and his worries. He was intent on only three things: the ball, the wheel, and the winning bet. He thrived on the suspense of the wheel's turning and the croupier's calling.

"Ein hundert gulden on lucky seven," Zishe said, piling the chips high and crowding out all around him. The table was now surrounded with a crowd of spectators as the word of this game spread through the casino.

"Sieben rote—seven red." An extended cheer came from the crowd and the croupier advanced the money. Heinrich was so delighted with Zishe's winnings he ordered drinks for everyone in the room.

"You'll break the bank yet," someone said.

"Funf hundert gulden funfzehn," called Zishe, and Heinrich immediately followed.

"Excuse me, my honored gentlemen," the man behind the wheel stuttered, "but you have reached the house limit, and I can't take your next bet until I check with our management."

The crowd slowly drifted away. Zishe thought he heard a change of music. It was quite unusual. The tympanies were booming, the symbols clanging, and the brasses trumpeting. Soon he realized it was the familiar *Horst Wessel Lied.* "Wen Juden blut spricht von messer*—when Jewish blood pours from the knife's point..."

Like a fire spreading, leaping from room to room, the people responded to the catchy tune. *"Heil* Hitler, long live the Fuhrer," they shouted, and they raised their glasses to drink to the party entering. Banners came from nowhere with welcoming praises to Hitler, Goebbels, Goering, and their party. The roulette and baccarat tables were abandoned by the guests and the staff. They lined up to get a better view while the concierge, the waiters, and the administration led the patrons to form a pathway for the important party. The domed conference room was soon crowded to capacity with the patrons of the two dozen gambling rooms. Zishe and Heinrich decided to join them, pressing themselves into the back of the room.

The clapping started as the officials in black uniforms paraded proudly into view. One by one they filed past the crowd, smiling and saluting. They proceeded to the specially constructed stage positioned strategically, under a swastika and a giant picture of the Fuhrer. Taking their seats, they waved to the thundering applause of an adoring audience.

"Honorable ladies and gentlemen," the head of the casino said, "I want to thank you from the bottom of my heart for the kind reception you are giving to the government." Applause and cheers went up throughout the room. "Unfortunately, due to the treaty forced on us by the traitors among us, Danzig was isolated and separated from our dear, beloved Germany." With his hands extended he calmed down the room. "Today you will be privileged to hear a solution to this unfortunate situation. Again, I thank you from the bottom of my heart. I will let the delegation tell you exactly what is happening and what we are to do. The next speaker, of course, is well known and dearly beloved, and without further ado I give you Herr Doctor Joseph Goebbels, Hitler's personal minister of propaganda."

A standing ovation greeted the small, slight man who walked with a limp. He waited patiently for the acclamation to end, scrutinizing everyone in the house.

"I have a message," he said, "from our Fuhrer, Chancellor Hitler, given personally to me to deliver to you. Our Fuhrer wants you and all German-speaking pure Aryans to know that wherever they live, whether in Austria, Sudetenland, Czechoslovakia, Poland, or Danzig, he considers himself personally responsible for each and every one of you." The applause was brusquely waved aside. "We know that, living outside the laws of our nation, you are at a disadvantage, but you can still follow the examples we provide. Stop treating Jews like human beings. Single them out, isolate them, just like you would a terrible disease. Marriage between Jews and Gentiles is out, and sexual relations are strictly forbidden. No Jew can be a German national or fly a German flag, and citizenship is out of the question."

He paused to drink some water. "Kick them out of your churches. There must be no taint of Jewish blood in our schools, governments, or organizations. There is no such thing as a German Jew. There can be no Jewish music, no Jewish books, and certainly no Jewish teachers in Germany. Give them the iron boot and burn all of their filthy possessions." He held up a sign. "'Germans be aware, do not buy from Jews.' We have placed these placards on all Jewish places with a Star of David in yellow and black to warn our population that dealing with Jews is stabbing the Fatherland in the back." He lowered his glance and moved even closer. "I urge you to follow our example. In Germany we have given the freedom to arrest any Jew to our heroic *geheime staatspolizei*—our gestapo. Your laws don't provide for it, but you can still organize and establish special units to provide that service for you.

"In Germany we have already begun the process of eliminating Jewry. Most of our towns and villages, we are proud to announce, are *Juden rein*. I urge you most strongly to hire no Jewish employees. We are rapidly imposing legal restrictions on Jews taking part in the trade industry."

Zishe remembered hearing of the wholesale appropriation of Jewish businesses.

"An individual's worth to the community is measured by his or her racial personality," Goebbels said. "Only a racially valuable person has a right to exist in the community. A racially impure individual must be eliminated. We must segregate Jews even in our schools. Please, dear people of Danzig, above all, do not allow your children to sit next to Jewish school children. They should be placed in a different part of the room."

✡ CHAPTER FOUR

Goebbels's speech was a tremendous success. Heinrich left to get autographs from the officials roaming about the rooms.

"Hello, Zishe." He felt a hand on his shoulder. He turned around to see Gretchen. Her face was even prettier than he remembered.

"What are you doing here? You surprised me."

"I came here with my dear friend, Freida, and her husband. They were nice enough to ask me to join them for an outing, and it has been rather a long time since I've been to the casino." She looked at him searchingly. "Don't you smile anymore?" she asked.

"Yes, of course." He relaxed his guarded expression to show her how pleased he was to see her. "You caught me in an off moment. I was listening to Doctor Goebbels and my mind was wandering."

"Are you here alone?"

"No," he said, "I'm with your brother, Heinrich. He was just here a little while ago."

"Hello, Gretchen," Heinrich said, returning. "Look what I've collected." He showed them the autographs of at least a dozen dignitaries. "Did you know that Zishe here is quite a gambler? He nearly broke the house."

Zishe acted as if to deny it.

"That's wonderful, Zishe. Congratulations."

The dance band had again started playing. "Would you like to dance?"

"I'd like that," she said, smiling. They both excused themselves and worked their way through the crowd.

The ballroom was charming, modeled after the great houses of the eighteenth century. It had a gilded ceiling, crystal chandeliers, and purple velvet curtains draped over large open windows offering a splendid view of the sea. The first dance was a Viennese waltz from Strauss's *Die Fledermaus.* Zishe took Gretchen in his arms, holding her firmly.

"I'm sorry I scared you off when you last saw me," Gretchen said.

"What do you mean?" Zishe asked, although he knew to what she was referring.

"Because I told you I loved you. I really shouldn't have said that."

"It was flattering, although it did scare me a little," Zishe conceded.

"I thought it did," she said.

"But you really don't know me." Zishe struggled to find the right words. "Times are unstable. I don't know what will come of it—or me."

"They say you're from Austria and you will someday be quite rich. But I don't think anyone knows you. There's something in you that frightens me, but I'm drawn to you."

"No one knows my past, and I prefer it that way. It makes life easier. But don't be afraid of me." Zishe hadn't spoken so seriously to anyone for a long time. It scared him to even open up this much.

It was nearly midnight. The concierge announced the last dance. The singer sang the haunting tune, *Lily Marlene,* a song that had begun in Germany during World War I. Zishe sang along, holding Gretchen closer. He felt the words and the music go down to the deep, hidden places where Gretchen touched him. His lips reached for hers and she responded. But then he pulled away and distanced himself. He had so much to tell her, but he was very afraid. He held Gretchen close and continued dancing with her. If she only knew how much I love her, he thought wistfully. The music cast its spell over him and he forgot his worries.

Later that evening, Zishe went home and looked at the letter from his sister again. He'd received it several weeks before. It reminded him where he really belonged. It was sad, but hopeful. He read it aloud yet again to himself, letting his lips relish the sweet sound of Yiddish.

Dear Zishe,

I hope and pray that all is well with you, as do Rebecca, Sarah, Joseph, Rifka, and Zindel. I wish I could send you good news, that everything is all right and that we are prosperous and contented. I postponed the writing of this letter for a long time because I don't want to upset you. Things have gotten worse by the day. Everyone in Poland is absorbing the propaganda from Germany. Polish-speaking German agents have been crossing the border, inciting riots, and advising the government on further anti-Jewish legislation. You know the Poles, it takes so little to enflame them. Already Jewish businesses in Przytyk have been painted over with Stars of David, with slogans telling Poles to avoid these establishments.

We have enough money to clothe and feed us and to pay for the children's tuition. But we're so afraid we no longer leave the house. Joseph and Sarah have both been severely beaten on their way back from school.

Last week a group of young hoods surrounded our house, shouting for hours words I would hate to repeat. They smashed all of the windows in the store. They went through everything, taking whatever they thought was of value while the police stood outside.

My main concern is for the children. I'm afraid to let them out of my sight. Last week Molly Liebman's daughter was beaten and raped. Golda Feldmen's three boys were tied up and tortured, and two of them might never walk again. And the Sugarman's son never came back from school, and they haven't heard a word from him since. Everywhere we go they taunt us, "Jew, Jew, go away. Go to Palestine where you belong."

I can no longer take care of the family and run the business. At the rate our money is going, it won't last long. We have to pay the police, the government clerks, the young hoods—all demand a payment just to leave us alone. We'll have nothing left in a few months.

Last week I heard from the British Embassy that we have been approved for six visas to immigrate to Palestine. Can you understand this, my Zishela? We are tired of cowering and cringing in fear; we can no longer take the beatings and abuse. I know Palestine is no picnic. The British are not eager to have us and the Arabs are no longer friendly, but anything is better than this. At least if we die in Palestine it would be with dignity, as fighting Jews defending ourselves and our family. And above all else, we would be buried in the holy soil of Eretz Israel. Our train leaves Warsaw on August 12 to Berlin, then to Hamburg. Our ship leaves on August 14 by way of Gibraltar via the Mediterranean to Palestine.

By the time you read this letter I will have told the family. We leave everything as is in Poland—our houses, our businesses. The Poles are only too happy to be rid of us. They can keep it all, and may they all rot in hell.

It would be my greatest happiness to see you once again before setting sail.

Please take care of yourself. You have always been very special to me and I still worry about you. Maybe I can even talk you into joining us.

I love you,
Lonka.

P.S. Kisses from the whole family.
P.P.S. Our ship is the Corde Cera, just in case you want to say good-bye to us.

Of course I will meet them, Zishe decided. How could I live with myself if I didn't give her my love and best wishes in person? And their departure coincided with a business trip he had already planned. What a fortunate coincidence.

He couldn't go with them to Palestine. He had too much to do here. He was amassing money. The money had bought him the correct papers and certificates—he was now officially a citizen of Austria. And now he knew he had to find a way to use the money to help his people.

CHAPTER FIVE

Zishe had always enjoyed traveling by train, and seated in his first-class compartment, he could appreciate the passing scenery even more. Germany was a beautiful country. It always amazed him how well preserved and immaculate the countryside was kept.

In front of him were letters and documents related to the business he was thinking of buying. He browsed through them, preparing himself for negotiations. *Die Fledermaus,* performed by Berlin's Staatsopera, could be heard from the radio mounted on the wall of the compartment. He tried to concentrate on the business documents, but the music only served to enhance his daydreams. His eyes drifted to his photograph of Gretchen.

"Have I told you how much I love you?" he said aloud, his finger tracing the outline of her face in the picture.

The train pulled to a stop and he was abruptly reminded where he was. He had intended to dine by this time, but he wanted to finish reading and filing his papers. He picked up a letter.

Dear Herr Holtz,

I am looking forward to seeing you soon. We have been very busy preparing the final package and have completed the last few details. All the appropriate documents, the complete inventory of equipment, materials, supplies, and salaries will be at your disposal. I am certain you will appreciate what this "gift from heaven" can afford us. Our engineers assure us that the production facilities can be easily converted to a variety of different uses. This can be done quite expeditiously. We have been fortunate in gaining important financial and political support, all of which we shall discuss in detail when we meet.

Looking forward to seeing you,
Herr Thyssen

Zishe filed the letter away and read the next one.

Dear Herr Holtz,

Your name has been mentioned to me with great praise and respect. As you must know by now, we are presently moving rapidly to increase our capacity to increase our nation's defense to a state of maximum capability. We need everything—machines, raw materials, factories, airplanes. I could go on and on, but let me get to the point where your financial and professional expertise could be of the greatest value for our country. To put it simply, we need uniforms. Not just any uniforms, but durable, practical, and (most important) designed appropriately to enhance and convey the image of our party and government.

Please do not underestimate the importance of this task. Our Fuhrer holds this in the highest regard.

Until we meet, I wish you a pleasant trip.

Yours,
Obergruppenfuhrer Steinholdt

Zishe added this letter to his files. Steinholdt, Hollman, Burghaus, Streisher—Zishe read through the stack of correspondence from officials who would soon be at his disposal, many of whom were Austrian with close connections to Hitler himself.

"Your table in the diner is ready. Please don't hurry, I only wanted to remind you." The attendant was polite and formal, and Zishe slipped the customary marks folded discretely into his palm.

"I will be there soon." Zishe closed his briefcase, placing it in the safe provided for each first-class compartment.

At the dining car, Zishe stepped up to the maitre d'. "I am Herr Holtz."

"Oh, yes, please follow me. It is a pleasure to have your company." The maitre d' showed Zishe to his table. It was a table for two but presently unoccupied. Zishe appreciated this; he could do without company.

Zishe liked to see the countryside slip by him, to hear the steady click of the wheels on the tracks. He couldn't get Lonka, Rifka, and Zindel off his mind. They were worlds apart. He had changed and he wondered how he could face them.

"Excuse me, Herr Holtz." It was the maitre d'. "I hope it will not be an inconvenience, but this table is reserved for two, and I have a most distinguished gentleman who wishes to dine. May I invite him over?"

Zishe looked up in annoyance but graciously nodded.

"Your grace, this is your place." The maitre d' slipped the chair back as a man in a bright satin frock with a red satin cap made himself comfortable.

"My name is Cardinal Rarkowski," he said in heavily accented German as he extended his hand with the palm straight down, expecting the respect of a kiss on it.

"I am Herr Holtz." Zishe shook his hand as he normally would any man. The cardinal was quite fat, with fingers like sausages, bedecked with sparkling rings. His skin was white with the unhealthy pink of someone who's had too many drinks. A cross dangled from his shoulders.

"May I ask what brings you here to our country?" Zishe asked out of politeness.

"As perhaps you know, I am the head of the church in Poland as well as a representative of the House of Cardinals, which, along with the Pope, represents Christ's church on this earth."

Zishe responded with a nod.

"I'm here on a religious, as well as political, mission. Chancellor Hitler and the church share many things in common. Herr Hitler is a Catholic, as are a large number of the members of his party. It is by mutual request that we have arranged a meeting. Since nearly half of all Germans and nearly all Austrians are of our faith, it is to our mutual benefit to cooperate with each other and to see how we can, shall I say, rid ourselves of the Jews."

Zishe was relieved when the waiter arrived to serve a large platter of pork, fish, chicken, and sausages. The cardinal poured himself a glass of wine, offering some to Zishe.

"Thank you, no," Zishe declined. The cardinal proceeded to consume large portions of what lay before him, but Zishe had lost his appetite. Poland and his sister were still on his mind.

Once off the train, Zishe walked in a leisurely, circuitous path that allowed him to see the city. He came upon shops that had marks of malicious mutilation, with the Star of David and *Juden* conspicuously painted on the buildings.

When he came to twenty-two Schubert Strasse, Zishe checked the letter to make sure this was the correct address. Herr Thyssen and his business associates were meeting him at noon at what appeared to be a deserted building. Most of the windows were broken or painted over with the word *Jude* and the yellow Star of David.

The building was housed in Arenstadt, a well-known center for textile manufacturing. Clothes, suits, dresses, and garments of every sort were produced here and exported to Germany and many other countries. Arenstadt looked like a small battleground, blood and debris still fresh on the avenues and streets. People in the street were polite but curt, rushing past signs of destruction as if they didn't see a thing. The city was a frenzy of production with factories working to full capacity.

"Herr Holtz?" Zishe turned around to see a man looking at him curiously. He tentatively extended his hand toward Zishe.

"Yes," Zishe answered, accepting his grasp.

"It is indeed a pleasure for me to meet you. I am Herr Thyssen. My apologies for all the broken glass and debris. Please, let's enter." Thyssen stepped in front of Zishe to protect him from stepping on some garbage on the ground. He guided Zishe toward the door. Thyssen was in his middle forties, with a suggestion of gray hair that gave him a mature, dignified appearance. Tall and narrow at the waist with broad shoulders, he was elegantly dressed in the latest fashion.

What seemed from the outside like a deserted building was actually a very busy establishment. Giant rolls of multi-colored fabrics were being turned into a variety of garments, with dozens of workers taking part in the many different stages of transformation. This factory seemed like a model of efficiency, every section specializing in only one part of the product as it was assembled on the long mechanized moving table.

"Allow me to introduce Herr Holtz," Thyssen said to the seven men standing around a table in a back room. They welcomed Zishe with a vigorous shaking of hands. Two of the men, Herrs Steinhart and Helholz, were dressed in civilian clothes as was Thyssen. The other four were in government uniforms.

"Gentlemen, I believe we can bring this meeting to order," Thyssen announced. "Herr Holtz, gentlemen, we have all worked hard to arrive at the position where we are, and I can only extend my thanks to everyone, here and in Berlin, who has given much-needed support. *Heil* Hitler." Several of the uniformed gentlemen slapped each other good-naturedly. "This city has been officially declared *Juden rein* so we may proceed to liquidate all Jewish-owned businesses immediately." Thyssen shuffled through the papers in front of him. Picking up a document, he continued. "This business, which manufactures garments, can be converted to produce uniforms for any branch of our government."

"No wonder this place smells so Jewish, I thought I detected the odor the moment I opened the door, the Jewish smell," a man in uniform named Hollman said. The stormtroopers laughed and Zishe winced, thinking of Lonka. He wondered what she would think of his being here.

"This business, as well as most of the other businesses we are in the process of liquidating, are owned by dozens and dozens of families. Each has only a small part ownership in the single enterprise, but they keep bringing their own kind from Poland or Rumania or Russia and sharing everything in common like a bunch of filthy Communists. How they live in such a despicable state is beyond me. So by getting rid of them, you'll be free of a few thousand filthy, emigrant Jews. Are there any questions before we get to the financial and organizational details?"

No one spoke.

"Please feel free to interrupt me if you have a question or any advice," Thyssen said smoothly. "I have brought together four gentlemen who, through their financial and professional acumen, will be able to unite all of these establishments into one organization, thereby increasing efficiency and profit. All to help our party, our country, and our Fuhrer."

"Have all of the financial calculations pertaining to reno-vation and liquidation been accounted for?" Oberfuhrer Streicher said.

"That is why we have our distinguished gentlemen with us now." Thyssen gestured toward Zishe and the three other civilians. "Herr Holtz will be in charge of all manufacturing, raw materials, and product designs. He will, in fact, be the head of the company. Herr Steinhart, Herr Helmholz, and myself will be more or less silent partners, supplying the in-vestment capital. We will of course always be ready to advise and help in any way we can with the success of this enter-prise."

Everyone looked quite pleased. No one asked any ques-tions. After a moment of awkward silence, Oberfuhrer Hollman said, "This liquidation, you mean to say we have to pay the Jews?"

"Well, Oberfuhrer Hollman, unfortunately, according to the laws now existing, we cannot take property without com-pensation." There was murmuring, a sort of disquiet. "Look, my friends, no one can tell us what we shall pay them." Thyssen smiled. "We tell them what they will get."

"If they don't accept?" Oberfuhrer Burghaus said.

"Then, Oberfuhrer Burghaus, they will get nothing, absolutely nothing. What we give them should be considered a gift. After all, haven't they really stolen this from us? May I ask the distinguished gentlemen for a vote of confidence?" All seven raised their hands. "Then I thank you with all my heart." He gestured expansively to the four uniformed gentlemen. "I know how busy you are and I'd like to thank you for coming this far and giving us your support. We will report all our activities regularly to you and the government. *Heil* Hitler."

In unison, the uniformed men stood at attention and saluted, exiting.

Thyssen, Zishe, and the other two financiers remained in the room. It was Zishe who asked the first question. "May I ask what price you were offering for the liquidation of these businesses?"

"You mean what we're willing to give to the Jews?" Hemholz seemed annoyed. "My suggestion is to offer them just enough money to transport them out of this country. With five thousand Jews and one thousand marks on the average, I would say five million marks should get them out of our hair permanently."

Steinhart, the accountant of the group, copied the figures into his ledger.

"Most countries will not accept them unless they can prove they can be self-supporting, and that would be a question of additional money," Zishe said. "We'll need a total of at least five million marks for liquidation, but then there's the money needed for renovation and at least six months of employee salaries. To be quite safe, let's assume it will take us a year to begin to show a profit. We should add another three million to our capital resources."

"Too much, way too much," Steinhart and Hemholz both voiced their objections.

"Herr Holtz is our expert in production and manufacturing. The extra capital would certainly provide a safe cushion," Thyssen pointed out. "I trust Herr Holtz. Can we put it to a vote?" Thyssen looked at each member individually.

"Let's go ahead." Steinhart was anxious to complete the proceeding. Reluctantly, all four hands were raised in approval of the amount of finance capital they'd provide for this investment. "One of us will have to tell the Jews of our ultimatum and make sure they leave within one week." Thyssen looked around the room for volunteers.

"I'll accept that task," Zishe said. The other three raised their hands in support. They shook hands, congratulating each other and wishing themselves good fortune.

## CHAPTER SIX

Zishe couldn't help admiring the charm and modesty of the house. It was in one of the better neighborhoods on the outskirts of Berlin, blending into the country forests. Beethoven's *Fifth Symphony* was being played on the gramophone for the guests in the salon.

This is the opportunity I've been waiting for, Zishe thought. If I gain their confidence, I may be able to get the money I need to save my people. Then he felt the fear that he was using them instead of helping them.

"*Ach,* Herr Holtz, let me introduce you to everyone." Oberfuhrer Steinholdt clicked his heels in sequence as he introduced Zishe. "Oberfuhrer Himmler, Oberfuhrer Heydrich, Oberfuhrer Hervoltz." He announced the names as if all were too famous to even be introduced by name. Himmler and Heydrich were the heads of the SA and the Schutzstaffel, or the SS, the two most powerful groups in Germany.

Too much is happening too soon. I never expected to become so involved, Zishe thought.

"Herr Holtz." Zishe turned to see Himmler's wife. "My husband tells me that you are in the process of organizing a large textile manufacturing operation for our country."

"Yes, that is correct." Zishe recognized Frau Himmler from the many pictures he'd seen of her posing with her famous husband, the head of the SS. Very Germanic with her blond hair and blue eyes, she was smaller than he expected and delicate as a lily.

"Ah, Herr Holtz. I've heard only praise of you from Oberfuhrer Steinholdt and also Oberfuhrer Hellmen." Himmler came to stand at his wife's side. He was short with close-cropped hair, small rimless metal spectacles, giving him the appearance of a pudgy, unimportant clerk who had been elevated to a position above his expectations. He seemed jealous of the attention his wife was getting. "But tell me, Herr Holtz, what will the Jews do when you tell them they will get next to nothing for everything they own? Oh, poor little Jews, poor little swine." He twisted his face grotesquely.

This is going to be some evening, thought Zishe.

"Ladies and gentlemen, Field Marshall Goering."

Everyone turned and applauded. Some raised their glasses, some saluted, and a few called out his name with *Heil* Hitler after it. Goering stood after Hitler in command. He was head of the German Air Force and had immense influence in all government departments. He smiled and waved at everyone. He was fat, and when he bowed, he did so with a flourish, extending his hand and tightening his stomach so it wouldn't hang down. He kissed the hands of the ladies and put his arm in a friendly embrace around the shoulders of the men.

"Ladies and gentlemen," Oberfuhrer Steinholdt said in a sing-song manner. "My dear friends, I would like to express my gratitude for your presence. Thank you, thank you, many thanks. If everyone would be so kind, we have to start the meeting on time. So please, ladies, feel free to enjoy the house. Our maids will be at your service. Gentlemen, let us retire to the smoking room."

"Very nice house you have, Otto." Goering sat on the largest, most comfortable sofa chair in the smoking room.

"Thank you, Field Marshall," Helmholz replied, seating himself opposite Himmler and Heinrich. Zishe and Togler sat on the opposite side, completing the circle.

"Excellent cheese, excellent wine." Zishe had heard that Goering loved to eat and drink. "Things are coming along famously. In fact, we are further ahead than expected with far less resistance." Goering smiled with each word. He plucked a few grapes off a bunch and popped them into his mouth. "No resistance to speak of. A few Communists, some Jews, a newspaper article. Nothing of importance. We have done this all under their noses. They respect power." Himmler and Heydrich were smiling admiringly. "We now have the strongest army, the strongest air force, and a very strong navy, particularly if we consider the formidable might of our submarines."

"A toast to our Fuhrer and our Field Marshall." Oberfuhrer Togler, standing, held his wine at an oblique angle. "*Heil* Hitler." Everyone stood, holding their glasses in salute.

"Let me come to a matter of paramount importance, one our Fuhrer personally feels has cosmic proportions and must be our first priority." Goering was puffing nervously at his cigar. His smile had disappeared and he seemed disturbed about how he was handling his words. "Let me start with practical matters. Our euthanasia policy toward mental and physical defectives has been quite well received with surprisingly little objection from home or abroad. Yes, a wonderful beginning."

Except for Zishe, everyone had a positive comment about this noble experiment.

"We are a master race, a pure Aryan race. But we could become weakened from within by inferior strains of our own stock. This first step is only a beginning, but it's an important one. We're focusing on the most efficient methods of disposing of unfortunates. Our doctors have been comparing lethal injection, carbon monoxide, and cyanide gas."

"I would think gas in large chambers would accommodate the most in the least amount of time," Himmler said with interest.

"Yes, Heinrich, gas seems to have the edge, but there are also the technical difficulties. Metal or concrete, pipes with liquid gas or pellets. We are fortunate our scientists are working tirelessly on solutions to these problems." Goering paused and smiled. "We're not talking here, of course, of Germany's defectives. That is a minor problem that could be solved quietly and simply in a less expensive manner."

Everyone was sitting at attention, hand on knees. Zishe wanted to participate, to make a good impression, but he was also afraid of what they were obviously planning. He moved forward, trying to gain an advantage and say something, but Goering was too involved in his speech to be interrupted.

"These are our guinea pigs, inconsequential in number. But we have to be prepared to handle millions as we expand our borders to include all the territories from England to France, from Norway to Greece."

"*Heil* Hitler, to our glorious thousand-year Reich," Himmler said with patriotic fervor.

"We are speaking of the 'final solution.' These are the very words the Fuhrer has spoken to me. Nothing goes on paper. This is strictly a secret matter. Everything will be communicated by mouth. The less written down, the fewer problems we'll have. This solution must be accomplished without the victim's knowledge until the final moment." Goering smiled. "There are five hundred thousand Jews in Austria and Germany, three and a half million in Poland, five million in the Soviet Union, and about three million in France, Greece, and Italy. I'd say we need to accommodate ten to twelve million."

Zishe sat completely still in disbelief. He had heard loose anti-Semitic jargon, but here was a definite plan to kill twelve million Jews by the most scientific means at their disposal. Gas, suffocation, death. His mind reeled at the reality of what these men were planning.

"Let me quote our Fuhrer as far back as nineteen-twenty-two: 'The annihilation of the Jews will be my first and foremost task.' Well, gentleman, our Fuhrer does not deal in platitudes; he deals in indisputable facts. We are now on the eve of the Last War, one that will establish a thousand-year Reich. Our forces are ready for any provocation, however slight. And when we strike back, we must be prepared to annihilate our enemies." Goering picked up a cigar, waving it over his head.

"There are sixteen million Jews in the world. How will we get to the last four million?" Still in shock at all he was hearing, Zishe thought Himmler sounded like an accountant who had misplaced a portion of his money.

"We'll get to them, my friends. We're only speaking of the twelve million in our immediate reach—those who must be annihilated and liquidated first."

"How long do you think that will take?" Oberfuhrer Steinholdt said.

"May I answer that question?" It was Himmler. "Let's say it will take our armed forces six months, at most ten to twelve months, to occupy Europe and the Soviet Union. With the final solution given our highest priority, our access—" He used his fingers as an abacus, turning over numbers and calculations while his lips moved to keep count. "Yes, fifteen months to gather, concentrate, and liquidate them."

Himmler grinned triumphantly. He had already disposed of twelve million Jews in his mind. "With the elimination of world's Jewry, we'll have removed the root cause of Bolshevism and their control of the world's financial markets. All the rest will be easy. Aryan supremacy will rise to the surface quite naturally."

Goering said, "How easy it will be. Two steps. First capture the Jews, second kill them. That will be the end of organized resistance."

The evening ended with the famous *Horst Wessel Lied.*

Driving back to his hotel, Zishe thought this is how evil looks, this is how it starts, in impersonal words and numbers.

Zishe awoke with a start in the middle of the night. The goose down blanket and the room reminded him he was still in Berlin. He touched his face and his arms to convince himself he was real. It couldn't have been a dream. It was more vivid than anything he'd ever seen, more real than the room, the bed, and himself. He rushed to the bathroom to verify his identity in the mirror. Last night, the party, the conversation, Goering, Heydrich, Himmler. He tried to remember every step from the beginning to the end. It was all too real. The final solution, gas chambers, the cold calculated murder of millions of Jews.

The meeting between the Jews who'd owned the factories and Zishe was to take place the following Monday, which gave him only forty-eight hours to prepare. His mind was completely absorbed with the manipulation of numbers, marks, *gulden*, dollars. He couldn't divorce the accounting, the finances from the people whose lives depended on the little bit of money they would receive for the property that was stolen from them. Five thousand lives in my hands. An awesome responsibility.

He got out of bed, dressed, and headed downstairs to order a taxi.

"Herr Holtz, your taxi is ready."

Zishe gave the bellboy one mark. He looked at his watch. "Five thirty," he murmured angrily. He was late. "Two fifty-seven Baumgarten Strasser, please."

"What are you going to a Jew place for, Herr Holtz?" Zishe could see the sneer and look of hate on the driver's face in the rearview mirror. "You should see what we did to it. I'll bet there's not a window left. And the paint—I have to admit, I'm one hell of an artist."

The driver was adorned with no less than six swastikas: one on his cap, one around his arm, one near his heart, and three on his lapels. Zishe was angry and impatient. "For God's sake, I have a business meeting. Get me to the 'Jew place,' as you call it, right away."

A puzzled look came over the driver's face. "Yes, sir. I'll get you there right away."

The taxi driver stopped the car across the street from Arenstadt's synagogue. There was too much broken glass to venture any closer. In the darkness, Zishe fumbled for his wallet.

"Thank you." Zishe placed the money in the driver's hand.

"Go easy, Herr Holtz, you might get hurt. Here." He offered Zishe a small flashlight. "We broke all the lights, cut the wires. Watch out for the ceiling, it got quite a beating. And the walls have very little support." He sounded genuinely concerned for Zishe's safety.

Some crude repairs had already been started. Slabs of wood panels covered some of the brick windows and makeshift logs supported some of the leaning walls and the crumbling brick facades. The place was not lighted, and he could barely make out the outline of a few people standing on the front steps near the door.

"Excuse me. I'm Herr Holtz," Zishe said.

"We were expecting a delegation, or at least a dozen people. Are you the only one?"

"I am the delegation." Zishe could now see who he was addressing. He was a short man with a slightly reddish beard, lost in an overcoat too large for him.

"I am Herr Shapiro. I used to be the rabbi at this synagogue." He gently pried the front door open. Zishe stepped inside. Hand-held candles flickered from a hundred places, each silhouetting someone waiting to hear the judgment. Zishe was guided to take his place in front of the Holy Arc, which was broken open with the Torah torn into a thousand pieces. It had been saved in seven sacred heaps of devotion. He stood alone, facing the congregation, hearing only the creaking of the temple's timbers and scattered weeping. Zishe stood as if someone had taken his tongue. He tried to clear his throat but a heavy lump was all he could feel.

"Magnified and sanctified be the name of God throughout the world which He hath created according to His will. May He establish His kingdom during the days of your life and during the life of all of the Houses of Israel. Yea, soon, say ye. Amen." Zishe cleared his throat. He was about to talk about the plans for liquidation, but instead he was intoning the Kaddish.

Suddenly Zishe was in another time and place. He was a boy who'd watched a brother and his friends being beaten by anti-Semitic bullies. Then he was at his brother's funeral. The windows were broken, men and women were weeping, and the candlesticks held by the congregation cast flickering shadows on their faces. Twenty coffins of different sizes lay open in front of the Holy Arc. He was standing over the body of his brother Leon and some friends, crying and reciting the Kaddish.

"Why did this have to happen? It was such a minor inoffensive incident," his father had said.

But now Zishe had business at the synagogue in Arenstadt. He blinked and came back to the present. "Yes," Zishe said. "Liquidation." His eyes were now accustomed to the darkness. The faces he saw could have been his mother, sister, father. They were the same faces transplanted in time and place. They were his people and he, as a representative of the Nazis, had to tell them how much they were worth.

It was hard to clear the lump from his throat, but it was six o'clock already and these people had been freezing for an hour.

"Ladies and gentlemen, thank you for your patience." Oh my God, did I say that in Yiddish or in German? He wondered. "As you've already been told, the German government has declared this town *Juden rein.*" There was a rumbling he took for a general affirmation. "The delegation of businessmen I represent has determined now what you will receive in compensation for your enterprise." He had used the euphemism "compensation," but they still gazed at him as a conqueror, one who was not to be trusted.

"Will one thousand per person be sufficient?" He'd expected some backlash, pleading, arguments. All was quiet. There was no astonishment or surprise. Nothing but beaten expressions, acceptance without protest. Zishe read their answer in their eyes. Their faces spoke a language that five thousand years had taught them.

"I understand," Zishe continued. "You do not trust me. I understand." A few eyes were blinking back in silent recognition. Can they tell I'm one of them? "One thousand marks will pay your fare to another country, and that's what you should use it for. If you decide to stay in Germany, this sum won't get you by more than one or two months, and it's very dangerous. Germany is doomed. You still have a chance at another life somewhere else. One thousand marks has been offered to you. I'll fund another ten thousand marks personally if you'll promise me you'll try to obtain visas to any country that will accept you and you'll get out of here immediately."

"Are you trying to bribe us to leave?" The rhetorical remark came from an elderly man.

As they filed past Zishe, the eleven thousand marks was handed to each Jew. Their leaders took the money necessary to distribute to those who had been unable to attend the meeting.

"Thank you. *Shalom.*" Each thanked Zishe and said good-bye in Yiddish. They must have recognized him.

Maybe there was a God looking after his people, but then why did He hide His face so often?

✡ CHAPTER SEVEN

There was so much shouting the brick walls of the hotel barely dampened the sound. Cars were honking, bugles trumpeting. It was like the beginning of a race. Several bands were converging from the border of the city to the giant plaza where the University of Berlin was located. Everyone was rushing to the celebration. Zishe began to run too. He was soon darting in and out of the crowd, gaining ground only to be stopped by a solemn procession of students with torches.

"What is this?" Zishe asked the man in front of him.

"We're burying the old, bringing in the new," the stranger said.

"Where?"

"*Unter den Linden Platz*, opposite the University of Berlin."

Burying the old? Bringing in the new? Zishe was impatient to get going. The procession was long and slow and he was getting cold. He jumped over the hood of a car, slipping sideways between two bicycles and raced the last two blocks without interference.

He arrived just in time. The plaza was surrounded by thousands of bright torchlights. Books of all shapes and sizes were piled high. Zishe edged close enough to read the authors: Thomas Mann, Heinrich Mann, Stephen Zweig, Arthur Snitzler, Eric Maria Remarque, Albert Einstein, Sigmund Freud.

The drumming started slowly in a mournful, staccato tone. "These flames," the announcer said, "burn the end of an old era and light the new. *Heil* Hitler, *Heil* Hitler. Long live the Fuhrer. Long live Germany. Long live the Third Reich."

"*Heil* Hitler," the crowd answered back.

The plaza soon became a mountain of fire. The crowds applauded and spontaneously sang their anthem. "*Wenn jude blut spricht von messers.*"

Zishe had seen enough. He was overcome with shame and fear.

"Herr Holtz."

The voice was familiar. Zishe turned to see Karl Franz, an old customer Zishe had fitted back at Weiss's tailor shop.

"Professor Franz. I would never have recognized you."

"Yes, I know. I must look awful."

Franz's glasses were skewed with one temple missing. Both lenses were missing, his face was full of blood and bruises.

"What happened to you?"

"It's all a mistake. They have..." Franz couldn't finish.

"Let's sit down. We'll talk." Zishe led him to a cafe next to the square. "Go ahead, it's all right. You can talk to me."

"Herr Holtz, they've burned my books." Professor Franz had been the head of the Department of Theoretical Physics and Mathematics at the University of Berlin. His work was acclaimed all over the world. He was a distinguished scholar as well as an outspoken supporter of Hitler. "Einstein, Bohr, Oppenheimer, and Franc I can understand. They're Jewish physicists. Their books are, well, they should be burned. But I am an Aryan." He was overcome with grief, and seemed dazed too. "Here, read these papers. It's beyond me. I have read them over and over. I have pleaded. I don't understand."

Zishe picked up one of the letters. It was addressed to Professor Franz from none other than Bernhard Rust, former Obergruppenfuhrer in the S.A., presently minister of all German science schools. Zishe had met him only in passing. He'd been an undistinguished headmaster who'd been dismissed for "certain manifestations of mental instability," as the provincial authorities at Hanover had put it. But in the bizarre world of party affiliations and loyalties, he was now at the top of his profession. The note was addressed without the usual titles: an ominous sign.

Memo to Karl Franz:

You are hereby dismissed from the faculty. All privileges will be denied. Return everything that does not belong to you. Your works are impure and corrupt.

They lean heavily on Jewish influence. Modern physics is an instrument of world Jewry. Einstein's theories, in particular, degrade German physics. Our pedagogical guiding star must always be our Fuhrer's Mein Kampf.

Only this book contains the truth, and by relying on it, we will have a pure German science. It is unfortunate that a man as educated as you, one who has supported the party from its start, should stoop so low as to use Jewish mathematics in your works. You are guilty of subverting German youth. Any attempt on your part to continue your activities will result in immediate discipline and imprisonment.

> *Heil Hitler,*
> *Doctor Bernhard Rust, Reich Minister of*
> *Science and Education*

Zishe folded the letter. Franz was trembling. "Well, what do you think? How bad is it?"

"It seems you have offended someone," Zishe replied.

"But who?"

"Aren't your books just numbers and abstract symbols?"

"Yes. There's nothing Jewish about them. If there is I will delete or rewrite anything they wish. I'll give a public confession to the errors I made because I wasn't aware how dangerous the Jewish physicists are."

Zishe was listening with only half an ear. He was again aware of the other realm. He saw Franz ready to begin life on earth. He saw him choose his parents, his talents, and his faults along with his circumstances. He watched in amazement as Karl Franz's life unfolded before him. Zishe saw all of his choices, the good and the bad, from birth through school—his friends, his likes and dislikes. From teacher's aide to full professor, then to the head of the department in an exclusive school. Marriage, children, money. Concern for others and generosity were consumed by his ever-increasing appetite for acclaim and position.

Karl Franz wanted to be the greatest and most important physicist on earth. He hated anyone who was better than him. He especially despised the Jews, who made up a significant portion of the world's preeminent physicists and mathematicians. Just the mention of Einstein's name made him sick with jealousy and pain.

All the spirits needed was an evil thought, a small opening to seize their opportunity. Zishe watched as Franz planned his first advance. It was only a minor position, but he lied about his competition. He made sure the authorities knew this was a Jew, and he falsely accused him of unpatriotic views. The spirits saw their chance and immediately gained an entrance. At first, he fought with some resistance. But over time it was easier to give in. He didn't need much coaxing. Before long, he didn't have a conscience at all. He surrendered his soul for a little increase in position.

Zishe was now in two worlds, the everyday and the transcendent. He didn't understand it. But Franz brought him back to the present.

"Tell me the truth. Don't spare my feelings. Am I a dead man?" Franz begged.

Zishe was watching a man crumble before his eyes. He wanted to be of help, but Karl had to learn this lesson by himself. He'd hurt a lot of people. He succumbed to temptation and pride and allowed evil to take over his life.

"Karl, take hold of yourself. I know nothing about your work or why they burned your books. How can there be a pure German science? How, in fact, can there be Jewish physics or mathematics? That's totally ridiculous."

"Einstein is a Jew. His mathematics is impure. I'm sure he falsified his proofs. I'll show him up. You'll see. All his relativity, all his fame, it's built on nothing but Jewish lies." Franz said as he stood up angrily and left.

Zishe could sense the fear in the atmosphere. The book burning, Karl Franz—they were just the tip of the iceberg. Packs of gangs were roaming about with hate and violence on their minds, looking for a fight. Hitler youth, stormtroopers, soldiers, even civilians without uniforms were waving flags and shouting profanities at any Jew in the vicinity.

Zishe saw an old Jewish man being harassed on the street. He went over to defend him. "Please, leave him alone. He's old."

A crowd of spectators was watching the Nazi youth terrorizing this poor old Jew. They'd removed his clothes and cut all the hair from his face and his beard. Zishe began to pull on them.

"I beg you, have mercy on him."

But they kept beating the man. Then a girl ran around the corner. Four Nazi youth were chasing her and she ran right into Zishe. Zishe held her protectively.

"Leave her alone," he said. "She's my girl." Then they were off, along with the crowd.

She started crying. Her body was shaking. "*Oy*, my God." She was staring at the old man on the ground. "Oh my God. That's my father."

"Quiet my child, my Jewish heart. He's dead," Zishe said softly in Yiddish.

She looked up at him, sad and frightened. He wiped the blood from her face and straightened out her hair.

"You are a Jew," she said timidly.

"Yes, but it's better not to talk."

She was clutching the yellow star she'd removed in her desperate attempt to keep it hidden. "They saw it before I tore it off. It was easier before they made us wear it." She was still shivering. "I can't stand to look at my father."

"*Sha*, just look at me. I will take care of his body. It must be given a decent Jewish burial. We need ten men, a *minyan*. I'll call a car for you. You need someone to care for your wounds." Zishe continued holding the girl and repeating the Kaddish while he looked at her dead mutilated father.

The funeral took place the next day. Zishe attended. It was short. The daughter, a rabbi, and a few friends were the only ones in attendance. The cemetery had been defaced with several layers of swastikas and the usual hateful slogans. The tombstones were broken with the names deliberately scattered to make it almost impossible to find the correct burial place.

The rabbi said all the customary things and prayed for the deceased in the traditional way, but it was done in haste. There was too much fear in the air. The rabbi ended his oration with a few uninspired condolences and then quickly departed.

Zishe decided to walk from the Jewish cemetery all the way to his hotel, an hour's journey. He walked in a daze, unaware of his surroundings.

A rock landed at his feet, and he found himself surrounded by five angry youths. He had nowhere to run—he was cornered. They soon had him pinned to the ground. The leader pulled the yarmulke off his head in disgust.

"You lousy Jew. You're a dead man. Isn't it nice you're so close to your own grave?"

They sifted through Zishe's pockets, threatening him with their knives.

"We're going to carve our initials on your heart, you filthy swine."

I'm going to die, Zishe thought. They tied his feet and hands securely to the iron railing. They took his wallet, his keys, and his money.

He knew they wanted to see him beg, but he wouldn't. They waved their knives, laughing.

"Who wants the honor?" They were casting lots to see who would get to cut Zishe.

The one with the big belly and the sadistic laugh won. He raised his knife and Zishe watched as it descended and then swerved, stabbing into the concrete by his side.

The boy cursed, gripping his wrist. It looked broken. "You lousy son of a bitch Jew."

The fat youth dropped the knife and took aim to kick at Zishe. Again he missed. His foot went into the wall. The force of the blow broke his toe.

"Come on, get him! He's all tied up—beat the living daylights out of him," the fat one said as he writhed in pain.

His companions advanced with their knives, but they had a strange look of fear in their eyes. Their blows were somehow being stopped. "We'd better go, something's not right."

"This Jew's spooky."

"He's got the power of the devil. Let's get out of here."

They couldn't get away fast enough. Their fear had turned to terror.

Zishe found he was able to loosen his ties easily and he gathered up his wallet and his yarmulke. He thought he was hearing things, a voice.

And then he saw her. She was right in front of him. Her eyes had a sparkle that reflected the light within her, and she stood as if she was floating.

"Zishe. You have been good to a lot of people."

He was still taking in her unearthly beauty. "Why are you here? Why are you appearing to me?"

"Because you have much to do. You will die to your present life only when it's time," she said.

"The toughs that roughed me up—you stopped them?"

"Yes, of course. Why look so bewildered? This was not the first time."

"There were other times?"

"Yes. We're always around, waiting until someone is ready."

"Ready for what?"

"For the time someone wakes up to the memory of who they really are."

"Are you an angel?"

"If that is what you want to call me."

"Yes, I know you. You're different yet the same. You've always been there when I needed you." He was on the verge of crying. "Yes, you and many more like you were taking care of Wilhelm, David, and all the other brave souls after they ascended. After they finished their mission on earth."

"We are always with you," she said.

"But why?"

"We are always helping whenever any difficulty arises."

"Then why was there no help for that Jew who was murdered, or for innocent victims of all those vicious pogroms?"

"They were all successful. They did not fail. Their mission was carried out to perfection."

"But why did they suffer so if they were on a mission?"

"That is what they chose. You should see them now. They are glorious."

"When do you come?" Zishe said. "When someone asks?"

"Not literally. We can tell when someone needs help to overcome some weakness. We know when they are truly asking to complete what they have started."

"What about those who cause all the suffering?"

"They have listened to a different voice. All souls have free choice. They all start out with a mission. But not all succeed. Nothing is guaranteed."

"Why do some souls go about choosing such terrible things?"

For the first time she was silent.

"Why?" Zishe asked, persistent.

"That is something you must discover for yourself."

Zishe was afraid she would disappear. He had so many questions.

"You are a Just Man, Zishe. There is always a Just Man on this earth."

Zishe didn't understand.

"One Just Man is all the earth needs. He takes our suffering upon himself. Into him all griefs are poured. He supports the entire earth."

Zishe thought, that describes Jesus not me.

"You understand," the angel said, growing brighter.

"Then why am I needed?"

"To keep the flame of Jesus's love alive."

"That couldn't be me. The things I have done—"

"Are of no importance," she said. "A Just Man has always been here. One more thing before I must go. There is much suffering ahead. A great deal of evil. You will be there in the middle. And you will be helped at each step. You will be given special gifts. Professor Karl Franz was a small example. You saw him succumb. You shall see greater things. Good-bye. We will meet again." She disappeared.

He stood silently, holding his yarmulke in his hands.

CHAPTER EIGHT

"Herr Holtz?"

He thought he recognized the voice. It was Frau Himmler, dressed in a long sequined black dress, pearls, and a gold brooch that accentuated the blondness of her hair. She cut through the crowd in front of the theater and walked over to Zishe.

"How nice to see you." Zishe extended his hand.

Himmler came up behind her. He shook Zishe's hand while he placed his arm protectively over his wife's shoulder. "A very special evening in honor of our Fuhrer. Wagner's opera, Tristan, and Isolde. Come join us. Our seats are not far from where the Fuhrer will be."

Zishe followed. Himmler had his own private guards who cleared the path for him. "Many things have happened since our last meeting. Wonderful news," Himmler said as they walked.

"Herr Holtz, General Poser, General Glick." Himmler knew everyone in their booth.

"Heil Hitler." Everyone stood at attention. The Fuhrer had entered. The ovation subsided only after Hitler sat down.

"Ladies and gentlemen." The lights dimmed. "This is indeed a special occasion. We dedicate this evening to our Fuhrer who has brought our nation back to its glory. To him we owe everything. May he live forever, may the Third Reich be the only power on earth. Heil Hitler." Another standing ovation, this time shorter.

Zishe was happy as the time passed quickly. He liked music but not Wagner. The atmosphere was stifling and oppressive. He could see Hitler from where he sat. The man was laughing and chatting as if the music was only a background.

At intermission, Himmler brought Zishe over to Hitler.

"Heinrich. Come, sit down." Hitler patted the chair next to him.

"*Mein Fuhrer,* this is Herr Holtz."

"Have a seat. Wonderful music, so very German. Nothing Jewish about it. That Wagner was a man ahead of his time. He wrote the libretto, all by himself. He had to first scrape off what the Jews smeared on our great culture. What a love story, that Tristan. Goes straight to the heart. And the power. That music's got backbone. Not like Jewish music. Mendelssohn, Meyerbeer, Offenbach. The world will soon be rid of that kind of music."

He spoke as if he'd known Zishe for some time. "Yes, we will soon be rid of their music, their literature. And of them. Every little Jew is already trying to hide all over the earth. But my reach is long, and I will find them. Their hour has come."

Zishe felt like a traitor sitting there with the Fuhrer, listening to him degrade his people without saying anything. His skin crawled with disgust. Then he began seeing wisps of transparent moving spirits hovering and dancing, entering and exiting through the top of Hitler's head.

Hitler continued to speak with ever-increasing hate, and the translucent spirits resonated with his words. Zishe was shown a review of Hitler's life. Every detail, every thought was projected while the Fuhrer talked. Zishe saw Hitler's birth and his childhood, which was not unusually harsh. He performed the usual childish pranks, but above all he loved being in control. The spirits hovered in profusion over him as a small child.

Zishe could see these spirits, but they couldn't see him. They were spirits without souls; they possessed only hate and an unquenchable thirst for material things. They were even trying to devour each other. Each wanted to be the most important.

It wasn't long before Hitler was exactly like them.

Is this hell they're coming from? Zishe wondered. He had seen where souls that have ascended go, but he had never been taken to a space or universe of hell.

He had only to think of the question and he was given the answer. Hell was empty, without any place or substance. It had no real essence.

The opera began again. Zishe sat back to watch the drama. Now he had seen evil. It was an illusion without substance that used people and created suffering.

Zishe wondered why the Jews had to suffer. There wasn't a spirit in the room that wasn't muttering something against them. Zishe was perplexed. Where is God in all of this? Why does He allow it?

"You will know when it's time. But here is a glimpse, to tide you over for a time," the angel's voice said.

The room became so bright Zishe thought he would go blind, but he couldn't close his eyes. He was shown all of Jewish history from the very beginning. "I have chosen you to bear the evil." The sound was coming from the light. "You are a lightning rod to absorb this evil so that the earth may continue and not be destroyed."

Zishe remembered the words of Isaiah: "Surely our griefs they bore, and our sorrow they carried. They suffered for our transgressions." He saw God had not forgotten. Evil had no face. It was the collective remnant of what was left after a soul had nothing substantial remaining. "That is why the Lord our God is one."

The opera started again, but Zishe couldn't concentrate. He was overwhelmed at what he had seen. He was glad to be in a position to fight for his people. He sent a silent prayer to God to give him courage.

The opera ended and Hitler left. Zishe followed in the crowds after him, feeling trapped.

Tomorrow I can see Lonka, he thought. At least tomorrow I can go back to being a Jew.

CHAPTER NINE

Zishe was on his way to meet Lonka. He was filled with doubts about the life he was living and how she'd receive him. His masquerade was a heavy burden. He wanted to abandon his position and his prestige and return to being the Jew he had always been. He needed someplace he could take his mask off and not be recognized.

He felt drawn toward the portion of Berlin that was still predominantly Jewish. He was walking and praying, asking God if there was in fact a plan for him or if he was just fooling himself, succumbing to the same evil that he saw in Professor Franz and Hitler. He needed time to collect his thoughts before he saw his sister.

He stopped at a little coffee shop.

"Can I get you something?" the waiter asked.

"Coffee and some strudel, please." The cafe was not far from the synagogue. A few Jews with yarmulkes on their heads were sitting at some of the tables.

A woman approached. "Is this seat taken?" She looked almost frightened.

"No."

"May I sit down?"

"Yes, please do."

She sat down without removing her coat, looking furtively around as if she was expecting someone.

"My name is Zishe."

"My name is Rachel." She looked at him as if he was a stranger, almost an enemy. "Nothing for me right now," she told the waiter. She kept fidgeting with her purse and self-consciously asked, "Do you live around here?"

"No, I'm just visiting. And you?"

"Just visiting."

Zishe recognized her Rumanian accent. There was a sadness about her. It was as if she was escaping but didn't know where to hide.

"You're not Jewish." She stated it as a fact.

"I am Jewish. You have no reason to be afraid of me," Zishe said in Yiddish.

"Thank God. I thought you were one of them." She looked up at Zishe, loosened the tight grip on her purse, and began to cry. "I'm sorry," she excused herself.

Zishe could not take his eyes away from her. He was seeing her entire life with every detail from her birth to the present moment. He wondered why God was showing him this.

Rachel was nothing like the others. Her life had been hard, with much sorrow. But she had never dwelled on hate or the thought of hurting anyone. She was born not far from Bucharest. She had two sisters and three brothers. Her desires were simple: love with a good husband and children. She liked the study of Torah, believed in God, couldn't stand Rumania because of the anti-Semitism. She came to Berlin thinking it would be better and was shocked to find it getting worse. She had thoughts of Palestine and was scraping to save money to go, but she'd just lost her job because she was Jewish. She was despondent, not knowing what to do. Suicide was tempting but she loved life too much and still hoped for a better future. She was a good woman, a decent soul, struggling to be good and honest.

Zishe could not see any great faults in her life. Some pettiness, some anger, but this was quickly dissipated by her love and faith. He felt a deep sense of compassion for her. This country had lost its kindness.

Then he was seeing into her future from the perspective that it had already been completed. He saw her choosing to go to Warsaw, thinking there were Jews there who could help her. She had just enough money for the fare, and she thought Poland was strong and wouldn't let the Nazis in. Jobs were scarce in Poland, too, but Rachel found work in a closely knit Jewish family. She was content but she missed her own family. She worked together with a man, David, whom she grew to love. They discussed marriage but decided it would have to wait for some future time when conditions were more stable.

War was imminent, and the letters from Rumania were even worse. The anti-Semites controlled the governments and were forming alliances with Germany. Rachel and David wanted to leave Poland, but they were told they couldn't without visas, which were impossible to get.

Rachel studied all the maps. She outlined possible countries in different colors. She was hopeful, but the answer was always no.

The news first came over the radio. Germany had invaded. David joined the army. Things were getting worse, but Rachel kept hoping somehow they'd be able to get away.

Poland was defeated in only four short weeks. David was captured, and when he was released, he could hardly walk without holding onto her. They had kept him as an example of what they would do to any Jew that ever raised their hand against them again.

Food and money were scarce. Each day more Jews were rounded up to work for nothing or to be shot. Rachel lost track of her family. Rumania was now a German ally.

The order that all Jews in Warsaw must live in the ghetto was immediately implemented. Rachel, David, and his family moved within the wall, taking only what they were allowed to carry.

Still Rachel believed this was a temporary phase of hatred; life would get better. David packed his bags and told her he was leaving for a job in a factory where the pay would be better. He'd been picked along with one thousand others. She watched him enter the truck under the watchful eyes of the Germans.

Others left too, never to be heard from again. There were rumors—but she didn't want to believe these stories. Some said they'd been packed like sardines in boxcars with no food or water, that they were taken to a place where they were undressed and made to dig their own graves. There was even one rumor going around about some incredible chambers where they murdered Jews with special gases.

Then she, too, was picked to go where there was a need for good laborers. She was promised better conditions and plentiful food. She joined the steady procession heading toward the station.

Zishe saw her death. He was shaken.

"Don't go to Warsaw," Zishe said, pounding his fist on the table. "Leave Europe. Germany will conquer Poland. The Jews are in great danger."

"Who told you about Warsaw? Who told you a thing like that?" she said, tightening her grip on her purse. She looked frightened.

Rachel got up and walked away. Zishe could see the fear in her eyes. She must think I'm crazy, he thought, unable to dismiss what he'd seen.

The hotel was only a half hour from the station. Zishe paid the taxi driver.

"Room three-oh-five—they are expecting me. My name is Zishe Holtz."

"The elevator is to the right."

Zishe decided to use the stairs. He was impatient and he felt full of energy.

"Lonka, it's me. Zishe."

"Zishe," she cried before he even opened the door. "Zishe." She was crying as she embraced him. "I knew you wouldn't forget. I told Zindel, 'You just watch, Zishe will make it on time.' It's been so long, so much has happened. You look different, very goyish."

"And you..."

"I look older. Look at my wrinkles. Hard times don't do much for beauty." She laughed. "Zishe, it's so good to see you."

"Zindel, I can't believe it. You, here in Germany. And in a little while, Palestine. A dream come true, no?"

Zindel said. "Zishe, come with us. Leave this stinking place before it's too late."

Lonka squeezed Zishe's hands.

"I can't."

"Why not? What's holding you down? You're not married; you have no children."

"I can't explain, Lonka. I have things to do."

"What could be so important? Money? That's not you, Zishe. Tell me the truth, what's holding you back?" she said.

For a moment Zishe thought he saw a movement, a momentary flash in the room. "It's a long story. It involves responsibilities, business—things I find hard to speak about."

"Zishe, the Jews have no chance here. But the Torah has promised we will be an eternal nation. All the prophets have repeatedly emphasized this. 'But fear not, O Jacob my servant, neither be dismayed, O Israel, because I shall redeem you from afar, and your children from the land of their captivity—for I will topple all the nations to which I have driven you.' I can quote any passage in our scriptures and get the same message."

"It's been two thousand years, and we still don't even possess the land," Zishe said.

"Be a pessimist, but first listen to me. We're still around. Two thousand years in exile, and we're still Jews. 'Yet even so, even while they are in the land of their enemies, I will not reject or spurn them, lest I break my covenant with them.' And the Exile, the Diaspora—the Torah predicted that, too. 'You yourselves I will scatter among the nations...leaving your country desolate and your cities in ruins.'

"Anti-Semitism," Lonka said with bitterness. "Even that the Torah predicted. 'Among those nations you will find no respite—you will live in constant suspense and stand in dread both day and night, never sure of your existence.... You shall perish among the nations, in the land of your enemies they shall consume you.' I am sorry, Zishe, but I feel this will happen soon. I am afraid for you."

The angel was there beside Lonka, hovering over her. It was the same angel who had shown him Rachel's future.

"Zishe, there is someone sitting next to you. Am I hallucinating?"

"No, Lonka. I am real. I am a messenger," the angel said.

"From heaven?" Lonka thought, staring off into space.

Zindel stared at Lonka and Zishe.

"Why are we blessed to have a messenger from God? We're simple people."

They were being shown Palestine. Two thousand years of desolation. Desert, plants, shrubs turned fertile, with trees, cultivated by Jews. Zishe was thinking of what he had been shown with Rachel. He was afraid of what lay ahead, afraid to believe in this vision.

Lonka said, "'You shall shoot forth your branches and bear your fruit for my people Israel, for their return is close at hand.' That's happening now, after two thousand years. Remember what Rashi, blessed be his name, wrote? 'When the land of Israel will yield its produce in superabundance, this will signal the approach of the end of the exile. There is no clearer end than this.' One thousand years ago—he wrote it that long ago." Lonka stopped speaking, but her eyes were still wide open, the vision of the future Israel still there before them.

He wanted to speak to her of the vision he'd had with Rachel and tell her the details of his present life, but he was afraid. He wondered again why he was being shown these things, why he was going through this.

"Angels—many more powerful than me—have misplaced papers, erased ink, written false documents, and created illusions to help you. You are a Just Man, and we have to help you with your present mission—but your sister, she deserves to know something of your life," the angel said to Zishe.

"Here, have some coffee." Lonka said to Zishe. "I don't want to press you, but why can't you come with us?"

Zishe took a few sips. "I am a Nazi—well, not officially, but I have collaborated with the highest levels of the party. I am wealthy, with businesses all over Berlin, Danzig, and Germany, most of which I have appropriated from their Jewish owners. My factories are important to Germany's armies."

Lonka's mouth was wide open. Even Zindel who was sitting quietly, shifted his position uncomfortably and nearly dropped his cup of coffee.

"Nazi? You? Do they know that you were once a Jew? I can't believe it," Lonka said, stammering.

"Of course they don't know I'm Jewish. To them a Jew is born evil. It's his blood they hate."

"Then why, Zishe?" Lonka stopped and turned around. "I just can't believe what you are doing," she said, and started to cry.

"To help Jews leave while there is still time," he said putting his hand on her arm.

"But you're a Nazi," she said, averting her eyes.

"Only on the outside. Call it camouflage. How else can I get visas, money, passports, and weapons?" Zishe asked angrily, turning away from Lonka.

"Weapons?" Lonka repeated.

"For those who can't get out in time."

"I wish to God I believed what you are saying—my own brother a Nazi," she said, shaking her head and sobbing.

Zishe put his arm around her. "I love you, Lonka. What I told you is the truth," he said, taking out his handkerchief and handing it to her.

"Thanks. I'm sorry I'm such a crybaby," she said, softly.

Zishe smiled. "Let me at least see the children before I go." He bent over and kissed them as they were sleeping.

"Good-bye, Zindel, Lonka. Until it's all over, if not on this earth, then—" Zishe pointed up.

CHAPTER TEN

"You're early. Have you been waiting a long time?" Zishe sat down next to Herr Weiss. They were at Danzig's finest restaurant.

"Half an hour. But never mind. I've lots to occupy my mind." Weiss seemed happy to meet Zishe, but there was a frown on his face.

"Is something wrong, Michael?" Zishe still felt awkward calling him by his first name.

"No, things are going along splendidly. Such good news from you. My, you've gone a long way. I don't know why you even bother to maintain a position in my business."

"You believed in me. You hired me as a nobody."

"But you're a big textile industrialist. Your uniforms are worn by every section of the armed forces."

"How is Frau Weiss? And Heinrich and Gretchen?"

"They're doing very well. Frau Weiss is now the president of the women's section in the Nazi party's local chapter."

"And you?"

"What about me?"

Something wasn't quite right. Weiss seemed nervous and afraid. Through his eyes, Zishe saw into the other realms. He could see that Weiss had been fighting with his wife. She wanted a divorce because she was afraid he was going to be exposed as a Jew. She regretted ever marrying him and argued that according to the Nuremburg laws, there was an escape clause for mixed marriages. If they divorced, Heinrich and

Gretchen could acknowledge the true German as their parent, renouncing their Jewish parent, and their blood would be considered pure. If he granted her the divorce, he could save his children.

"Do the Nazis know you're a Jew?" Zishe said suddenly.

"No, I don't think so. My God, those records should have been thrown out. My family disowned Judaism so long ago—how could anyone draw such a false conclusion? Of course my wife knows. It's difficult to hide your past, especially in Germany, where everyone keeps records." Weiss was fidgeting, and he looked as if he wanted to slip beneath the table. "I converted a long time ago. My family tree reads like Hitler's or any one of those pure Aryans.

"It reads Jew, like you and me. Converts don't count, no matter how far back. They'll get you and then me." Zishe's voice was loud and tinged with anger. "What about Gretchen? Does she know you're Jewish?"

"She knows." He was crying.

"Would she disown you if you divorce Frau Weiss?"

"Her mother is adamant. Gretchen must renounce me and sever all ties."

"Have you spoken to Gretchen about any of this?"

"She loves me—I am her father. But you know how religious she is. I can't blame her if she doesn't want to become a Jew."

Zishe could see in Weiss the disintegration of a human being. Too many compromises. Too much hunger for power and money. And above all, a furious denial of anything Jewish. "Is Gretchen at home? I'd like to see her."

"She's home."

The house looked different. With its red buntings and swastika flying, it could have been the headquarters of the party.

"Come in, Herr Holtz. The ladies are expecting you. Right this way. They'll be with you in just a moment."

The butler brought Zishe to the drawing room. The maid came in with a platter of pastries and tea.

"Thank you." Zishe poured himself a cup. The heat felt good on his hands. Frau Weiss and Gretchen came in. He stood up. Gretchen looked beautiful. "Frau Weiss, Gretchen."

Frau Weiss curtsied. She'd changed. She looked harder. "You know we have filed for a divorce, Herr Weiss and I?" she asked without preamble.

Zishe showed no reaction to this.

"Oh, it's been a very long time coming. We never were interested in the same things. It's all for the best. As far as the business—we'll have to speak about arrangements later." She glanced at Gretchen. "Oh, you two must have a lot to talk about. I have some things to do. How about dinner tomorrow night? Can I count on you to join us?"

"Yes, thank you." Zishe stood up as she left the room.

"I've missed you," Gretchen said. Zishe had expected a happy response, but she was crying.

"It's your father," Zishe said.

Gretchen nodded.

"I've already seen him. He's also very unhappy," Zishe said.

"Has he told you? Mother doesn't want you to know the real reason because it's so shameful, but—do you know?"

"Everything."

"Mother, she's so ashamed and furious. She says Jews are the cause of everything bad." Gretchen paused to regain her composure. "I am Jewish—unless I renounce my father and claim only my mother. If I don't, I will be classified as a Jew." At that word she could barely control herself. "Me a Jew— now I have to hate myself."

"Have you made your decision?" Zishe said.

"No. I love my father, but to be a Jew..." Gretchen's voice trailed.

"Like Jesus or Einstein," Zishe pointed out.

"Aren't you in agreement with the party? I mean, I've never heard you say anything against the Jews."

"I'm not a member of the party."

"But I thought—"

"I conduct business. I make money. They like fancy uniforms, and I design them well. I keep my opinions to myself." Zishe watched Gretchen struggling with her decision. He watched as she averted her eyes, the tears trickling down her cheeks. Zishe could imagine her thoughts. She must be brave to have withstood the steady stream of anti-Semitism she had heard from her mother and friends.

Gretchen's lips were moving as if in prayer. Her face appeared more serene. She looked up at Zishe, her eyes still moist.

"God is love. How can I hate? I love my father. Why should I disgrace him? I've known Jews all my life, they aren't evil. All that is wrong. Anyway, Jesus was a Jew—I should be proud I am one too."

Zishe was relieved. There was no hate inside Gretchen.

"What do you think about them? You must have some opinion." Gretchen caught Zishe off guard with that question.

"The Jews are an ancient people. Every hundred years or so, someone tries to exterminate them. They've outlived all their enemies, and this time will be no exception."

"Aren't they supposed to be God's chosen? And didn't God give them the Torah?"

"How do you know about the Torah?"

"I've read a lot, especially since I saw that figure in the Mariakirsche. The expression on that face and the words. They were so beautiful."

"That statue of Jesus and his words?"

"Yes."

Zishe couldn't forget that day. It was the day that she'd told him she loved him. It seemed so long ago.

Gretchen stood up to offer Zishe some more tea.

"Thanks, but I need to go."

"But my father—you haven't given me any advice," she said, pleading.

Zishe turned to her, but he didn't know what to say.

"This choice will be the most important one of your life," he finally said.

"The most important?" Gretchen said, looking helpless.

"I love you, Gretchen. That's all the help I can give you." He held her hand and kissed her. Then he quickly left.

The Jews in Europe would be decimated unless Zishe acted immediately, using his influence to warn and aid as many as he could. Of course, his life would be at risk but no more than any other Jew's in Germany. First he had to make contact with an organization that had courage and foresight. There were several groups he'd been following. They had different religious and political views, but they were united by one goal—saving as many Jews from destruction as they could.

Zishe was bitterly realistic about the fate of European Jews. Most would die, but those who escaped would ensure their culture's survival.

Zishe heard of Mark through the grapevine. Mark was part of a rebel Jewish group that believed Jews must use arms to defend themselves, but that it was too late to prevent the slaughter in Europe. After a great deal of effort, Zishe managed to get in touch with Mark.

Zishe knew what was said about him behind his back. He was trusted by the Nazis but not by the Jews. It took a lot of work before Mark would even consider a meeting, and Mark set up the conditions.

"We'll meet in the church. You won't know what I look like, but I'll know you. Just sit alone, and if it looks safe, I'll contact you." Mark's note was curt, scribbled on a piece of brown paper, with the time and the church circled in red.

Zishe was patient. He sat through a sermon, all alone, waiting.

The choir had just finished when Zishe decided he'd waited long enough. He stood and started to leave.

"Zishe."

He turned to his right and there was a man in his twenties with a mustache and a goatee. "I'm Mark. Keep looking ahead and be seated. And you'd better have something important to say," Mark whispered.

His German was good, but the way he spoke gave away his origins. Zishe guessed he was from Vilna, Lithuania.

"What do you know about me?" Zishe said.

"Austrian, businessman, on friendly terms with Goering and all the other fascist pigs. An opportunist—someone who would sell his own mother. You probably know every detail of what is going to happen to the Jews," Mark said, spitting out the words like bullets. "If this is a trap—or anything close to one—you're dead. So get to the matter quickly. I have no time for Nazis."

"I've done a good job if I can fool you. Your group knows power. You're not cowards—guns, weapons—they're a part of your philosophy. Jews must defend themselves," Zishe said.

"Quick, out with it," Mark said impatiently.

"This is not a trap. I am a Jew. Never mind how I got into such a position of power," Zishe said in Yiddish, hoping it would help him.

"Big deal—so you speak Yiddish. You're either a Nazi who can speak Yiddish, or a Jew who has sold his soul."

Zishe was hard-pressed to continue. What proof can I give? No matter what I say, he'll doubt it. And why should they trust me? I can't blame them if they don't accept my offer.

"I can see why you are suspicious. My own sister mistrusts me," Zishe said, sighing.

"Stop whining. Time is running out," Mark said, thrusting a pistol into the back of Zishe's head.

"You have no choice," Zishe said, fearlessly. "You have more to lose then I."

"In what way?"

"You kill me and there will be no escape for hundreds of thousands of Jews," Zishe said, turning around, his eyes glaring.

"I'll take a chance. I have no choice," Mark said, placing the pistol back in his coat. "But I still don't trust you. I wish I could read your mind, but I'm not God or an angel."

And then the angels appeared. Twenty-four—they were in every pew, some even on the altar, and a few hovering near the ceiling.

And Mark was seeing them too. Mark's eyes opened wide, and his face was like a child's, full of wonder.

"Angels," Mark said. "Like from the Zohar—I can't believe my eyes."

Zishe and Mark were smiling together ecstatically, taking in this heaven on earth. And the angels were telling Mark to trust Zishe.

Mark turned to Zishe. "I stopped believing in angels and God so long ago. I believed our destiny is in our own hands. But this—" Mark lifted up his hands. "How much will you help us? Will you stop this wave of evil? Will you change their minds? Will you give safe passage to every Jew?"

"Listen to me, Mark—we've got to act on our own. Believe me, we have very little time. The Nazis are out to destroy us. Hitler is preparing a holocaust, a shoah for Jews."

"How can you help us? Money, connections? Where do you come in?"

"First money. You'll need lots of it. For ships, railways, all types of transportation. We've got to get Jews out of here."

"To France? Holland?" Mark said.

"No. Europe is not safe—those countries will be gobbled up in a hurry."

"Then where? Palestine? America?" Mark asked.

"Yes. And England is also safe." Zishe gave a detailed account of what they had to do.

"Is this where you come in?" Mark said.

"Yes, as long as I have my cover."

"Weapons, guns, grenades—" Mark was ahead of himself.

"Hold on a minute." Zishe was overwhelmed by Mark's plans.

"For Palestine," Mark said. "To make Israel a reality. But they will also need them here. They can't just go to their graves like sheep. Those who are willing to fight should have weapons."

"Yes, for those who are willing. God helps those who help themselves. Let's get going," Zishe said.

"Next week. I'll let you know the place and the time," Mark said.

Mark started to leave, but Zishe stopped him and said, "I'll bring money. *Shalom.*"

Zishe felt a sense of pride. To be a Jew and risk everything for the Jews, to help, that made him feel alive.

Mark skipped across the street, waving. He disappeared around the corner.

"Thank you—thank you. *Shema Yisrael adonoi elohenu.* I put my life in your hands. Praised art thou, our Lord, our God, and God of our father. God of Abraham, God of Isaac, and God of Jacob..."

Zishe's heart was light, and he felt he could endure anything, even the guests who'd be at Frau Weiss's dinner party. He was so grateful. God had plans for him.

The bus stop was nearby but he wasn't in a hurry. He decided to walk. He stopped to buy a paper on the way.

"Hitler demands immediate apology for maltreatment of Germans in Poland," the headline said.

Zishe only skimmed the articles. The paper was full of threats. "Germany warns." "Hitler denounces the traitors that separated Danzig from Germany. World Jewry, he says, will have to pay for this conspiracy." He folded the paper and put it away. It wouldn't take more than a visit from a brigade or even a few colonels for Danzig to become part of Germany. Still, Danzig was not yet in the Third Reich. At least the laws were still different. Jews didn't have to wear the Star of David. They still could hide their identity. But the German eagle could swoop over the city any day.

Zishe worried about Gretchen and felt helpless. She was in a difficult position. She had to decide whether to be a Jew or a German. There was no middle ground. He was so preoccupied he nearly passed by the Weiss house.

"Zishe. How nice to have you over," Frau Weiss said. "Come, let me introduce you to our guests." She was dressed as if she was twenty, in the latest fashion from Paris. She looked very svelte, much thinner than Zishe remembered, until he

124

saw the outline of her corset. She looked as if she was going out of her way to announce she was now available.

Poor Herr Weiss, Zishe thought. He'd probably give anything not to be a Jew.

"Colonel Wolff and Frau Wolff, Colonel Bingle, and Frau Bingle," Frau Weiss said.

He had never seen her so pleased and in such good humor. Her husband's departure must have been a great relief to her.

Then Gretchen appeared. "Hello, Zishe," she said, taking his hand, eyes cast downward. She was dressed in blue, with shoes and necklace to match, and a small blue comb in her hair.

Zishe took her hand and they sat down together. "I like blue," Zishe whispered to her.

Gretchen smiled. "Thank you."

"The news is so exciting," Frau Weiss was saying. "My organization, that is the women's section of the party, have been discussing the imminent addition of Danzig to the Third Reich."

"Since we're both military men, Colonel Bingle and I applaud such an action," Colonel Wolff said.

Colonel Bingle added, "And Germany's threat to Poland…"

"Completely appropriate," Colonel Wolff said, nodding.

This evening could turn out to be long and boring, Zishe thought. Zishe had to say something. "I hear your Jews have to wear armbands of identification?" Zishe looked directly into their eyes.

"Yes, that's true," Colonel Wolff replied.

"Why?" Zishe said trying to make them uncomfortable.

Frau Weiss frowned.

"I suppose to protect Germany's interests," Colonel Bingle offered.

"The Fuhrer himself ordered it," Colonel Wolff said with authority.

"Do you think there will be war? Britain is making all sorts of noise about Poland," Frau Weiss commented, changing the subject.

"Our Fuhrer knows how to play these games. I leave it in his competent hands." Colonel Wolff's's words were applauded by all but Zishe and Gretchen.

Frau Weiss was relieved dinner was being served. At least it would occupy their time. This group was not very talkative, in spite of all her efforts.

Dinner was served. "May I offer a toast?" Colonel Wolff stood up with a glass of wine. "To our Fuhrer and the Third Reich."

"*Heil* Hitler." The response was mechanical. The eating began in earnest. The maids made sure everyone's plate and wine glass were filled.

Zishe's plate remained untouched; he was not hungry. He began seeing Bingle and Wolff's lives unfold before him and he wondered why he was seeing this. Then Zishe noticed Gretchen was also experiencing this vision.

She put her hand in his, pressing it tightly to show her excitement. Zishe now saw the angel. She was trying to get his attention.

"Gretchen needs to see how difficult it is to live as a Jew. This view of these two should help her be more prepared," the angel said to him. The angel disappeared, her words still ringing in Zishe's ears.

Gretchen and Zishe saw Colonels Bingle and Wolff stationed in a small city in occupied Czechoslovakia. There hadn't been much action. The Czechoslovakians had put up little resistance.

It was Sunday and both were in church. Their mutual love of Jesus gave them a sense of communion and a special friendship. They walked together to a small cafe across the street from the church. The sun and the drinks made them feel good. They talked about where they'd be sent next—Russia, England, or France. Bingle had no illusions about war. He knew it could be brutal. So far he'd done little fighting, but the thought of going to Russia frightened him. Bingle was concerned about how the Jews were being treated and he expressed this to his friend. Wolff kept saying, "But those are our orders. The Führer knows best," even though he, too, had doubts.

Then they were assigned to reinforce the Polish police. Bingle couldn't stand the treatment of the Jews there. The Jews worked hard but were treated brutally by both the Poles and the Germans. He began to speak out. "No whips, no physical abuse. Keep your insults to yourself. These are people not dogs."

Bingle kept thinking of Jesus. "Do unto others as you'd have them do unto you." He saw Jesus in every face.

Angels rejoiced at every one of Bingle's decisions. Gretchen's mouth fell open when she saw the angels.

Colonel Bingle was called to answer for his soft treatment of the Jews. He was given a special assignment to prove he could carry out orders.

Instead of angels, Gretchen and Zishe now saw smokey wisps, vicious, cursing, ready to become a part of Bingle.

But Bingle saw through the deception. He believed Jesus would have him love the Jews. The evil spirits were very angry as they dissipated.

The next day Bingle reported as ordered. He was put in charge of an SS Death Head unit, which operated secretly behind the lines. The few paved roads were in disrepair, making the ride there bumpy and difficult to maneuver. Bingle was shown to a red brick building covered with ivy.

"My name is Captain Buerger. Let me show you the facilities. Your assignment will be to administer justice. Most of the work will be done by Jews who will be watched by German guards."

They walked toward a large converted truck, which was more like a van. It was specially constructed. Two rear doors could be hermetically sealed. The inner walls were of sheet metal, with no seats. The floor was covered by a wooden grating with straw mats on top. Two peepholes between the driver's cab and the van were the only way to view what was happening after the doors had been closed. Two tubes came out of the cab from the gas generators where the driver sat and were hidden under the wooden grating.

"Impressive, no?" Captain Buerger patted the truck. "Come, sit in the cab with me. Here—these buttons control the gas flowing into the rear."

Bingle saw an open truck driving a load of Jews to the spot.

"They enter the building from that door."

"What for?" Bingle's fears were coming true.

"They are told they need delousing. After they are naked, they are told to enter the van that is ready with the doors wide open. This is the point our guards need to take action."

"Why?"

"Because at this point they realize they are to be gassed. The final few steps are always accompanied by screaming. It's difficult, and we must use force to seal the doors. We drive them a hundred yards or so, stop the van, start the gas generator, and after fifteen minutes or so they're all dead. You can watch through the peephole if you like."

"And the Jews who help?"

"Oh they're grave diggers—they're a funny lot. No one will touch them. They're like lepers. They wait for the delivery over there." The captain pointed out to a spot about a mile away. "That's where we dump the bodies. In layers. Very efficient. These gravediggers can empty a van in fifteen minutes. Then it's ready for another hundred Jews." The captain smiled with satisfaction. "Just think of it as a job, for the Fuhrer. These Jews are like animals. They don't have feelings like us. We're doing them a favor. Picture in your mind how much better the world will be."

Zishe and Gretchen could feel Colonel Bingle's pain. A war was going on inside him between the angels and the evil spirits trying to gain control.

"Colonel Bingle, the Jews are undressing. You are to supervise the first gassing."

Men, women, and children were undressing, folding their clothes neatly. "Lay your clothes so you will know where they are after you return," Bingle said. Most were shivering from the cold. Bingle had been given a whip to use on them. Just another order. He was a soldier and he'd been trained to obey.

"Please, through that door," he said.

"We're going to die. No, not in that van. Oh, my God," voices wailed.

"Your whip, Colonel Bingle. Use it. Get them in," the captain shouted.

Bingle heard the *Shema*, the holy prayer, from every mouth. Orders came flying from all directions while Bingle stood paralyzed.

"Get in. Get in that van," the captain said. The whip cracked and snapped, and Bingle heard the hiss as the doors were sealed. The screaming became muffled, but the pounding of desperate fists could be heard.

"What the hell is the matter with you?" the captain said seeing the expression on Bingle's face.

"Jesus is in every one of those people. He's being crucified all over again," Bingle said.

He didn't realize how fast he could run, but Bingle passed ten soldiers before he got to the van. He grabbed the driver out of the seat and took the van. Bingle drove into the woods until it was dark, and the dense foliage could hide them. Then he opened the doors.

"It's all right. Please get out, leave."

The people looked so frightened. "Run! Please believe me, I don't want you to die. Run for your lives!"

He watched the Jews as they ran away without clothes. Huddled together, they disappeared into the woods. "Dear Jesus, please help them. Please help all the Jews," he prayed.

The soldiers soon caught up with Bingle. They marched him off to prison. His trial was brief. Sentenced for treason, he faced a firing squad with his soul at peace.

The angels surrounded Bingle. Zishe and Gretchen were overwhelmed by the vision. The Bingle of the future had triumphed over evil.

Zishe looked at his watch. It had only been a few seconds since the eating began. He caught Gretchen's eye. Then their attention turned to Colonel Wolff. While he was with Bingle, he listened to Bingle's concerns about the Jews and agreed with him. But then they were parted, and Wolff was sent to the city of Krakow. He was assigned to patrol the streets, enforce the laws, and watch for any sign of Polish resistance. He was effective and respected without being unduly harsh and was considered to be in line for a promotion.

"Colonel Wolff, I have been looking over your file. Excellent."

"Thank you, general."

"It seems you have earned the fear and respect of even your enemies. That is good. I believe you are the man for this assignment. They will listen to you."

"They?" Wolff questioned.

"The Jews. Oh, it's a small matter. We have to move them to a small camp."

"Yes, sir. Thank you for your trust," Colonel Wolff said.

"Starting tomorrow, you'll have two hundred men to help you. The trucks will be ready. It is important to do this quickly, before they suspect or offer any resistance."

They arrived early the next morning. Trucks, soldiers, rifles, and dogs, all ready to move at the slightest command. Wolff still had some doubts, but these Jews were different. They were dirty, dressed like paupers, and speaking a funny language. Maybe Hitler had a point when he spoke of "hygienic measures to ensure racial purity," Wolff thought.

He would have to give the orders to begin. He felt guilty. This was their home. He would be firm but gentle.

The dogs' barking made the Jews scream. They ran in every direction. They hid behind doors, in attics, basements, anywhere to avoid being caught. They act as if I am out to harm them, Wolff thought. Can't they understand? This is just another order. Why do they have to behave so? He remembered Goebbels: "Treat them with respect and they will spit on you. They are like vermin, they multiply unless they're squashed."

"Shoot them if they resist. That's an order," Wolff said. He was surprised—it hadn't been that hard. A barrage of bullets hit its targets. Twenty corpses were dragged to the center of the square. Thousands and thousands of Jews came out of hiding and got into the trucks.

After the Jews were gone, everything became very quiet. He still felt a little guilty. What would Jesus have done? he thought. Love your enemies, turn the other cheek—well, those were fine sacraments, but he preferred to think of Jesus throwing the money lenders from the temple. Yes, that would be his example—violence for a sublime purpose.

He was feeling better; he had done his job effectively. "These Jews, they're not even cultured. They smell. Hitler wasn't wrong." This would be easy.

The triumphant sounds of evil could be heard vibrating with the light. They smelled victory within their reach, fighting and cursing among themselves for possession. Gretchen could see evil at work. It hovered greedily around every thought.

"Excellent job, Colonel Wolff. I couldn't have done better myself. Your discipline under fire shows that you have great potential. We need men like you to control the Jews, otherwise they will undermine our Fuhrer and the future of the thousand-year reich," the general said later.

Wolff took in every word with pride. He liked to be praised. "Thank you, general. I have only done what I was told. It is my pleasure to be able to serve my Fuhrer."

"I will be sorry to lose you, but you have been requested by Obergruppenfuhrer Grusshart himself. Our loss is their gain. Here are your orders. *Heil* Hitler."

"*Heil* Hitler." Wolff saluted and left the room. Obergruppenfuhrer Grusshart. Wolff tried to remember where he had heard the name. Wolff knew Grusshart was the commandant of the camp where they detained Jews, but he couldn't remember for what purpose. He brushed aside his suspicions and opened his orders.

"Second in command—immediately—grave responsibility." Wolff read on with increasing excitement. "I'm going places. I wish I could tell Bingle." He missed him most at times like this.

The next day he drove past the guards, straight to the headquarters at the camp.

The camp was surrounded by barbed-wire fences and guards posted at strategic locations. He could see hundreds of figures in the distance, but it was hard to make out their dress or their features.

"Good to have you with us, Wolff."

"My pleasure, Obergruppenfuhrer Grusshart."

"Call me Hans. There is no need for titles here. We'll be working together very closely. This is a very special operation."

Wolff was beginning to like what he saw. This was a place of power.

"Let me show you around. This is quite an enterprise. You'll have no trouble with the Jews. You'll be surprised how docile they've become."

Wolff followed without a word although he had many questions.

"You'll be in charge of these." Grusshart pointed to a group of emaciated Jews wearing prisoner's clothes.

"Yes, sir." Wolff felt sorry for them. They were lucky he would be their guard. He would be good to them, compassionate. He watched as one of the guards abused the prisoners. I'll put a stop to that when I'm in charge, Wolff thought.

Wolff wandered into the yards. He needed to see the prisoners up close. "What's your name?"

"Shalom Friedman, sir—number five-three-zero-one-five." He removed his cap, snapped it against his thigh, and came to attention.

Wolff looked into his eyes—they weren't even human. This man reminded him of a frightened animal. "Why are you here?" Wolff said, trying to be kind. He had to move back, the smell was too awful.

"To work, sir."

"Did you do anything wrong? Maybe you stole or killed someone?" Wolff said.

"No, sir. Nothing like that."

"So, you don't think you deserve this."

"No, sir."

"Am I correct in assuming you feel our army would imprison innocent people?"

"I don't know, sir—I was told—they brought us here," the man said, stuttering.

Wolff was losing his patience. If this man was innocent, he would come straight with an answer and not have to beat around the bush. Maybe he had no conscience at all. He looked as if he was hiding something. Wolff had to believe in his position. He wanted to succeed, but he also wanted to feel he was just.

The face, the long nose, the mannerisms of an ape—subhuman—those scientists were quite right. Wolff walked around the man, full of moral indignation. I once believed Jews were our equals, that they had the same moral persuasion, but I never imagined that they could be like this, he thought.

"You look like an intelligent man. What did you do before they sent you here?" Wolff said.

"I am a rabbi."

"You mean you were." Wolff thought his tone was impertinent.

"I *am* a rabbi."

"Then pray, do something brave, let's see if God still listens to you."

"*Shema Yisrael Adonai elohenu...*"

"Enough, stop."

"*Shema Yisrael Adonai elohenu...,*" the rabbi continued without hesitation, as if the world depended on the prayer's completion.

Wolff felt his blood surge with anger as he took out his whip. This arrogant bastard, Wolff thought. To think they're still around after they crucified Jesus.

Wolff continued the beating until the praying stopped and the prisoner was dead. Wolff marched through the yard with his whip, making sure everyone understood.

Zishe watched the evil spirits applaud Wolff's thoughts. They liked his thinking, his anger, and especially the way he used his whip. They were thrilled they had been allowed to participate in such a cruel beating.

133

Gretchen couldn't believe how easily those vibrating remnants of evil had gained an entrance. She was amazed how they took advantage of the slightest opportunity to establish their position and incorporate themselves into the victim's mind.

Zishe felt impatient now. He was going over a mental list of people who could help him get money and visas for the Jews. "I'm sorry, I must go." Zishe got up and put on his coat.

"Thank you for coming. I know you have important things to do," Frau Weiss replied.

"I'll walk you to the door," Gretchen said.

At the door, Zishe pulled her close to him. He was silent; words seemed useless after what they had just seen. She'll make the right decision, he thought as he went down the steps.

CHAPTER ELEVEN

"Hotel Schloss, room number five-forty-five. Tell Herr Thyssen, Herr Holtz is in the lobby."

"Herr Holtz, Herr Thyssen will be right down. He asked me to tell you how surprised and delighted he is that you have come tonight."

Zishe sat down. He really knew very little about Thyssen. They had a few meetings, but he never could get past the surface.

"Herr Holtz. Good to see you."

Zishe's thoughts were interrupted. "Good to see you," he said, standing. He stared at Thyssen.

"Oh, the uniform," Thyssen said, looking down at his clothing. "You look surprised."

"Yes. I thought you were a civilian."

"There are no more civilians. Not within the party circles. Every businessman must be an example. It's nice you have come for a visit, but I can see there is something else on your mind."

"I need access to the company's funds."

"I thought you had it."

"Not all."

"Well, of course, most are commingled with other industries in a complex arrangement that goes all the way into the government's treasury," Thyssen said.

"We have an enormous opportunity," Zishe said, looking for a way to catch Thyssen in his own greed.

"Enormous?"

"Yes, very big. American money, lots of it, ready to be invested."

"With us?" Thyssen said.

"They want action. They like our efficiency. They see Hitler has brought stability to Germany," Zishe said, reeling him in. "Shipyards, airplanes, cars, that's where they want to put their money."

"Their sympathies are with us?" Thyssen said in awe.

"Yes. Many of their most influential men, such as Lindberg and Ford, have supported us."

"Yes, the pilot and the car manufacturer. Very intelligent men, very progressive. Any idea of the amount?"

"Yes. They will match us fifty-fifty. They want to see us support them."

"Well, they can trust us," Thyssen said emphatically.

"They want to see our cash. They want to be sure that we are financially sound, sort of like collateral. A goodwill gesture."

Zishe felt seedy. If Thyssen had any brains, he thought, he would send his own team of investigators to verify this information.

"Here. The key, the special code, my name and fingerprints—this will put the funds at your disposal."

"I'll contact you when I hear from the Americans."

Zishe was up early the next morning. He was eager to get started. He had run through the plans until he felt at ease with how he would proceed. The government treasury was in the heart of the business district. The entire operation should not take more than a few minutes. Just a few numbers, names, codes, keys, and fingerprints, and a check worth millions would be in his possession. Then he would have to deliver the check before the authorities could suspect anything was amiss. Mark had given him all the proper directions.

Zishe entered the bank, trying to act as casually as he could. One false move, and the gestapo would be all over him.

"Herr Holtz?"

"Yes." Zishe showed them the fingerprint and the number, and the manager accompanied him into the inner chambers of the bank's secret clearing house. Zishe immediately went to work on the sequence that opened the doors to the funds.

Two hundred million marks.

Zishe sighed with relief as he walked through the outer door. It had been easier than he had thought. He was now very rich, with a check in his pocket that would allow the Jews to escape.

A taxi drove him straight to the address where Mark's friends would be waiting.

"It's Zishe," he announced at the door.

"Come in, it's cold. Mark will be here in a moment. Meet Tobias." The woman, who Zishe remembered as Gilda, pointed to the man leafing through a book standing by the sofa.

"Hello. Mark was right—you look very goyish. But he assured us that he had some special evidence that you were all right," Tobias said.

Tobias was lean and tall, with a mustache and very thick glasses. He had a perpetual frown, and he squinted when he wanted to examine anything of importance.

Mark came into the room.

"You work fast," Mark said without greeting Zishe.

"Not nearly fast enough to keep up with the way the world is changing," Zishe replied impatiently. He paused. "How many people can you get out of the country at a moment's notice?"

"Twenty-five thousand. Some have visas, some don't, but with enough money we can slip them past some greedy officials," Mark replied.

"That's good enough for now. And weapons? Guns?" Zishe said.

"Machine guns, rifles, pistols, grenades—all ready to be loaded. The ships are waiting; the men and women have already been trained. Some are here, most are already in Palestine." Mark gave numbers and details effortlessly.

Zishe pulled the check from his pocket. "Here."

Mark kept staring at the figures as if they were carved in stone. "There is a God," he said.

"Weapons," Zishe said. "Where will you store them? Who will be able to use them? Do we even have a group, a militia, anything in Europe?"

"Too difficult, too much territory. Who will believe us anyway? They laugh at us. Don't you know what they call us?" Mark asked.

Gilda looked up helplessly. "Jewish fascists, that's what they call us, because we believe in fighting for our rights. They say we're making the problems with the Germans. That is all we hear." She threw up her hands in a gesture of helplessness.

"Our only hope is Palestine. We have to get Jews to leave, to convince them that this is not their home, that they will be murdered. Most won't listen. And you, what will you do?" Mark said.

"I am going to stay. I know we're doomed, but everyone has his mission," Zishe said. "I've got to go." Zishe turned to Mark and embraced him. Gilda and Tobias had tears in their eyes as they watched Zishe leave.

The church of the Sacred Heart was in Langfuhr in a district with a large Jewish population. Zishe had agreed to meet Gretchen there. When he arrived, she was already in prayer. Zishe slipped silently into the place she had reserved for him.

"I love you," Zishe whispered in her ear.

Gretchen put her hand into his.

"Why did you ask me to meet you here?" he said.

"I have to prove something to myself." Gretchen turned to listen to the bishop.

"Our Father, who art in heaven, please look down upon us in our hour of need." The bishop was looking up at the ceiling. "Our Fuhrer needs all of us to help him. Make his wishes come true, free our nation from those whose aim it is to destroy us from within. We ask in Christ's name that you bless our Fuhrer, along with all who have unselfishly devoted their lives to him."

Zishe could see Gretchen's nose wrinkle.

"Can you smell smoke?" she asked.

"No."

"I can smell it, I can even tell where it's coming from." Gretchen looked around for the exit. "Zishe, come let's go. Quick!" She tugged at his arm and pulled him behind her down the aisle through the door.

"I still don't smell any smoke," Zishe said.

"It's coming from there." She pointed toward the sea. "Hurry. It's only a few minutes from here." Gretchen held onto Zishe's arm. "I smell it. There it is."

Zishe had a sinking feeling in the pit of his stomach. The synagogue was burning. Some Jews were trying to put the fire out, while stormtroopers stood by drinking beer and laughing.

The fire department got there after the synagogue was already in ashes. The firemen pretended to be sorry, joining the Nazis in a rousing chorus of the *Horst Wessel Lied.* *"Wen juden blut spricht..."*

Gretchen hid her face in Zishe's chest. She was sobbing and shaking. "I knew it."

Zishe could barely hear her words. He wondered how she'd known, what had made her leave her church to see a synagogue burn down.

Zishe had to get her out of here. "Taxi," Zishe said, flagging down a cab.

"To your home?" Zishe asked Gretchen.

"No. I want to be alone with you. To your hotel." Gretchen cried for the entire ride. It was as if she'd left something behind her in the synagogue's ashes.

"We're here." Zishe cradled her in his arms.

"I'm all right. I'll be fine." She stopped crying. She walked with Zishe through the lobby and up the stairs to his room.

Zishe had Gretchen lie down on the sofa. He sat beside her, brushing the hair out of her eyes. Gretchen took Zishe's hand and stroked it as she gazed into his eyes. "I love you very much. I don't want to ever be without you."

Her eyes shone with such care Zishe knew he would never stop loving her. "And I love you. We will always be together, nothing will ever separate us," he said.

"Zishe—I don't know how to begin. I am afraid you'll think I'm seeing things, that my imagination is too vivid. But if you don't believe me, no one else will." Gretchen paused before she continued. "You won't think the less of me if what I say sounds bizarre or farfetched?" she said, taking Zishe's hands.

"It happened in the church," she said. "You were there with me. I saw it all. Everything laid out in magnificent splendor, with a lot of ugliness beside it."

Zishe moved closer.

"I'd been praying, saying the rosary, when I came to the part 'Father who art in heaven.'" Gretchen dabbed her eyes with her handkerchief. "The heavens opened—I wish I could describe it more eloquently—and I saw myself there. It was me, more me than what you see. Oh, I wish you could've seen me there."

Gretchen's eyes were glazed but ecstatic. "My soul, uncluttered and eternal, before I was born. Before I'd chosen—yes, chosen."

Gretchen was trying to find words to describe what was not meant for this world. Zishe could sense her frustration, but thought it'd be best to leave her alone and not to interfere.

"I was there even before God created the earth. Even before there were any other worlds," she said. "Before universes and other realms even existed. We were there with God together with every soul ever created."

Gretchen pressed Zishe's hand in hers. "This is the part that's so odd. I was among the souls that had chosen to come to earth as Jews, even though we knew how hard it would be." Gretchen paused. "There was one soul I felt I would meet someday. In a way, he reminded me of you."

Zishe wanted to say something, but he could sense she was still not quite finished.

"Then I was ready. I decided this was the time and the place where I was needed the most."

Zishe felt himself perspiring.

"That is not all. Zishe, I have to tell you everything, even the horrible ending. I am a Jew, and I will meet my death together with millions of Jews in special camps built to murder us."

"Would you make this choice if you hadn't had this vision?" Zishe said at last.

"That's a choice I made thousands of years ago. I cannot deny my father, that is a biological fact. If he is a Jew so am I. The Nuremberg laws are made by man, not by God. Hiding behind my mother's skirts would be living a lie and I can't. Life is short, anyway—who knows how long I'd live even if I denied my birth?"

"And your religion, your church? Jesus?" Zishe uttered the name that had been used against Jews for so many centuries with some hesitation.

"He, too, was a Jew—a very brave Jew. His soul was so brilliant."

"But the Jews have been charged with—"

"Crucifying him. I know how false that accusation is and all the suffering it has caused for us."

"Then your faith hasn't changed," Zishe said.

"My faith is stronger than ever. In Jesus I can feel the presence of God. To me they are one and the same."

Zishe was amazed how Gretchen's mind worked. She saw through the usual veils that covered the truth. "You saw the synagogue burning?"

"Yes, while the bishop was abusing the Jews. It was as if God was speaking to me."

Zishe suddenly felt very awkward. Gretchen had been so honest. He wanted to be completely honest, to tell her everything. That he was a Jew, that he was only posing as a Nazi to help his people. He even wanted to tell her how he was working with others to try to save as many Jews from annihilation as possible.

God has revealed to both of us the same terrible news of the future destruction of his people. Zishe was in agony. He was afraid if he told her all he was doing, he might be putting her into more danger. It was going to be hard enough for her now that she was declaring herself a Jew. I must leave her alone, he decided. I must put as much distance between us as I can.

And he already had planned numerous business trips, ostensibly to help German interests, but always to places where he could be of the most help to his people.

"My being a Jew—does it matter to you?" Gretchen said.

"Yes, it matters." Zishe looked straight into her eyes. "It matters more than you think." He paused. "It matters because now I know that we will always be together."

"Together?"

"Yes, together. But please don't ask me to explain. That much has been revealed to me. All I want you to do is trust me for a while, no matter what you hear or see. I know it will be hard, but I can't tell you any more."

Zishe had her in his arms. He kissed her and held her tightly. They were silent. Both knew that something solemn had occurred, that words of explanation were no longer necessary.

"I have to go. I won't even write to you. It's be too dangerous. When the time is right, I'll contact you. Always remember, no matter what, how much I love you." And Zishe called a cab to take her home.

CHAPTER TWELVE

It was Saturday, and Zishe was feeling lazy. He had nothing to do that couldn't wait until later. When he heard the knock at the door, he thought it was the bellboy with his breakfast. He opened the door, a tip ready in his hand.

"Zishe."

"Mark," Zishe greeted in surprise. "Come in. You look awful. Is something wrong?" He motioned for Mark to sit.

"Poland has been invaded. German divisions are now crossing the border," Mark said.

"When did this happen?"

"A few hours ago. Haven't you been listening to the radio? Danzig has gone crazy. Every street has a parade. Bands are roaming everywhere, celebrating, even smashing windows." Mark looked distraught.

"And Danzig?" Zishe was considering the possible implications.

"Danzig has declared herself part of Germany, part of the Third Reich. They're crazy as hell. The Fatherland—it's all they can talk about!"

"I'll be ready in a minute. I want to see this myself." Zishe quickly got dressed to go out.

"They're dancing, hugging, kissing like madmen. Where is that German composure they brag about?" Mark said as they went out onto the street.

Two arms suddenly caught Zishe around the neck. A drunk woman clung to him, her lips on his mouth thrusting herself into him. "*Liebling,* don't you want to celebrate? We're free at last." She was pretty, but he pushed her away.

"Look at that man," Zishe said, pointing to a man who was about age sixty, paunchy, smoking a cigar, and singing Germany's praises. He was dancing. "This is the day he's been longing for."

"The music—the noise, I should say. What direction is it coming from? Crazy assholes—singing their hearts out. Teutonic knights—yes. I like that—from the grave alive. 'Woe all the world, make way for our gods. Wotan, Thor—those I worship—destroy those who defile your sacred home. Heaven has pulled Germany up to make her great.' I can see their gods arising, demons from the deep," Mark said. He shook with anger.

"They're just in love with themselves. Nothing mystical about that," Zishe said.

Zishe had never seen the private side of Mark. He was always so filled with purpose, so involved in politics. Devoted to his goal, he was driven by anger and love, but now he and Zishe were affected by the mob.

"Hey! Lighten up, save that energy for where it counts. You should be proud of yourself—Germany needs more like you. Straighten that tie, wear that swastika like a man. That old Jew's no match for you. Here's some money—the beer's on me." Zishe dished out coins to an old man sitting on the sidewalk.

"I am not a Jew," the old man said vehemently. With beard, hooked nose, stooped shoulders, black coat, and blood oozing from somewhere in his clothes, he continued to berate Zishe. "Who knows what a Jew is? Maybe I am one and I don't know it. The Nuremberg laws suck you in. One-half, one-third, one-fourth, one-eighth Jew—all depends on who counts."

With the laughter of a madman, the old man vanished.

"Let's join the parade," Zishe said, laughing and hurting from inside. He pulled Mark to the front where there were flags and pretty women.

"This I like." Zishe pointed ahead. "We love our Fuhrer," he said sarcastically. "This banner tells of a great love affair.

Kiss them, embrace everyone. Sing Mark—this is one crazy day. Feel like them, you will learn more today than you ever knew. This is your enemy in love."

"Wenn den juden blut spricht...," they sang with sadistic joy.

Five hundred marchers propelled their bodies forward. "Danzig is Germany. Germany is Danzig. Yes, today is the start," they screamed. The mood had caught even Mark. He was marching arm in arm with the masses he despised.

"Germany, Danzig, Fatherland, Fuhrer—down with the enemy. *Wotan,* strike them dead." Zishe mouthed the platitudes his spirit hated in an insane patter.

"Make way, the conquerors are here." The people exalted.

Strutting, with goose steps in proper time, head and helmets inclined, rifles upright, arms at their sides, German soldiers invaded the narrow streets with trucks, artillery, and large cannons. Danzig offered herself as a willing sacrifice, in love with her conquerors. *"Heil* Hitler," the crowd shouted and women smothered the soldiers with kisses and roses.

"Nero, Danzig is burning, play your trumpet." Zishe shoved a bugle at Mark.

"You're crazy," Mark said.

Zishe struck a villainous pose and Mark blew a tune, some old nursery rhymes, part Jewish, part Rumanian, out of tune and very loud.

A chorus of troopers joined the fun, bellowing to Mark, "Hurrah to the Fuhrer. Blow that bugle. To the Fatherland, the Reich. Praise God and Christ, and don't forget *wotan."*

The night came too soon for the crowd. Danzig sagged. Lights blinked. Flowers and paper littered the streets where the stormtroopers hung around, some singing, "Glory be to all. If only there were more days like this, more Danzigs to be conquered."

Zishe had to drag Mark away. "Too much wine, too much victory. I know you don't drink but you're inebriated with life. That happens before death."

"Death? Who's dying?" Mark asked.

"Danzig. Europe," Zishe said. "That was a dirge. The last dance of death, free to anyone who wants to join. Far better than crying. Leave it to the Germans."

Zishe was irritated now. The celebration, the girls, the old man—they all played on his nerves. "Mark, let's get going. It's late. One taste of victory and then a frenzy will follow—and sooner than you think."

"If only I wasn't a Jew," Mark said, then looked ashamed. "If only this was a victory for the Jews in Palestine."

Stragglers and lovers wandered unchaperoned through the city. Zishe and Mark made their way back to Mark's home. Their plans became important again.

"The money, Zishe, two hundred million, it's being used to send Jews to Palestine, Panama, and Argentina. We still need guns and bullets. But there are so many more people, now with Poland under attack. Over three and a half million Jews left behind. Oh, God, how many can we get out? And if we can't get them to believe what's happening to them, what's the use?"

"I'm going down two to three weeks from now. On business," Zishe said. "I'll ride the rails in style. Don't forget, I'm part of this."

"I guess I got too used to you as a Jew. Pardon, Herr Holtz. This little Jew owes you an apology. *Shalom.* I'll send messages—you'll be met. They'll tell you what to do, who to see."

"Thanks, Mark. I'll check with you before I go."

"*Shalom,* Zishe. God be with you."

"Three weeks and we're nearly finished. A few more days, a little mopping up and Poland is ours. Warsaw, how you will love it. Like Paris, only sweeter. I hope those bombs didn't destroy its beauty. And the girls are so pretty," General Steinem was talking to his comrades.

Zishe was the only civilian on the train.

"They'll send their cavalry. No fun shooting them down." The general spoke with evident pleasure. "One warning shot and they come out running with hands covering their heads."

The group laughed.

"I hear the Russkies are worse. These Polacks are fierce in comparison." Surrounded by the officers of a conquering army, General Steinem was enjoying the cuisine provided by the dining car of this special train to Warsaw.

"Is everything in order?"

"Yes. My compliments to the chef."

"From our finest restaurants in Berlin." The maitre d' was standing with attentive respect.

"Ah, Herr Holtz. How fortunate to be part of this future," General Steinem said with a sigh.

Zishe watched the countryside slip away. It had been a while since he'd been there, but there didn't seem to be any change. Cottages in disrepair, rickety rails that even the best German trains couldn't ride smoothly on.

Zishe breathed in. He hadn't missed Poland. When he left he'd thought he'd never return. And he'd never thought he'd return in this way, powerful and in disguise.

"You're so quiet, Herr Holtz. You must have a great deal on your mind, what with materials, uniforms, medical sup-plies—quite a fancy bit of logistics," the general said, interrupting Zishe's reverie.

"Yes. Many things," Zishe agreed.

"Where will you be staying?"

"At Hotel Warszawa, at least for the first night."

"And then?"

"I don't know. There are too many uncertainties—ordi-nances, army positions, communications."

"Yes. The war—nothing is for sure."

"Yes—absolutely."

Zishe thought of the plans to meet Mark's friends. His contact's name was Zloty.

"Excuse me, general. I have some papers to finish—de-tails, nothing important. We should be in Warsaw in an hour at the most. Enjoy your meal. I'm sure we'll meet later."

Zishe moved through the diner toward his compartment. Alone, he skimmed through his notes. He reminisced about Warsaw—the smells, the politeness, the fights. The city of Jews and Poles.

The car was waiting for him at the station. "Hotel Warszawa, Herr Holtz?"

"Not yet. To twenty-five Slovik Street first. It's just a little bit out of the way."

"Yes, sir."

The streets, potholed and scattered with debris, made travel inconvenient. "The Jewish section, Herr Holtz?"

"Yes, I believe you're right. Wait here. It might be an hour or so." Zishe left the car and driver on the street.

Red brick two-story buildings with frilly overhanging potted ledges, crammed into yards without space, lined the street. People went about in a flurry of activity.

"Please. Excuse me." Zishe slid through the maze, dodging the people. He ran up the steps, skipped the first floor and stopped, knocking on the door.

"Who's there?" A voice said in Polish from behind the door.

"Zishe. Mark's friend."

There were skittering steps, voices consulting, arguing. Then the door opened. "Zishe, Mark's friend? We have no connection—some mistake—you have another in mind." The man was wearing a black coat and hat, his green eyes barely visible.

"Mark told me you could help."

"We still know nothing." Then he turned behind him and said, "Mark?" A woman came to the door.

"Last name? Maybe I can recognize."

"Liebowitz—"

"What's he done? Something wrong? Police?" The woman shivered in her thin cotton dress. Her lips could barely pronounce the Polish words.

"I have come a long way with this message." This time Zishe spoke in Yiddish.

"Now I understand. Of course, Mark. From Danzig."

"Can I come in?" Zishe said, almost pleading.

Zishe was lost here in his own world. He could sense their fear. "I have come to help you. Germany is not playing around. I might look like a Nazi, but I am a Jew. I am telling you the truth."

They parted to let Zishe enter.

"The Germans have a plan to kill every Jew," Zishe said. No movement. They just stared.

"If you stay here, they will murder every one of you."

"A madman, a regular *meshuggener,*" some muttered.

There were now thirty in the room. "We have connections. Visas to Palestine. Money," Zishe said. "We need to get the message through. Please help me. The future of our people is what we are fighting for!"

"Too hot. Too much sand. The Arabs hate us," they said in unison.

"Yes, hot. But there's the possibility of freedom. You'll have guns to defend yourself."

"Farming! We have lost that memory. Maybe they need tailors, shoemakers, jewelers," a shy boy of twenty said.

"You can learn. Others have."

"America, I have cousins there. France, I have relatives. Holland, Peru, Colombia," the crowd said.

Now he was getting somewhere. Hope ignited the desire to live. "The idea is to get out, not to choose your favorite place. Forget France, Holland. They'll be trampled by German armies. America, South America, Africa, Palestine—at least there you'll have a chance."

"Give the Germans a chance. They couldn't be much worse than the Poles. And who says they're out to kill us? Beware, young man, you're spreading rumors that could come back to haunt us," a man hissed. He was wrinkled and scowled. Bitterness emanated from him.

"Maybe he's right. Why start trouble? Let's wait and see," another voice said.

There was pounding on the door. "Open the door or we'll break it down."

"It's the Germans—quick, let them in," Zishe's host said.

Guns smashed through the wood, followed by four boots. Two soldiers stood menacingly tall.

"Herr Holtz. I told them who you were, but they went ahead anyway." Zishe's driver was eclipsed by the stormtroopers.

"What have we here? An illegal meeting of Jews?" The leader's glared menacingly as weapons were waved indiscriminately around the room.

"This is Herr Holtz. The head of supplies," the driver said.

"Can I ask you the meaning of this? I am here to investigate delicate matters that should be of no concern to you." Zishe flashed his badge.

"Oh. My apologies. I didn't know to what your driver was referring. You know we have to be so careful," the leader said, his disappointment obvious.

Weapons were lowered. Helmets were taken off in a show of respect.

"Give your names to my driver. You shall be put on report for trespassing and entering with complete disregard of orders."

The stormtroopers left. Zishe turned back to the Jews who were staring at him, frightened.

"What is happening to our world? Who can we believe? We have to put our trust somewhere, but where?"

"Listen to me and get away," Zishe said. Some nodded, others hesitated. "Start working, spread the news. Funds and visas will come, but you must hurry."

Zishe rose. "*Shalom.*"

"*Shalom,*" they responded.

"To headquarters." Zishe's driver gunned the car. "Take your time, drive around. I want to see the sights.

"But, sir, I thought you were in a hurry."

"Canvassing, only canvassing. I need to confirm the condition of the roads, the obstacles."

"Yes, sir."

"Straight, then turn left. Go five blocks and then turn right."

Zishe hadn't forgotten the neighborhood. Faces hadn't changed. Marriage, birth, death. Events were celebrated and ancient traditions were kept.

He saw the rabbi and they recognized each other. Then a familiar peddler. The car rumbled through the ghetto and Zishe searched through hidden memories of stores, homes, the synagogue. A crowd of children eyed Zishe, before the school vanished past the windows. Was that Morris from so long ago?

"Out of the way, you damn Jew," his driver said to a Jew and his goats on the roadway.

"Sorry, officer," the Jew said. "Goats are stubborn creatures. This won't take but a moment, sir."

The driver stepped out of the car and took out his pistol, ready to shoot. Zishe jumped out of the car and struck his hand down, surprising the driver. "I was just going to scare him."

"Don't you ever do that again," Zishe said angrily. "Now to headquarters."

The car glided to a stop in the spot assigned to Zishe. Soldiers were posted at doors, entrances, and rooftops.

"Herr Holtz, my name is Colonel Kube. I will be at your disposal during your stay in Warsaw. It will be my duty to carry out your orders and make your stay here profitable."

Colonel Kube looked young for his job, perhaps twenty-eight or thirty years old. He had close-cropped blond hair and chiseled features more granite than handsome.

"Exactly what have you done so far? What kind of experience do you have?" Zishe asked this clean-cut, mechanical being.

"Hitler youth with personal commendations from the Fuhrer. Tank commander, first to cross into Poland. Temporarily in charge of policing Warsaw's Jewish population."

"That's enough—your credentials are impeccable." Zishe felt hate race through his blood.

"Is something the matter, sir?"

"Nothing. I'll call you when I need you."

"I have been asked to brief you. But I'm sure you need rest. Some refreshments. I will be waiting on the second floor. That's where your offices are."

Zishe saluted and walked away. He'd nearly lost his temper. Hate does that, he thought. It's like a fire, a volcano erupting. He went into the officer's club and poured himself some coffee. He wished Gretchen was with him.

Zishe had a restless night. Colonel Kube kept reappearing in nightmares, terrorizing Jews in the most sadistic ways.

He awoke to the telephone ringing. It was Colonel Kube. He was to bring Zishe to see the Jews who worked in the manufacturing plant.

"The Jews are waiting. I told them you would be there to give them some encouragement. They're scared. They've heard all sorts of rumors. We need to allay any suspicions. All we want is order and good old-fashioned work."

The captured Jews were in the streets with suitcases, bags, and boxes. They dragged their possessions from here to there, wherever they were shoved or directed. They looked like lost sheep.

Zishe could feel their despair. Then the screaming started in the crowd close to the entrance. A woman screeched with terror. The sound was punctuated by the snap of whips and batons. He ran toward the horrible noise, dodging his way through the crowd. Colonel Kube was walking over, and as soon as he did, the screaming stopped. The soldiers pulled back and a woman lay silent.

Zishe could see some bruises and a few marks, but there was no blood on the victim. She sat up, dazed. The angels were surrounding Colonel Kube. Zishe could hardly believe his eyes.

There were twelve soldiers surrounding her, with blood dripping from their hands, clothes, batons, and whips. They looked puzzled.

Then the woman smiled blissfully, got up, and walked away.

Zishe saw how troubled the soldiers looked. They'd probably never seen someone recover so quickly.

Zishe couldn't move. He felt tears forming in his eyes. It was the angel.

"You were with Colonel Kube? I don't understand."

"We go where we are needed. You can't judge a person by their appearances. You can't always understand what a person's mission is."

"The future," Zishe said. "It looks so bleak for millions of Jews—to be murdered just because of some crazy lunatics."

"There is more help than you think."

"But the murders, the plans—can they be stopped?"

"Not entirely. But their plans can be thwarted. They will eventually be defeated."

Zishe was not comfortable with that answer. He still kept thinking of the suffering involved.

"This is only a very small part of the story. Remember there is a world to come that stretches into eternity. Those who die righteously sanctify that world. It's called *Kaddush ha-Shem*. They bring forgiveness to the whole world."

"And those who torture and maim? Those who chose evil?" Zishe questioned.

"Divine justice includes also judgment of those who do evil. They will get their reward in a world made just for them."

Zishe wished he had enough wisdom to understand everything he'd heard.

"I came here to try and contact Jews, to save as many as I could, to warn them and give them visas and money." Zishe felt his strength returning. "Can you make them trust me? Can you make them listen to me?"

"We're sent to help those in need, but only those who are willing to be helped—who are trying to fulfill the mission they chose," the angel said.

Now Zishe could see angels moving about, mixing in with the crowd, helping wherever they could. Some were with soldiers, some were with Jews.

"Jews listen. Hear me out. I will help you." Zishe had no fear. He spoke in a loud clear voice that anyone could hear. "Get out of this country. Tell everyone that Jews are in great danger. You will need help. I have visas and money."

Zishe went through the crowds answering questions, telling them where they could get the necessary papers.

The soldiers went about their business, apparently not noticing anything unusual. In fact, they seemed to be going out of their way to be more courteous.

CHAPTER THIRTEEN

The ride back to Danzig was quiet and uneventful. The signs of destruction were less evident. Poland seemed to have returned to normal.

But Danzig was still celebrating. Swastikas were flying at full mast from every corner. The streets were crowded with sailors, soldiers, and a newly arrived contingent of Germans. Weapons, from cannons to anti-aircraft guns, were everywhere,

Zishe wanted to know that Gretchen was all right. And he knew he could only get that information from her mother.

"Hello, may I speak to Frau Weiss?" Zishe hated to use the telephone. It seemed like such an impersonal way of talking. "This is Herr Zishe Holtz. Yes, she knows me well. She's changed her name? Frau what?" Zishe could hardly hear the name. "Frau Steinmetz. All right—whatever she calls herself— just let me speak to her. Anna, yes, this is Zishe. I've been in Poland with the army. Yes. Very interesting—I'll tell you all about it when I see you. Tell me, is Gretchen home? You don't know? Well, I can come up for just a few hours. All right, I'll be there tonight. Good-bye."

Zishe had suspected this might happen. He wondered where poor Herr Weiss was.

Zishe arrived at the family's house and rang the doorbell without enthusiasm.

"Come in," Frau Weiss said. "A guest of mine is dying to meet you. You must tell us all about Poland. I'm so proud of our army. Finished in just four weeks. How wonderful." She walked arm in arm with Zishe into the parlor. "You will love him," she said as she started her introduction. "Herr Holtz, Captain Kastner."

Zishe extended his hand as the captain stood up.

"I've heard so much about you. I'm honored to meet you."

"Captain Kastner is our new chief of police, now that we are at last a part of Germany." She made no attempt to hide her affection. She brushed his hair and stroked his hands, as if he belonged to her.

"Please tell us about Poland," Captain Kastner said.

"Not much to tell. I'm sure you've seen the news reels. We won. There is no more Poland. Gretchen," Zishe said to Frau Weiss. "How is she?"

She seemed startled to hear her daughter's name. "Oh, Gretchen—she's a very silly girl. You know she's not Jewish, but she insists on saying she is."

"My very thoughts. How could she be a Jew with a mother like you?" Captain Kastner smiled but looked concerned.

For a moment Zishe thought they would embrace each other, but they only held hands.

"Heinrich. Pretty soon he'll be right up there with the party heads," Captain Kastner said.

"When he heard his father had a Jewish background— why, he was furious. The thought of it made him sick. Thanks to God for our Fuhrer's wisdom. His laws are necessary. I don't know what I would have done if my children could not choose whose bloodline they followed," Frau Weiss said.

"And your husband?"

"He is not my husband." She was full of indignation, with her hands clasped to her heart as if those words hurt her.

"What Anna means is that the marriage is voided. We have disposed of those dreadful laws forced on us by the Jewish international conspiracy."

"May I then rephrase my question? Where is Herr Weiss?"

"He's indisposed," she said.

"Indisposed?"

"Stutthof—that's where he is. That dirty Jew—that's where he belongs." Her voice was full of anger.

156

"The concentration camp? Isn't that the one about twenty miles from Danzig?" Zishe continued as if he was interrogating her.

"Yes, that's where he is. And on my orders." The captain spoke in an officious tone.

"Why?" Zishe said.

"Because he resisted the law. He is not allowed to do business in Germany. That goes for all Jews." Frau Weiss's tone changed. She acted as if the entire affair had been beyond her control.

"I understand. You did it out of love for your country, out of patriotism." Zishe knew he had to handle her carefully. She could still be useful to him. "And Gretchen?"

"Here is her address. Maybe you can bring her back to her senses. She will listen to you. Such nonsense. She doesn't know how bad it is to be a Jew," she said.

Zishe thanked her. He tried to keep his remarks short and courteous. Promising to be in touch, he apologized for his haste and casually dropped some important names. Zishe knew how easily they were impressed. The captain wouldn't let him get away without at least a toast to their friendship, the Fuhrer, and Germany.

Events were moving along much faster than Zishe had expected. The changing laws and their brutal enforcement made him realize how transient friends could be.

He could tell this Third Reich wouldn't last. But many innocent people were going to be hurt. Zishe couldn't let himself dwell on that. He had too much work to do. He had to obtain Weiss's release from Stutthof. He'd have to go there in person. The SS could be very brutal, and Zishe knew Weiss wouldn't last very long.

Twenty miles was not very far, but Zishe let the soldier drive. The swastika-emblazoned car looked impressive. Zishe had made sure they knew he was coming and that Weiss would be available. He did not want to waste his time. He had seen the gestapo at work.

"There it is, Herr Holtz. About a mile away." The buildings cast a faint silhouette against the sky, flat boxlike buildings enclosed by a high barbed-wire fence.

Zishe showed his papers at the gate.

The camp was stark and ugly. A few inmates were shoveling dirt from one pile to another. A guard stood by, his rifle slung casually on his arm, watching the car drive toward him.

"Where is the visiting room?"

The soldier pointed to a hut attached to the main barracks.

"I am Captain Geiss. We spoke earlier." He was dressed in the khaki uniform of a prison commandant. He bowed, keeping his heels at attention, then thrust his arm into the air in the standard salute.

"I thought Herr Weiss would be ready, as we agreed," Zishe said, looking around.

"Corporal, be quick. Bring Weiss out." The captain said, shouting at the guard as if he was at fault.

Zishe didn't recognize Weiss at first. His head and face were completely shaven. His face was gaunt, and his hollow eyes kept staring ahead into space, as if he was unaware of what was going on around him. "Michael, it's me, Zishe."

"I knew somebody by that name." He finally allowed his eyes to settle on Zishe. "He looked like you—but that was a long time ago."

"It's the same Zishe. Your partner. Everything is going to be all right."

"All right," he repeated mechanically.

"You'll come with me. I'll get you out of here."

Zishe walked over to Captain Geiss. The captain had already obtained his instructions from the gestapo to release Weiss into Zishe's custody. "Don't worry about his clothes. I'll dress him at home."

The driver led Weiss by the hand, as if he was blind, warning him of obstacles ahead.

"Let's get going." Zishe was impatient and very angry. Those imbeciles, he thought. He looks more dead than alive. He had a hard time constraining his fury. He wanted to talk, but Weiss sat perfectly still, his eyes wide open but oblivious to his surroundings.

Zishe knew that Weiss would need help—first to recuperate, then to emigrate.

Zishe had arranged for a nurse to stay with him at an apartment. He'd also found a doctor who was willing to treat Jews. The soldier helped Zishe get Weiss into the bed.

"Thanks. I'll call you if I need you."

The soldier saluted and left.

The nurse bandaged his wounds. Weiss offered no resistance, still unaware of what was happening.

"Order anything you need," Zishe told the nurse. "Food, medicine, just tell them to charge it in my name."

"He'll need lots of food. He hardly weighs anything. He must have been starved, besides the torture." She couldn't help crying.

"This man's in shock," the nurse said. "We're seeing more and more of this since torture has become routine."

"Will he recover, do you think?"

"Yes, in time, maybe. He'll start to talk when he feels safe, and maybe he'll begin to recognize things, little by little."

"Thank you for coming to help me. You're very brave, caring for a Jew."

"I must help God's people."

She was a kind woman, a devout Christian, as was the doctor. Zishe wished there were more Christians like them.

Danzig plunged into Nazism with the ardor of a long rejected bride trying desperately to make up for lost time. It was hard to see through all the debris where Jewish houses and businesses had once been.

The gestapo and police used any excuse for an arrest. There were also the mobs, the Hitler youth, the stormtroopers. All out for a laugh and to prove their patriotism. The Jews were an easy mark.

Zishe spent a great deal of time traveling from city to city: to Frankfurt, Vienna, Warsaw, Lodz, Krakow. The war and the need for his products were making him rich. His factories extended from border to border, including Poland, Austria, and the Sudetenland. And Zishe continued giving money to the Jewish underground.

The weeks slipped by and became months. Weiss was getting better but still not making much sense.

Zishe missed Gretchen. He had to fight the urge to contact her. Any premature move could alert suspicion and place her in danger. He would have to be patient and wait until it was safe. Then he saw her on the street. She was wearing the yellow Star of David on her coat, and people kept their distance. He knew it was time to get Weiss out of the country, but he had to get in touch with Gretchen first. She had to leave, too.

He wondered how he could approach her. He had her address and knew where she worked. He'd asked Mark to watch over her. Zishe didn't think she had any idea of what it was to be a Jew. He'd told Mark that if anything happened to her, he should contact him.

Mark lived a few blocks from Gretchen's place. He shared his apartment with several friends. It was small but comfortably arranged.

Zishe explained the situation as best he could.

"You're acting like a nervous bridegroom," Mark said. "Just go to her. Explain everything. Tell her what you're doing."

"I don't know if I can. But I have to get her out of the country with her father."

"They want to leave?" Mark said.

"The father barely knows his own name. They broke him. And Gretchen—I don't know what's going on with her."

"She wears that star like a medal of honor. She doesn't even try to hide it. I think she really is happy to be a Jew. Funny how you can never figure people."

"Figure people?" Zishe questioned.

"Yes—I always figured a Christian would rather die than be a Jew. I mean, the stuff they're told about us."

"Well, you figured wrong. Don't put them all into one basket."

Mark accompanied Zishe to Gretchen's apartment building.

"Room three-oh-two. Her lights are on."

Zishe rang the bell, but there was no answer.

"Try knocking," Mark said.

"Who's there?" It was Gretchen's voice. She sounded suspicious.

"Zishe Holtz," he said.

"Is this some kind of joke?" Gretchen's voice sounded hard and irritated.

"Gretchen, it's me, Zishe. The Mariakirsche, the Church of the Sacred Heart, the statue of Jesus." The handle jiggled, and the door opened just wide enough to let a sliver of light out. Gretchen looked at them. After a few seconds, she unbolted the chain. She tightened the belt on her robe and straightened her hair.

"Can we come in?"

Gretchen seemed stunned and relieved. "Come in. Please excuse my appearance."

Zishe was surprised how strongly attracted he still was to her. Her suffering only added to her beauty. "This is my friend Mark."

Gretchen focused on the Star of David stitched on Mark's coat. "Have a seat."

"It's been a long time."

"Yes, a very long time." Gretchen answered listlessly.

"Your father—"

"He's dead I think," she interrupted. "They took him over to Stutthof. My mother did it. She had the gestapo take him away. She told them that he'd been spreading sedition and was involved in illegal acts. Her new boyfriend is head of the police. I tried to visit my father, but I wasn't allowed."

Gretchen spoke with great composure, relating the details matter-of-factly. Zishe noticed a tear that she quickly wiped away.

"What can I do for you?" Gretchen looked straight at Zishe.

"You have to leave." The second he said the words, Zishe wanted to bite his tongue. He had meant to suggest this more subtly.

"Where can I go?"

"Your father is alive. He's reasonably well," Zishe said.

"In Stutthof?"

"No, at the place I got for him. He's been there for months with a nurse. Physically he's all right, but his mind—he's not the same man you knew."

"You got him out? Why?"

"Because he's my friend. He believed in me. Because I love you. And because I am a Jew like you." Zishe heard the words, hardly believing he was saying them.

"Why did you hide it?" Gretchen's voice was cold and angry.

"He's saving thousands of his people," Mark said.

Zishe felt like a fool, like a schoolboy in front of a teacher, trying to prove what he was telling was the truth after habitually lying.

"You're known as a Nazi," she said.

How humiliating, he thought. Like being known as a murderer. He felt sorry for himself. For a moment he would have given anything to be free of his present position, even if it meant that he'd have to stop helping thousands of Jews. Zishe brushed that thought out of his mind.

"I love you too much to see you hurt," Zishe said, trying to hide the tremor in his voice. "I am involved in illegal activities." He paused, trying to regain his composure. "Espionage, stealing, impersonation, falsifying documents, supplying weapons to Jewish partisans—I had to keep secrets. I knew it would only be a matter of time before the authorities caught up with me. I feared that they might also suspect you. It has been very hard to keep away from you," Zishe said, softly.

Zishe noticed the change in Gretchen. Her face was suddenly full of joy, almost radiant. Her eyes opened wide.

Zishe looked up. All twenty-four angels, the ones that had appeared to convince Mark, were lighting up the room with a heavenly glow.

"Just like when we saw them before, the same angels that appeared when we saw Colonel Bingle and Colonel Wolff's future lives." Gretchen's voice had changed. It was now excited and ecstatic. She was staring into space. She pronounced his name, the way she used to, as if she was discovering him for the first time. "Zishe, just like the angels in the church that day when I watched myself come to earth."

Gretchen put her hand out to Zishe. She was crying with happiness.

"Yes, Zishe is a Jew. He is a Just Man. He has saved hundreds of thousands of Jews, and he'll save even more. The Nazis can't see what he does—they are blinded by their egos," the angel said.

"Look." Gretchen stepped back in awe. The angels spread out a scene before them.

All three watched as Jews arrived in Palestine, England, and Africa, escaping certain death. They watched Zishe and Mark's efforts bear fruit in the many lives saved.

"Now you know why you must leave with your father," Zishe said.

"And leave you to die without me?" Gretchen said. It was said as a challenge.

"You must leave. I have to stay and die with my people."

"Then my mission is with you. I can't leave."

"Your father will leave tomorrow. I've arranged it. His visa is ready," Zishe said.

"Where to?"

"To Palestine."

"That's good. Maybe he'll learn to become proud of being a Jew," Gretchen said.

Zishe wanted Gretchen to stay, to be with him, but he did not want her to suffer. "You have chosen a very difficult role," he said. She tried to interrupt but Zishe continued. "Please, Gretchen. Just let me say this once and then I will never mention it to you again. To be a Jew here is going to mean torture and death."

"That's my choice."

"But I don't want you to be tortured with me. When they find out what I have done. The money I have diverted. The secrets I have divulged. The bribes, the Jews who have escaped."

"I know," she said. "I love you, Zishe."

163

"But they will punish you too," Zishe said, pleading.

"I can only die once, but we have the world to come. Eternity before us—isn't that what we're here for? To complete our mission? Don't we have a higher responsibility and a special covenant, to die for the sanctification of the divine name? *Kaddush ha-shem*—isn't that the pure offering?" Gretchen said, taking Zishe's hands.

"I love you, Gretchen." They kissed in spite of Mark's presence.

"Here's my address," Zishe said, writing it down.

"I'll be there tomorrow to say good-bye to my father." Gretchen unlocked the door for them. The streets were dark. The clouds were heavy. Only a few dim lights illumined their path.

✡CHAPTER FOURTEEN

Zishe was worried. He had expected Gretchen at eight and it was already ten. His imagination was getting the best of him. The thought raced through his mind that maybe the gestapo had seen her with Mark. He kept looking at his watch, pacing back and forth.

Weiss was moaning in the bedroom. Occasionally Zishe heard him speak to imaginary companions. Zishe was worried about his behavior. His movement out of the country had to be kept secret.

"Herr Holtz? There is someone at the door," the nurse said as she dressed Herr Weiss.

"I'll get it." He went to the door eagerly. "Gretchen! At last! I was getting worried."

"I knew you'd be concerned. The stormtroopers are having some type of celebration."

"Did they see you?"

"No, but they're looking for Jews. I had to go the long way around."

"I forgot—"

"You're not used to me being a Jew," she interrupted.

"Not quite." Zishe helped her remove her coat.

"Hold me, Zishe." For a few seconds they felt safe in each others arms. "I can read your thoughts."

"Let's see how good you are."

"You're getting ready to be a representative at an international meeting in Geneva. Germany wants to put on a good

165

face to deflect the rumors that they're killing Jews. Let's see, the United States, the Soviet Union, Switzerland, Sweden, Japan, Hungary, even members of the occupied countries France, Holland, Denmark, Norway, and Italy will be there."

Zishe laughed. They thought alike. He was happy he now had nothing to hide from her. "But you forgot that every thought was also filled with you."

"You're also a good flatterer." She curled her lips into a half-smile.

"We have so little time to be together. Every moment is precious." Zishe sighed. Their lips touched lightly.

"Herr Weiss is ready," the nurse said as she entered the room. "Try to speak softly—he's still easily shocked."

Gretchen entered the room where her father was sitting. He looked past her while he chatted to someone she couldn't see.

"Father, it's me, Gretchen."

"Yes—we were thinking of you. Isn't that so?" He grinned into empty space.

She picked up a chair, set it directly in front of him, and sat down. "It's good to see you," she said.

His eyes flickered, as if he was trying to refocus his thoughts on the person in front of him. "Gretchen." He stretched out the word. "It's really you."

"Yes, it's me."

"Your mother divorced me, put me in a camp. They beat me. They made me do all kinds of horrible things."

"I know, Father. But you'll be in Palestine in a few days."

"Palestine? But that's for Jews. I'm a Christian, a German."

"You'll be well taken care of."

"I don't want to be a Jew. I converted to Christianity a long time ago. They're mistaken. Your mother doesn't understand. I was treated like a Jew in Stutthof—like the others. I tried to make them understand I'm not really a Jew. It's all right to treat real Jews that way, but I'm not like them."

He was crying and his hands shook.

"Father, trust me. You can be anything you want in Palestine. But not here. If the Nazis call you a Jew, then in their eyes that's what you are," she said sadly.

"Nobody understands. If I could just speak to Hitler myself. He's so intelligent. Maybe Goebbels—that's a magnificent man, or Goering or Himmler. Of course they'd understand. Just give **me** one more chance. They'll let me have my business back. I'll be a German again. Yes, that's what I will do."

"Goodbye, father. I love you." Gretchen kissed his forehead, put her arms around him, and then left the room.

"I'm sorry you had to see him in this condition."

"Thank God he'll be out of here soon." Gretchen reached for her coat.

"You're leaving?" Zishe sounded disappointed.

Gretchen nodded sadly. "It's true then, the meeting in Geneva?" she asked.

"Yes."

"When they ask if those rumors about the treatment of Jews are true, you'll be in an awful spot. I'll pray for you."

"Do you still go to church?" Zishe said. He knew how much that had meant to her.

"They won't let me in—no Jews allowed." She spoke as if it no longer concerned her. "I'll pray for you." She paused. "I always do anyway."

Zishe started to follow her down the stairs.

"No. I'd rather say good-bye here. It's so hard."

Ever since he'd first heard about it, it had been Zishe's plan to go to Geneva. He had to lie and slip money into many hands to persuade the officials in charge to let him go along. "Just as an observer," Zishe told them.

At first they had protested, claiming that he had no expertise in such matters, that his specialty was uniforms. He didn't have the proper credentials to face the representatives of so many of Germany's enemies.

"We need someone who we know we can trust to support our policy concerning the Jews. Of course, we also need someone who they will consider impartial, whose professional status is removed from the army. You at least have never been known to say anything against the Jews."

Now that Zishe had permission to tag along, he had to think carefully about how he could use this opportunity to tell the world what was happening. He realized he had few options. Orders had to be followed. The window of escape was narrowing very rapidly. Germany had changed from a beer-brawling mob of stormtroopers and Nazi supporters, to a highly efficient professional apparatus. Bureaucrats, scientists, and administrators followed orders without question.

This was Zishe's first flight in a military aircraft. He arrived in Berlin in less than two hours. He was met by the three men who would represent Germany at the conference.

They introduced themselves as if they were pulling their names out of a hat. "Glad you're aboard. We need all the help we can get."

Zishe had trouble telling who was speaking, or whether they spoke in unison. Dressed meticulously, their civilian clothes made them look harmless and gave them a cultured, international appearance. They looked like ambassadors of peace and justice. Zishe was sure the gestapo had rehearsed them.

"Zishe Holtz," he said. "From Danzig."

"Danzig. Wonderful city. You must be so proud."

"Yes."

"Please step forward, gentlemen," the pilot said, walking up to the group. "The airplane is ready. We're cleared to depart within the hour."

Zishe was relieved to get going. He'd asked for a special seat so he could be alone to prepare for the conference.

The conference was attended by reporters from all the countries that had business or political involvement with Germany. Zishe and the three representatives sat under the German flag in the spaces provided for them.

"Herr Holtz, I'd like you to meet Bishop Thiered and Bishop Ernst. They have been sent by Berlin to answer any questions that might be related to religious fears," said Herr Mueller, a German delegate.

Both men were important spokesmen for their respective denominations, Bishop Thiered from the Lutheran church and Bishop Ernst from the Catholic. Zishe had heard them speak before. Both were eloquent, succinct speakers. They were vigilant in their support of the government and had been only too willing to oust every converted Jew from their respective congregations.

The delegates were trying to find their seats. There was an air of excitement in the room. Zishe could see the silent negotiations as the countries lined themselves up according to their alliances.

The countries recently occupied by Germany were well represented. Zishe looked closely at them. Poland, Norway, Denmark, France, Yugoslavia, Czechoslovakia, Holland, Belgium. Collaborators, he thought with disgust.

"Don't bother to answer any questions." Mueller leaned over to Zishe. "We'll take care of that ourselves. Maybe a short speech at the end, something inspirational coming from you that would add just the right touch of confidence to our position," he suggested.

"The conference will come to order." The chairman thumped the podium with his gavel. "This conference has been called by unanimous consent. We are here to address certain alleged complaints that have been directed against the present government of Germany concerning the treatment of Jews in Germany and in the occupied countries. We are here to determine if there is any truth to these accusations."

Zishe listened as each country got up to speak. They couched their questions in the most docile, vague, and diplomatic language they could muster, hardly seeming to accuse Germany of anything. They referred to rumors and quoted sources they implied might not be entirely reliable.

Zishe was furious. This is monstrous, he thought. They're letting Germany get away with murder. This isn't even a slap on the wrist. Now Germany can see how little the world really cares about Jews. This is just the signal they need to go ahead with their plans.

The German delegates had no need to refute such watered-down charges.

The delegate from Poland was particularly impressive. He even lashed out against the Jews themselves for allowing such malicious lies to cast aspersions "on one of the most enlightened governments history has ever produced."

A Jew tried to speak without success.

"You're out of order," the chairman said. "You do not represent a country. If you don't sit down, you will be thrown out."

Germany diplomatically allowed all the countries to voice their opinions. Zishe listened to the evasions as each country tried to avoid any involvement.

"Thank you for your patience," the chairman said to Mueller and the rest of the delegation. "I believe we have settled this matter to the satisfaction of the entire conference. Germany is not directly responsible for any anti-Jewish activities that might have taken place in their territories. The political policies of Germany are not anti-Semitic."

Applause greeted the chairman's speech. The delegates were anxious to leave. The smiles of satisfaction on their faces were a sign of the relief they felt at finding there really was no problem to solve.

The chairman motioned with his hands to indicate he had something else to say. "We have not heard a word from our German delegation. They haven't had a chance to defend themselves. I believe we would all like to hear what they have to say."

Mueller advanced to the podium as the delegates quieted down. He stood silently as though deep in thought. "Ladies and gentlemen," he said finally. "We're deeply grateful to have you as our friends. Your quest for truth and justice is a tribute to the new order, the new world that will soon become a reality. We didn't have to come. We had nothing to hide. We even let you decide. We are completely exonerated, as we knew we would be. We're sorry you had to waste your precious time on the Jewish conspiracy's repeated distortions and lies."

Scattered applause greeted the remark, with the delegates from the occupied countries clapping the loudest and longest.

Zishe knew he would not be called on to speak, but he had to make a move. He felt his heart pounding in his chest as he stood. The audience rose to applaud Zishe as he took his place at the podium. He was surprised by the reception he was given. Mueller's mouth dropped open, but he stepped back and let Zishe through.

"I have something to say," Zishe said, although he wasn't sure what he was going to say to this audience. They were so willing to let Germany off the hook. If he told the truth, he wouldn't be able to work from within any more.

"The world," he said, "is troubled by hatred, rumors, and jealousy. We face many difficulties."

Zishe knew there was not a moment to lose. Germany is about to attack Russia. The Jews living there will be trapped. That thought gave Zishe the courage he needed. This would be his last chance to warn the world of Germany's diabolical plans. He took a deep breath, and with both hands grasping the podium, he looked intensely at the audience.

"I am a businessman, a manufacturer of textiles. I've produced clothes of all types and uniforms. I am successful and rich. My businesses are very profitable," Zishe said. "I am not a Nazi. I have no official position with the government of the Third Reich. I have never taken an official position or spoken on anything political before. I have kept my opinions to myself."

Muttering could be heard from the audience. Zishe could hear the uncomfortable shifting of positions.

"The leaders of Germany have confided in me about the real nature of their plans. These are not the same as those they have expressed in public."

"Traitor. Liar." A few of the delegates were becoming agitated.

"I have traveled throughout Germany and Poland through the courtesy of the government and the army. What I say is based on what I have seen and heard." Zishe relaxed his grip on the podium, grabbed the microphone and walked toward the edge of the speaker's platform. He waited until there was complete silence, even turning around to quiet the German delegation's nervous whispering.

"Hitler has a plan. Goering has a plan. Himmler has been assigned to carry it out."

Mueller started to stand, to protest, but Zishe stared at him and he sat down.

"All Jews are to be liquidated. Exterminated." Zishe paused just long enough to let the response die down. "At this very moment Jews are being murdered, by special Einsatzcommand groups attached to each army unit. Jews are being forced to dig their own graves before being shot or buried alive."

Zishe stopped to see the effect his words had. He continued. "*Vernichten arbeit*—work them to death. This is being carried out through forced labor under conditions where Jews will die like flies. Jews are taken from their homes and transported to camps where they can be disposed of more easily." Zishe glared at the delegates. "Preparations have been in place for years. Mentally deficient and insane people have been used as guinea pigs to find just the right combination of chemicals and chambers that will expedite the murder of Jews most efficiently."

"Nonsense, rubbish!" both bishops said, shouting their disapproval.

Zishe turned to them. "Hypocrites. You know better than that. Where are the Jews you have kicked out of your congregations? Those whom you called Christian before? Where are they?"

Their faces became red.

"In cattle cars, in concentration camps. You've sent them to their death. The final solution, that's what you call it. Camps with special gas chambers are already being built to accommodate the Jews arriving from all over Europe and soon from Russia." Zishe's voice cracked with emotion as he addressed the delegates. "Something must be done if you have any conscience at all. If you leave them to die, the world will never be the same again. It will be hell. You are responsible. This is your choice." Zishe could see he'd hit a nerve. The conference had quieted down.

"Remember—what you allow to be done to the Jews will come back to destroy and haunt you, too."

Zishe heard the words of Jesus coming from him. "'I tell you the truth, whatever you did for one of the least of these brothers of mine, you did for me.... Whatever you did not do for one of the least these, you did not do for me.... Then you will go away to eternal punishment, but the righteous to eternal life.'"

"How dare you quote Jesus, desecrate his words!" Bishop Ernst was irate and he looked as if he would strike Zishe.

"Yes, bishop, those are the words of Jesus. And his brothers are the Jews—just like he was and I am."

"I knew it. You're a Jew—a dirty Jew." Bishop Thiered said with contempt.

Mueller and the German delegates stormed out of the room. The conference was in shambles. Delegates were shouting at each other and at Zishe. Accusations were flying. Guards had to break up the fights that were starting everywhere.

CHAPTER FIFTEEN

Zishe knew he no longer had a home; everything he owned would be confiscated. If he returned to Danzig, he would most likely be arrested as soon as he crossed the border. As he walked the streets of Geneva after the conference, he knew he couldn't stay there. He wouldn't be of any use in Switzerland.

He searched for an inn where he could get food and a place to hide until he could figure out what to do next.

"Hey, German."

Cap tilted, unbuttoned coat and shirt exposing his chest, the man reeked of alcohol. "You, German," he repeated, his hot breath clouding the cold air. He approached Zishe, stumbling and reeling.

Swiss Deutsch, mixed with French, twisted the drunk's thick tongue.

"I need to find an inn. Here's some money," Zishe pulled some change from his pocket, "but first find me a good hideaway, a quiet place. Then the money is yours."

The drunk grunted and tried to grab the money but clutched only air. He lost his balance and landed on the stones.

"First the inn."

"Okay, follow me," the drunk said thickly.

Zishe felt the cold air; he'd left his coat back in the hotel.

"Shema Yisrael Adonai Elohenu Adonai Eh'oth." The drunk wove through the streets, singing. *"Yis-gadal d'yis-ka-dash sh'mayra-bo."* The voice was rich, deep, echoing off the

walls. *"Yori-bon o-la v'ol 'ma-y adah-t hu mal-ko me-leh-mel-he-yon."*

Am I hearing voices, or is this the drunk singing Hebrew prayers? Zishe wondered. He listened and followed. The song wandered with the drunk through the narrow streets. Tears were pouring from Zishe's eyes as he tried to catch up with him.

"Yis-ga-dal d'yis-ka. Shalom—a-ky-hem-mal-a-ha-he-sha-raysmel-a-hay-el-yion."

"Here's your inn," the drunk said. They stopped in front of a brick wall at the end of the street.

"This is a dead end."

"My money." The drunk stretched out his hand, as if he had done his job.

"Your money—for a brick wall?"

"No money—no inn." The drunk had his hands folded in front of his chest in defiance.

Zishe handed the money over. The drunk immediately put it into his pocket.

Zishe started walking away, thinking he had been cheated, when a sudden impulse made him turn around. The brick wall was still there, but now there were windows and doors, with soft lights glowing warmly inside. He could even smell a roast cooking. "Le Juif —the Inn of the Jew." The French words hung from the door.

"Let's go in," the drunk said. He sparkled.

"An angel. I should have realized, your singing."

"We're always around." They entered and were met by many more angels.

Zishe sat down and food was brought to him. The drunk was the most glorious being Zishe could remember ever seeing. Azure, purple, gold, silver, amber—a kaleidoscope of colors were coming from him.

"What now? Where do I go from here?" Zishe said. He knew he had to return to Danzig.

"Your decision is correct," the angel said, reading Zishe's mind.

"I know I'm going to die. I've been told. I am a Just Man. I must take suffering upon myself so the world will not disintegrate from all the evil that is being unleashed." Zishe knew he would die, but how, when, and where it would come about he didn't know.

"We will support you," the angels said in one voice. "We are here to help."

"Thank you," Zishe said. "Tomorrow, I will leave for Danzig."

The angels saw the question in Zishe's eyes. "Be at the main railroad station at four o'clock in the morning. The international sealed train will leave at that time. No one can inspect or search it. You will be safe until you exit. You will have a new passport."

"*Shalom,*" was all Zishe could say.

"*Shalom,*" the angels said.

Zishe showed the Swiss police his passport and his ticket.

"Danzig," the policeman said. "That is in Germany, for your information."

"Yes," Zishe replied.

"Well, if that is what you wish," the policeman said uncertainly, looking worried. "But I must inform you that you will have no protection. The moment you exit the train, our jurisdiction ends."

"I understand. You have made yourself clear, and I thank you."

Zishe counted the hours by cities and towns. Berne, Zurich, the border. Each click of the wheel brought him closer. Castles, forts, the forest—history passed by through the windows. Crusades, wars, the plague—reminders of yesterday eulogized in statues and squares.

Munich. On the front page of a newspaper fresh from the press, Hitler was glorified. Then Zishe recognized his own picture above the words "traitor" and "Jew." No mention of exactly what he had done. There were a few words about him stabbing Hitler in the back and defaming the Third Reich but nothing else. How unfair, Zishe thought sarcastically. Not a word about swindler, embezzler, spy, or how he had pulled the wool over their eyes.

Zishe laughed to himself. They were embarrassed to have someone outsmart them, to have to admit they were not invincible. They'd probably erase his history, burning any pictures of him. He was probably number one on the gestapo's most wanted list.

The train didn't even stop at Nuremberg. Zishe thought of that great valley a few years ago with thousands of Nazis and Hitler accepting their adulation. What would the knights of old have thought? he wondered. Are their ghosts still clanging around watching this new clown using their town?

Berlin—a brief stop. No passengers on or off. A few letters and a station full of soldiers waiting to embark for Russia. The war had begun in earnest.

Zishe spotted a few Jews being loaded onto boxcars. They were branded with yellow stars.

"Next stop, Danzig," the conductor said.

Zishe turned to see the last Jew disappear from view. As soon as he was home, he too would have to wear a yellow star.

"You'll be just another Jew, for a little while." Zishe remembered the angel's words. He couldn't remember much more. "Just long enough." Zishe repeated the words to himself.

He fell asleep and his dreams were filled with angels. He remembered traveling to a realm where the flowers were like gems, alive and glowing with love, telling him he was a Just Man and all would eventually be well.

Danzig.

Zishe reached inside his coat to feel his new passport. He'd need it when he went through customs. Zishe pulled it out and leisurely thumbed through the pages. Schlomo

Glatzman. Right underneath his picture, it said, "Occupation tailor. Born in Lemberg." And it had a capital J.

Getting a new passport and new name had been easy enough. Money could still buy documents for practically any purpose. Schlomo Glatzman. Zishe had to remember his new name. He had to prepare himself to be a Jew again. He walked through his memories, remembering how it had felt, the fear and the joy. He felt the bulge in his side pocket. His fingers traced the contents before he pulled it out. A yellow Star of David. Zishe fingered the embroidered borders. He remembered the look on the tailor's face when he'd ordered these badges of shame. He'd be arrested on sight without these stars. But he would wait until he got to Danzig to put them on.

Zishe thought of Gretchen and Mark, and how good it would be to see them again. Zishe could picture Mark in a kibbutz, working to make the hot desert sands fertile, blooming with rich crops and flowers. He could feel the warmth in his daydreams.

"Danzig. Please exit if this is your destination," the conductor said.

This was no time to dream. Zishe pulled his luggage from the overhead rack. The passengers were moving forward toward the open doors. Zishe pulled out the arm band.

"Please move forward."

"Yes," Zishe replied as he fumbled trying to pull the arm band into position while holding onto his luggage. He could see the passengers back away from him as if he had a plague.

He felt transformed by the arm band, turned from a prince into a toad. Zishe tried to extricate the cloth of the second star to wear on his coat. It had become caught on the bottom in his pocket.

"Move, you dirty pig," the man behind him said.

The words of defamation shot through Zishe, completing his transformation from Nazi to Jew as he hastily pinned the star to his coat.

Customs waved everyone through with a smile and a salute, until they came to Zishe. "Anything to declare?" the officer said.

"Nothing."

"Nothing?" The officer said sarcastically. "Let's see, Jew. Open it up. We don't have all day." Zishe opened the bag as fast as he could. "Take every single item out. Spread them in front of me." The officer waited until all of the contents were neatly stacked in front of him. Then, placing his foot on the stand, he kicked everything all over the station.

"You're free to go, Jew. Pick it all up," the officer sneered.

Zishe dodged between moving feet, underneath the stands, and around tables, trying to find his scattered possessions. He humbly excused himself as he stooped in front of the passengers' feet.

That was some initiation, Zishe thought. I'll be lucky to get through the streets alive.

Zishe walked away from the station, avoiding the main streets. He knew where he could go without attracting too much attention. He would have to walk—public transportation was too dangerous. He would try to make his way to Langfuhr. Maybe he'd be lucky and find Mark and Gretchen without too much effort.

Shouts came from every building along the way. It was especially hard to contain his rage when the children surrounded and blocked his way. He had to patiently wait until they tired of their game and let him proceed on his way. He knew they were waiting for an opportunity. One touch, one false move, and they'll come running after me, he thought.

Even the back alleys, the side streets, were not safe. But the thought of seeing Gretchen again kept him moving.

He was down the block from her house when he saw her. She was walking in the opposite direction. Zishe started running. He wanted to call her name, but he was still too far away. Suddenly, Gretchen turned around.

"Zishe," she said.

"Gretchen," he said breathlessly. They embraced without fear or shame.

"Come, let's go back home." Gretchen's eyes were moist, but her voice was strong. "You, too?" She touched his star.

"You must have read the papers," Zishe said, as they entered the room.

"Yes," Gretchen said as if it were of no importance. "Just a little notice that you betrayed your country. A Jew, that's all." She turned to Zishe. "You must have given them hell at that conference. They want to destroy you."

Zishe laughed.

"How did you get off the train?" she said.

"I am Schlomo Glatzman." Zishe showed her his passport.

"Looks like you."

"Of course, it's me," he said. They both laughed. "I've missed you. I couldn't wait to see you."

"I thought I'd never see you again," Gretchen said, crying.

Zishe cradled her in his arms, rocking back and forth. He couldn't talk. He knew this moment wouldn't last, but he wanted it to be something he could remember when they were parted.

"They're rounding all the Jews up. There are only a few of us left, and they know exactly where we are." Gretchen spoke in a grave voice, but without fear. "Zishe, we don't have much more time. This will probably be our last...."

Zishe understood and held her close. He kissed her breasts through her clothes.

"Let me," she said, unbuttoning her blouse. Zishe explored each part she exposed. "This will be forever, even though it will be the first and the last." Gretchen pulled Zishe toward her.

"In death we will continue—on and on, with love that will never end—timeless."

Zishe saw the realms, angels and all. "Do you see it, Gretchen?"

"Yes, my love," she replied.

Their flesh moved together with each touch until he was swallowed deep inside her. They tasted heaven together and a feeling of peace descended. Then they fell asleep in each other's arms, as if all their cares had ceased.

## CHAPTER SIXTEEN

The next day came too soon. Zishe had dreamt of Gretchen all night, and when he awoke with her beside him, he thought he was still dreaming. He let her sleep while he lit the stove and prepared a pot of coffee.

Gretchen woke up. "It smells good." She got out of bed. "I've never seen you cook before."

"Some cook—I just boil the water and pour it through the filter."

"You're silly," she said.

"And you're right." He laughed and drank some coffee. "It gets me going first thing in the morning."

"You're telling me all your secrets, your bad habits. Maybe I'll find you less charming. I might even become disillusioned."

"So then I'll just have to find someone who's less picky," he said, smiling.

She started to giggle, and Zishe pretended that she had wounded his pride. Then they both fell into each others arms.

"What will I do without you, now that I have you at last?" Gretchen brushed back his hair. "I don't look pretty in the morning, do I?" Gretchen asked, pretending to pout.

"More beautiful than ever before. Now I can never let you go." Zishe was trying to memorize her face, to capture this moment.

"What will happen to us?" She kissed Zishe's forehead. "What will happen to the world we know of? Oh, don't mind me—I just want to hear myself talking to you." She sighed and let him go.

"How many have been rounded up?"

Gretchen started to wash the dishes but stopped. "I'm sorry, Zishe. I guess I just wanted to pretend a little longer that we were in another world, that there would be a happy ending."

She started crying, but abruptly forced herself to stop by taking a deep breath and moving away from Zishe. "Most are gone—they've only left a few of us. I don't expect they'll leave us alone now that Germany has invaded Russia."

"Where?" Zishe barely finished the word before Gretchen interrupted.

"Stutthof, Auschwitz, Birkenau, Belzec, Sobohor, Chelmno. Does it really matter? To their deaths, that's where."

Zishe had never heard Gretchen speak like this. Her soft voice rose with her anger until it seemed to accuse the whole world. "Say something. Tell me that what I am saying is a lie, an illusion. That I will soon wake up and find the world full of peace."

Gretchen could no longer contain her sadness. She rushed over to Zishe. "Please hold me," she said as she dug her fingernails into his flesh. "Never leave me again. I want to die with you, no matter where. Promise me, tell me it will be so."

"I promise we'll be together—we'll die together." Zishe had no doubt that his words were true. He had never been so sure of anything before.

Zishe didn't know exactly how he would start his new life. He had some money with him, but that wouldn't last very long, maybe a week or two. Finding work would be difficult, especially since there were no longer any Jews in business, and he doubted if many places would dare hire him.

Gretchen still had some work, but that was temporary and undependable. She worked as a maid and cleaning lady, and sometimes even helped sorting vegetables in a small grocery. They'd let her work only because they had known her family. She could see the fear in their eyes every time the police or gestapo came near.

"I've got to leave for work. I'll be home at seven." Gretchen had already dressed and was ready to leave. "I can't wait until tonight. I love you so much." She kissed Zishe and started to leave, but turned around. "Be careful. Avoid public places, and make yourself as inconspicuous as you can."

Zishe smiled reassuringly. He watched her through the windows as she walked down the street. "I'll try to find Mark first. I hope they haven't taken him away," Zishe muttered to himself. "No, Mark's smart. He knows how to make himself scarce. He'll last longer than most. And he has all those contacts."

Zishe felt reassured. He looked at his arm band and his coat. He had no choice, he'd have to put them on. If he was stopped without them, he would go straight to jail.

Zishe walked through the streets, trying to appear as casual as he could. He'd gotten used to hearing the curses. He didn't even bother to turn around. As long as he was left alone, he could bear the taunts.

He made his way to where Mark lived, grateful it was not far away.

Zishe hadn't remembered the house being in such disrepair. The stairs had large cracks along the edges where the rails were embedded. The walls were chipped, the windows broken, and yellow paint was splashed on the door, forming the word *Jude* with a Star of David. They're labeling houses too, he thought. Soon they'll be making their marks on our bodies.

The bell didn't work, but it was easy to open the door because the lock was broken. All Zishe had to do was use his shoulder to push the door aside. "Mark?" Zishe said.

His possessions had not been disturbed. Zishe walked through the kitchen and into the bedroom. Mark was sleeping soundly in the bed, his head wrapped in bandages. Zishe tiptoed until he came close enough to hear Mark's breathing.

It was hard to believe this was the Mark he'd known. His mouth was swollen and several teeth were missing; his eyes were circled by large black bruises. He was moaning in pain and mumbling incoherently.

185

Zishe hated to wake him up. He decided to wait. Looking for some diversion while he waited, Zishe looked around until he came upon some newspapers. Zishe turned the pages. There was a picture of the newly married Frau Weiss and the police chief. What a pretty picture, Zishe thought bitterly. She's certainly in a hurry to climb the political ladder.

"Zishe."

Mark propped himself into a sitting position. His bandaged head, black eyes, and swollen lips made him look like a clown.

"Mark." Zishe threw the paper aside. "What have you been up to? Looks like you aren't doing so well."

"No, not well at all." Mark held his head between his hands. "A few stormtroopers and Hitler youth, only ten or twenty." He laughed. "Those are better odds than most get.

"The Jews, you mean," Zishe said.

"Yes. There's not many of us left—a handful. I don't know what they're waiting for. If you ask me, this is their way of torturing us." Mark started to cry.

"That bad?"

"Worse."

"Tell me, Mark, how many did we help?"

Mark's face relaxed, and he spoke with pride. "One hundred thousand. At least that, maybe more. And the weapons—they have enough to die fighting. And Gretchen?"

"I saw her to work this morning."

"Good. She's a brave woman."

"I need to do something. I want to help."

"There's nothing. Just sit and wait until they pick us up. I've seen so many go. By police cars, trucks—they're brought to the trains. Away from the main station, where no one can see. Where they used to keep the cattle. It's all so easy—the rails go right through."

Mark started to drift off to sleep and Zishe decided to let him rest.

There were still some Jews in the streets. Zishe could tell who they were by the way they tried to camouflage their movements. But this only made them more conspicuous.

He was getting good at avoiding dangerous situations. He'd been on the other side, he knew how they thought. It felt good to outfox them, at least as long as he could.

Zishe passed by the Mariakirsche. He could still remember his first date there with Gretchen. The smell of the flowers in the garden brought back pleasant memories.

He stepped into the church. A few people were at their prayers. He walked past the pictures, and the statues until he came upon the simple carving that had affected him so profoundly.

"So that is Jesus." Zishe reread the words. Truly a Just Man, Zishe thought, wiping the tears from his eyes as he remembered being here with Gretchen.

Zishe looked at his watch. Seven-thirty. It was later than he thought. Gretchen must be worried.

Zishe walked down the path. He was still far from home. A bus swung around the corner. He'd have to take a chance. Walking would take him too long.

"*Jude.* Back there." The driver motioned to some empty seats far away from the other passengers. Their eyes followed him with contempt.

Zishe was grateful to be alone in the back of the bus. But he had to pass through the rest of the bus to exit. The chorus of insults followed him out, along with a few kicks. Zishe held his sides where he hurt the most.

It was dark. He could run with relative safety. A few more blocks and Gretchen would be in his arms.

Zishe ran past the house. He hadn't recognized it in the dark. There were no lights to guide him. He stopped, turned around, and searched.

Zishe looked at the house again to make sure he was correct. Zishe walked back with a sinking feeling that something was wrong. He ran up the stairs. The door was ajar. He tried to switch on the lights, but they wouldn't work. He lit a match.

The room was a mess. Everything was either broken or out of place. Gretchen was gone and the signs of struggle were everywhere.

"They've got her. They've taken her away," Zishe said. His voice was full of rage. "The railway—the cattle station." He was sure she'd been taken there. He had no time to waste.

Zishe leapt over the pavement. In his rush he nearly tripped down the steep stairs between the streets.

The cattle cars were outside the city, just far enough to be hidden from view. It was curfew time. It was forbidden for Jews to be outside. The darkness hid his flight, but he'd have to pass through the main station. Then he remembered the path that circled around through the park and bypassed the station.

It was dark. Zishe had trouble finding his way. He had to grope between the benches and the trees. He could smell where he was going. It was good cattle left such a foul trail. He never thought he'd be glad to inhale it.

The odor carried him to his destination, where his feet followed the path cleared by his hands. There was a light between the bushes. He was closer than he thought. He could now see the faint outline of the trail.

He was making too much noise. His breathing was labored, and the branches snapped beneath his feet. He stood still trying to catch his breath.

He could hear the soldiers shouting commands and the barking of the dogs.

Zishe crept through the park, avoiding the bushes, and trying not to make noise.

"*Jude, herein.*"

Zishe knew they were loading the cattle cars. He'd seen that done before. He knew the procedure. First the orders, then the dogs, and, if there was any hesitation, then the whips. He kneeled and peeked through the bush that blocked his view. About a thousand Jews. Fifteen boxcars. And a hundred soldiers with whips, rifles, and dogs.

He could barely make out the silhouettes of the moving figures. A dozen times he thought he saw Gretchen, but a dozen times he was disappointed.

The sparsely lit platform cast dark shadows, and the flash-lights sweeping through the crowd seldom lingered long enough for him to recognize anyone.

There she is—it's Gretchen, he said to himself. The soldier kept the light in her eyes, as if he was trying to blind her. She was ready to embark, pushed by the soldiers and the crowd.

The soldiers were shouting and too distracted to see Zishe come from the bushes and step in line. A whip tore into Zishe's back, propelling him even further into the crowd. What a lucky blow, Zishe thought as he stood with only four people between him and Gretchen. He watched her picked up by the guards and shoved into the car. She didn't even look back.

"Nearly full," the soldier shouted as they prepared to close the door.

The car was already so full of people that Zishe thought he'd suffocate, even though the doors were still open.

Zishe's heart raced. He could nearly touch Gretchen.

"Shove the rest in. They don't mind each other's company," a soldier said, laughing.

Zishe was the last. He felt the door slide against his back, taking a piece of his jacket with it. He heard a loud clang and the bars snapping shut.

It was now quiet except for the laughter outside. There was no crying, no one spoke.

Zishe could see the back of Gretchen's head. She was wedged between people on all sides, with not enough room to turn around.

Air rushed in through the solitary vent as the train started to move. They'd been standing still for over an hour. The noise of the rails drowned out the few that now were starting to cry. It was too dark to be able to distinguish the people in the car. Occasional flashes of light illuminated faces for only a fraction of a second.

Zishe found he could slide his body, an inch at a time, to change his position. It was a slow process, but he had nothing better to do. He'd often have to wait until some light was available, if only for a moment, to be sure he was still headed in the right direction.

Zishe felt no fatigue. He was grateful to be here. He belonged with these people. He had to accept their fate. He thought of all the suffering, and then he thought of that statue of Jesus. Zishe could see Gretchen's profile. He had to slide in front of the person at his side, then swivel on his heels until he stood just at an angle in front of her.

Gently, gently. It's good to be thin at a time like this, he thought as he made the final movement. He felt Gretchen's body at his side. He could hear her breathing and her praying. She kept repeating the rosary. It was barely audible, but Zishe could make out the words.

The train rolled through a town. Zishe could tell because of all the lights.

"Zishe," Gretchen said, blinking. Tears rolled down her cheek. "Why?" She took his hand in hers and kissed it. "Your promise. You kept it. We'll never be separated."

"Which camp?" Zishe said.

There were hushed whispers, but no one knew exactly where they were going.

"Zishe, you must be tired." Gretchen stroked his cheek.

No water, no food. Even the dead had to keep standing. They tried to keep their spirits up by singing. That worked for only a short time—it was getting difficult to breathe in this cramped space with only one vent for two hundred people. The air was filled with the foul smell of waste and vomit.

"How many more hours? Days?" The questions never ceased.

"They can kill our bodies, but not our spirits. This is not the first time they've tried. If one of us survives, only one, and the world hears, we will have won," Zishe said aloud.

"*Shema Yisrael adonai Elohenu adonoi eh'oth.*" Gretchen's voice rose above the crowd, above the stench. Zishe marveled as the rest of the car joined in the prayer.

✡ CHAPTER SEVENTEEN

Four days out and the doors were still locked. Nearly a third were dead, and the rest took turns holding each other up.

"I see something, straight ahead." A child had been hoisted on the shoulders of the tall man next to the vent.

"Describe it to us," the tall man said.

"Buildings—people moving about—striped suits. Soldiers and large chimneys with black smoke.

"The name? Which camp is it?"

"I don't see any words."

Zishe could feel the train being switched to some side tracks, slowing, coming to a stop. Dogs were barking, guards shouting.

"Open the doors, open the doors!" a few desperate prisoners cried. They could take it no longer.

"Stop them. Put your hand over their mouths, or we will all be in trouble!" the others said.

Zishe could hear some muffled voices screaming.

Three hours later, the doors finally opened. They were unloaded like cattle by the whips and the soldiers.

"Women over there," a soldier said. Zishe watched Gretchen being taken away. The selection began.

"They kill people here—they kill people," said a man with the deranged look of the insane. His bones were visible under his striped prison clothes.

A guard came after the man. He wouldn't budge. He kept repeating his warning until the bullet went through his head.

This way, that way—fingers pointed to buildings. The strong were saved; the weak went to the gate near the smoke stacks.

Zishe was assigned to a work detail. All day long he dug large rocks from the ground and carried them to the edge of the camp. They were piled into a wall to hide what was going on in the camp.

Zishe worried about Gretchen. He wondered if she'd been chosen or gassed, if he'd ever see her again.

The guards beat the inmates when they fell or if they appeared lazy. Zishe watched how the guards went after certain types—the proud, the weak, those who looked the most Jewish, those who looked up at the wrong moment.

The German guards were terrible, but the Poles and Ukrainians were even worse. What a German guard would ignore meant death at the hands of a Polish guard. The Ukrainians liked to pretend they were cossacks and the Jews were their horses. They made the Jews neigh and strut while they rode on their backs. They were especially bad when they'd been drinking.

The trains never stopped bringing prisoners. They came from Greece, Yugoslavia, Russia, Poland, unloading their human cargo and turning around to bring more.

There was a man called *Der Kleine*, Small One. He could crawl through spaces only a rabbit or rat could navigate. He knew all sorts of things. For a few cigarettes or a piece of gold, he could find out anything you wanted to know.

"I saw her," he told Zishe. "She's working collecting clothes, shoes, and hair. She wanted me to let you know she's alive."

"Thank you." Zishe handed him a cigarette.

"Sorry. That's the best I can do," *Der Kleine* said sadly.

"At least I know she's alive."

The days were long and the nights too short. Zishe was always hungry. The bread and watery soup weren't enough to maintain his strength for the grueling tasks he had to perform. If not for the black market, the underground commerce that thrived under the eyes of the guards, Zishe would have starved to death months ago.

The Ukrainians liked vodka and gold. If someone could get friendly with the inmates who stripped the bodies and pulled the teeth, a little gold could go a long way.

Zishe was alert at all times. He knew that one false move, one mistake, meant instant death.

Zishe saw Mark and Yosi in the crowd as the train was unloaded, but he couldn't find out where they were sent. It was a few months before he met up with Mark.

"Mark," Zishe said.

Mark looked up in surprise, then continued working. Any suggestion they were talking would be met with severe discipline.

"Sorry I left in such a hurry," Zishe said, trying to smile.

"I thought you'd dodge them longer than that. Gretchen?"

"Gretchen's here. She's alive."

"They still don't know who you are?"

"No. I was Schlomo Glatzman until they tattooed this number on me. Now I'm number one-four-zero-zero-two-nine-seven."

"They must be searching all over for you. You got them real good," Mark said, laughing bitterly.

"What could be worse than this?" Zishe said.

Zishe shifted his position to get a better view of the guard from the corner of his eyes. "You came out with another friend of mine. Yosi."

"The Communist?"

"Yes."

"That's all he talks about—the people's revolution. The Russians coming to free us."

"He's okay. Tell him I'm here."

Mark picked up a large rock and walked away.

Zishe kept working as darkness fell over the camp. He said a prayer for Gretchen and his two friends.

Each day started with roll call. This could take a few minutes or a few hours, depending on how well the guard thought the Jews performed. "*Mutze* on, *mutze* off." The caps were taken on and off at the guard's commands, ending with a smart slap against the thigh. Over and over again. The command had to be obeyed by the inmates until the guard was satisfied they'd mastered it. Today roll had lasted only a half hour. The camp was expecting someone special. The prisoners had been busy putting everything in order for days.

A procession of seven cars entered through the gates. Zishe recognized the man with the steel rimmed spectacles sitting in the front car and looking like a poor imitation of Hitler. It was SS Reichsfuhrer Heinrich Himmler. Maybe he won't recognize me, Zishe thought. He remembers me in fancy clothes with more flesh on me. I'll blend in nicely with the rest of the inmates.

Himmler halted the procession. He was to inspect the premises.

"Roll call order—attention—*mutze* off," a guard ordered. The prisoners ran to their places, snapped to attention, and slapped their caps against their thighs.

Himmler held his baton at his side, walking stiffly and looking each prisoner in the eye as he filed past with his entourage behind him. He would stop abruptly in front of some inmate, appearing to have spotted something suspicious. Then he'd suddenly continue on his course, as if he'd found what he wanted.

Zishe watched him approach. He could feel his heart pounding against his chest, but Himmler stared him down as he had all the others, then continued on without any hesitation.

Suddenly Himmler stopped short and retraced his steps, landing squarely in front of where Zishe stood. "Don't I know you?" Himmler said.

"No, sir."

"Your number?"

"Number one-four-zero-zero-two-nine-seven, sir," Zishe said.

"The name attached to that number." Himmler said to the commandant.

"Schlomo Glatzman," the commandant said after looking in the book in his hands.

"Interesting. He looks like another Jew I had the misfortune to know." Himmler was breathing into Zishe's face. "Fingerprints," he said to the commandant brusquely.

"In the office. We have the ink and the special pad," the commandant replied.

Himmler moved a step closer to Zishe.

"Zishe Holtz, if I am correct. The hair, the eyes, the nose, especially the mouth, exactly as I remembered," Himmler said, frowning and looking intently at Zishe.

Zishe kept his composure, keeping his eyes fixed straight ahead.

"You tried to make a fool out of us." Himmler said. "You'll pay for that." Himmler could hardly contain his rage. "In a very special way." He grinned sadistically at Zishe. "Get him out of here."

Himmler continued his inspection while two guards hustled Zishe out of line. They made him run by prodding him with their batons.

Zishe knew his fingerprints would match. The Germans were very efficient with records. He didn't have much time.

"Thumb." The soldier said, pressing Zishe's finger against the pad. "At attention—no movement. Not until we get the photos." The guard looked at Zishe with contempt.

Zishe let his thoughts wander. He was prepared to die, but the suspense made him feel uneasy, as if he might not withstand the ordeal.

"Shema Yisrael Adonai elohenu." Praying always made the time go quickly. Zishe felt close to God, but never closer than when he knew he was doing His will. "Watch over your people. Let them live in peace. May they survive this genocide. Dear God, they are innocent. Please don't hide your face."

Zishe wanted to cry, but his eyes had dried up. Nothing came out and he stood staring into the corner where he'd been told to wait.

"I knew it the minute I saw him. The fingerprints match."

The door flew open and Himmler strutted in. "You son of a bitch—you thought you could get away with it!" Himmler slammed Zishe's head against the wall. "You scum, you pig of a Jew!" Himmler shrank back as Zishe felt the blood run down his face. "Jewish blood. Filthy, disgusting." Himmler looked as if he was about to vomit.

"Get him out of here. For now," Himmler said with a sneer.

Zishe was put back to work, but instead of carrying rocks, he was carrying bodies. He knew this was just the beginning of what Himmler had in store for him. He had little time to think as he dragged the still-warm bodies from chambers full of excrement and gas.

No relief, no rest, no stopping, on and on, all day long. Each batch, two hundred souls, took thirty minutes. Zishe made sure every dead soul received the holy Kaddish. Even cleaning the excrement off the walls, floors, and, when he could, off the bodies, he did as an act of purification and prayer. Zishe sometimes thought he could even see the souls rising with the gas and ashes from the chimneys.

But Zishe kept wondering about Gretchen. He wondered where she was, what they'd do to her, to Mark, to Yosi if they found them. It wouldn't be long before the Nazis would discover who they were.

Passover was getting close, but there was little joy or anticipation. Even if they were allowed to celebrate, there were no matzos, no wine, no *hagaddahs*.

Easter came first this year and the Jews were put to work making Easter eggs, trimming the bushes, preparing the grounds, and constructing a special stage with a medieval setting. The commandant was very religious and serious about Easter. He said he was "doing a little piece of Christ's work here on earth."

The soldiers and guards all forgot their differences on this special occasion. They were all Christians; they all believed in Christ and his resurrection, even if some disagreed on the date.

"Another week until Passover, Zishe, and then we can thank God for freeing us from Egypt," Itzak said.

Itzak had a strange sense of humor. He and Zishe were "death Jews." They were kept separated from the rest. When they weren't carrying corpses, they were restricted to a small brick enclosure without windows. They'd been at this job for six months.

"That's three hundred and fifty thousand bodies. Now, if I were paid by the piece, I'd be a rich man," Itzak said.

"Then we would celebrate by escaping," Zishe said, smiling at his own joke.

"Yes, from here to heaven." Itzak took the joke in stride. The Germans called the gas chambers "the road to heaven."

"Give me a hand—this one's too heavy." Zishe couldn't lift this corpse—it was a man with layers of fat, as if he'd lived well.

"German Jew. Probably just discovered he's Jewish," Itzak said. "Probably never knew what hit him. I'll bet he's at least seven-eighths goy. Poor fellow—I wonder which hit him harder, being gassed or being branded a Jew."

Zishe bent under the weight even with Itzak's help.

"*Schneller*, or you'll be next," a soldier said, laughing at the emaciated inmates carrying the corpse like ants.

"Easter," Itzak said.

"So what?" Zishe said.

"The crosses—there's three of them in the yard."

"So what? Most of the guards here are Christian. They have pastors and priests attached to every unit."

"But they're planning the real thing," Itzak said.

"The real thing?"

"Yes—three Jews for Jesus and the thieves. Something about a passion play. The actors will be Jews," Itzak said. He spoke as if it didn't matter to him. "We've all got to be there. We get a holiday. We get to watch the whole performance for free."

"Then we'll have to watch the whole bloody thing," Zishe said, adjusting the corpse in his arms.

"Yes. And it could take up to eight hours or more." Itzak seemed resigned to the whole thing. "All I know is that Hitler loved it when they last performed it at Oberammergau. Do you think any of it is true? Did we really do that to Jesus?" Itzak had a worried look on his face.

"To a Just Man? No," Zishe said.

Itzak looked up suddenly. "Jesus—a *Lamed-vov?*"

"Yes. That's why the Romans got rid of him. A Just Man can be very dangerous. He upsets the world. God speaks through him."

Zishe started on his run back to the gas chamber with Itzak right behind him. They rested for a few minutes before the chamber was unlocked. This was a gift they weren't used to. After the screaming had stopped, Zishe pulled on the bar as Itzak helped.

"Harder—put some muscle behind it," a guard said, ready with the whip.

Zishe gave one final shove and the door hissed open. The bodies tumbled out. "No wonder we had a rest. There's more than three hundred bodies in there. They must have suffocated even before the gas was turned on," Zishe muttered.

This time they didn't have to wait for the gas to clear. They started with the bodies that had fallen out.

"Evil can't stand the messenger from God. It makes them afraid," Zishe whispered. "The Romans couldn't stand that. They had to shut him up."

"But the Jews. They're blamed for crucifying Jesus," Itzak said, dragging the last body out.

"Not at first. Only centuries later. The Christian Jews had been scattered. Their writings were in the church's possession. The church now was Rome."

Zishe started on his run. Itzak was breathing harder than usual.

"Jewish writings?" Itzak said, whispering.

"The new testament was written by Jews," Zishe shouted, making sure no soldiers were around.

"Then why do they hate us so?"

"Because they no longer understand how Jewish Jesus is."

Zishe couldn't reach high enough to place the last body on the pile. Itzak scampered up the corpses as if he was climbing a mountain and completed the peak with a small child.

"Zishe, get up. The next shift—we're on."

Itzak had to shake Zishe to get him awake. Four hours' sleep was not enough.

"They're coming too fast—one train after another—they must be losing the war—and they're desperate to finish murdering every Jew," Itzak whispered as Zishe rubbed his face.

Zishe rolled out of the cot he shared with three others. If one moved the others also had to shift.

"We'll all be killed. They wouldn't dare let anyone live who's seen what they've done," Itzak said.

"Why such gloom? You're sounding as if we're already dead," Zishe said. He was already dressed.

At the chambers, the diesel engines were pounding away, spewing forth their poison. Zishe crawled in first, trying to hold his breath while he grabbed a child and carried it away. He'd learned it was best to start with lighter weights and to avoid staying too long in the chambers at first, at least until the gas had dissipated.

Itzak was behind Zishe carrying another corpse.

"Did you run out of talk?" Zishe said to break the unusual silence.

"I might as well let you know." Itzak moved closer while working the pile of corpses before them. "You're Jesus. Himmler has picked you out."

Itzak ran. The guards looked particularly suspicious this morning.

"When?" Zishe said when he caught up with Itzak.

"Tomorrow." Itzak climbed back into the chamber. "They're shutting down the engines for the occasion. They want all the Jews to watch. Even the new arrivals," Itzak said quietly. When the chamber was nearly empty, it was like an echo chamber.

"They're going to watch the show while I'm dying?"

"They've combed the camp and the new arrivals for musicians, craftsmen, actors. They've been relieved of all work while they're rehearsing. Violinists, cellists, trumpeters—they have a whole orchestra." Itzak looked at Zishe. "The audience will include some of the most famous members of their party."

"Don't I get to rehearse my part?" Zishe said, trying to lift his spirits.

"No one speaks. The priest and pastor recite the whole thing while the Jews silently go through the motions." Itzak shrugged his shoulders and shook his head, hoisting another corpse out of the pile.

✡ CHAPTER EIGHTEEN

Zishe woke early the next morning. Except for snores or coughs, it was quiet. The diesel engines had been turned off. There would be no work today, no bodies to carry.

"Everyone up and out. Single file to the yard. We'll have roll call for an hour or two, then we have a special show. A little education for you Jews," a guard shouted.

Zishe jumped from his cot and lined up as ordered.

"You, stay here. The rest out." The guard hit Zishe with the butt of his rifle. The inmates marched out.

Zishe was cold. He was shivering, alone with the guard in the barracks.

"Captain Father Martin, Captain Pastor Binder," the soldier said, announcing their arrival. They were dressed in officer's uniforms with large crosses on the coats.

"This is Zishe Holtz—the Jew who tried to pose as one of us." The soldiers pointed to Zishe. Father Martin walked over while the soldier was speaking.

"Let's get to the point." Father Martin seemed impatient and a little nervous. "The performance will start in one hour. Reichsfuhrer Himmler and his guests have already arrived. You're to be Jesus. I'm here to coach you. You must know where to stand, where to move. The other actors will guide you. We'll do all the speaking."

"You'll stand among the disciples," Pastor Binder said. "Then you'll be arrested—they'll hit you and take you away. Then you'll stand in front of the Sanhedrin. From there you'll be bound and placed in front of Pontious Pilate. Then you'll be crucified."

Zishe felt as if he were being instructed on how to behave at his own funeral.

"That's all. Have him dress—the cloak is in this package." Father Martin handed a package to one of the guards. "He's on in one hour."

Father Martin started leading the group out but suddenly stopped and turned around. "This is a very sacred play. We are celebrating our Lord's death, his murder by Jews like you. Any mistakes, any disobedience, will be considered sacrilegious—and every Jew will pay dearly for it."

Zishe sat down now that he was alone. Even the guard had gone. He wondered if Gretchen would be watching and if he'd have to see her watching him die.

Then he remembered God. *"Shema Yisrael Adonai elohenu."* It felt good to pray. He wanted the Kaddish to be constantly on his lips. Not one corpse escaped his benediction.

He wondered why God was allowing this to happen. Perhaps this place was too ugly for His presence. Maybe that's why He hid His face.

"Here put this on." The guard returned and had Zishe put a white cloak on. Zishe tied the rope around his middle. His hair was long, not shaved like the other inmates.

"The sandals."

They were stuck in the package. He removed his battered shoes and put them on.

"You look just like Jesus," the guard said, in awe.

Zishe slid his hands along the cloak. He was already feeling the part and forgetting he was a "death Jew." He felt alive.

He walked out of the door with the guard at his side.

"This way." The guard guided Zishe toward the road that twisted past the soldiers' barracks.

Zishe saw the crosses on a mound as he rounded the corner. Five thousand inmates stood in rows at attention. The guards wandered among them to make sure they stayed there.

Near the front, a pavilion had been built, which was now occupied by the invited guests and their wives. The crosses were hung over the stage where the play would be performed, while the orchestra played in the pit beneath the stage.

"Hurry, get him up here. We're getting ready to perform the first scene," Father Martin said through a loudspeaker on a podium. It was attached to the stage but elevated to give it a more panoramic view. Pastor Binder was climbing the ladder, getting ready to take his turn in the recitation.

"And so, when Jesus had finished his discourse, he said to his disciples, 'Ye know that after two days is the Passover, and the Son of Man is to be crucified,'" Father Martin said in a deep reverent voice. The music in the background swelled. "Then he assembled together the chief priests, and the scribes, and the elders of the people, unto the palace of the high priest, who was called Caiaphas, and consulted him that they might take Jesus by trickery, and kill him."

As Father Martin spoke, the chosen inmates donned clothes to depict priests, scribes, and elders. They acted out their roles, milling around, looking sinister and secretive.

"But they said, 'Not upon the fast, lest happily there be an uproar,'" Pastor Martin said.

Zishe entered and let a woman anoint his feet. He looked over at the Nazis seated comfortably in their chairs.

"Then one of the twelve, called Judas Iscariot, went unto the chief priests and they covenanted with him for thirty pieces of silver. And from that time he sought opportunity to betray him."

Father Martin's voice was harsh with hate as he said Judas Iscariot's name. The Jew who portrayed Judas wore a false large hooked nose, a wild black wig, and a black coat. He rubbed his hands together with glee while laughing in a shrill, cackling screech. The priests and Judas danced a dance of joy in time to the music.

Zishe appeared in scene after scene, without faltering or losing his place, even getting to eat in the Passover scene—the Last Supper.

Father Martin continued. "Now when the evening was come, Jesus sat down with the twelve. And as they did eat, he said, 'Verily I say unto you, that one of you shall betray me.' And they were exceedingly sorrowful and began every one of them to say unto Him, 'Lord, is it I?'"

At this point, the Jew portraying Judas Iscariot contorted his face into something that looked like a vulture and with a sweeping movement hid his face in his cloak.

"And he answered and said, 'He that dippeth his hands with me in this dish, the same shall betray me.'" Father Binder paused as Judas Iscariot quickly uncloaked his face and dipped his bread in the dish. He laughed out loud.

Zishe's heart sank.

Pastor Binder said, "'Take, eat. This is my body.' And he took the cup and gave thanks. 'Drink ye all of it. For this is my blood of a new testament, which is shed for many, for the remission of sins.'"

Zishe broke the bread handed to him and sipped the wine. He continued playing his part almost unconsciously, unaware of where he was or what he was doing. The music was beautiful, almost haunting.

He heard only bits and parts as Father Martin and Pastor Binder alternated, each trying to outdo the other in reverence and devotion.

Zishe, with the disciples around him, went to the edge of the stage to kneel and hear Pastor Binder's voice calling out Jesus's prayer.

"'My Father, if it be possible, let this cup pass from me; yet not as I will, but as Thou wilt.'"

Zishe was profoundly moved by those words. Only a Just Man could say such a thing, he thought.

"And while he yet spoke, Judas, one of the twelve, came and with him a great multitude with swords and staves from the chief priests and elders of the people. Now he that betrayed him, gave them a sign saying 'Whomever I shall kiss, that same is he, hold him fast.'

"And forthwith he came to Jesus, and said, 'Hail master,' and kissed him. And Jesus said unto him, 'Friend, wherefore art thou come?' Then came they and laid hands on Jesus and took him."

The Jews bound Zishe and led him away. The disciples fled; Judas snickered.

"And they had laid hold of Jesus, led him away to the high priest where the scribes and the elders were assembled. Now the chief priests and elders and all the council sought false witness against Jesus, that they might kill him, but found none."

Zishe remained bound while the pastor described the trial. Each word emphasized how innocent Jesus was and how evil the Jewish priests and people were.

"And the high priest arose, and said to him, 'Answer thou nothing?' And Jesus held his peace."

Father Martin continued the scene.

"And the high priest answered and said unto him, 'I abjure thee by the living God that thou tell us whether thou be the Christ, the son of God.' And Jesus said unto him, 'Thou hast said. Nevertheless I say unto you, hereafter shall ye see the Son of Man sitting on the right hand of power and coming in the clouds of heaven.' Then the high priest rent his clothes saying, 'He hath spoken blasphemy. He is worthy of death.'"

Zishe watched the poor inmate who was playing the high priest struggle to tear his clothes into little pieces.

"Then did they spit in his face and buffet him and others smote him with the palms of their hands saying, 'Now tell us, thou prince, who is he that smote thee?'"

The Jews in the play knew they were being carefully watched and the blows they gave were supposed to land and wound. They hurt Zishe even more than the daily beatings of the prison guards. He staggered to try and keep his balance. He was blinded by the blood pouring from his scalp, and he could barely hear the words.

"When the morning was come, all the chief priests and elders of the people took council against Jesus to put him to death. And when they had bound him they led him away and delivered him to Pontius Pilate, the governor."

Pontius Pilate appeared wearing a steel helmet. He was dressed regally in bright red and white clothes beneath a steel vest.

"And Jesus stood before the governor, and the governor asked him, saying, 'Art thou the king of the Jews?'" And Jesus said unto him, 'Thou sayist.'" Pastor Binder paused, looking over the crowd. "And when he was accused by the chief priest and elders, he answered nothing. Then said Pilate unto him, 'Hearest thou not how many things they witnessed against thee?' And he answered him never a word, insomuch that the governor marveled greatly."

Zishe tried to concentrate on the story, although he had heard it often before. It carried a powerful hidden message beneath the hate.

Pastor Binder spoke as the music paused.

"Now at that feast the governor was wont to release unto the people a prisoner, whomsoever they chose. And they had then a notable prisoner called Barabbas. Therefore when they were gathered together, Pilate said unto them, 'Who will ye that I release unto you? Barabbas or Jesus, which is called Christ?'"

Zishe's mind was wandering, the words of Binder fading in and out.

"The chief priests and elders persuaded the multitude that they should ask for Barabbas and destroy Jesus."

Zishe tried to listen, but Pastor Binder's voice was being directed toward the prisoners and Nazi officials.

"'Whither of the two will ye that I release onto you?' They said Barabbas. Pilate said unto them, 'What shall I do then with Jesus, which is called Christ?' And they all said unto him, 'Let him be crucified.'"

Zishe's head cleared, and his heart skipped a beat. The cross in the middle was meant for him.

Pastor Binder continued. "And the governor said, 'Why, what evil hath he done?' But they shouted the louder, 'Have him crucified—crucify him.'"

The entire stage was now filled with throngs of Jews. They were now screaming in unison, "Crucify him" moving threateningly toward Zishe.

Pastor Binder was acting as a conductor, waving his hands to indicate the timing and intensity of screaming.

"All inmates join in." Binder motioned toward the five thousand Jews, dressed in the pinstripe costumes.

The orchestra repeated the same refrain over and over again, until all the Jews were screaming together.

"Crucify him, crucify him."

Zishe had never heard so many voices shouting together. They screamed as if they meant it. There was hate and anger in their faces.

The shouting went on for ten minutes until Father Martin hollered through the microphone, "Enough!"

The crowd was used to taking orders. They stopped as soon as they heard Father Martin's voice. The orchestra began to play a new theme, and Father Martin continued.

"Now when Pilate saw that he couldn't prevail, but rather a tumult was made, he took water, and washed his hands before the multitude, saying, 'I am innocent of the blood of this man. Now it is your business.'"

The Jew playing Pilate dunked his hands in a wash basin held by a guard. He looked at the audience while washing his hands.

Zishe thought, Poor Jew who has to play this part. He has to make Pilate look so innocent. He looked around and, from the expression of the Jewish faces, he could see he was not alone in his thinking.

"Then answered all the people," Pastor Binder spoke these words very slowly, as he pointed to the inmates standing in the yard, indicating he wanted all of them to join in, "'his blood be on us and our children.'" He spoke in an angry voice.

The actors on stage repeated the same line, over and over again, soon being joined by five thousand more Jewish voices.

"His blood be on us and our children."

"Louder, with more feeling! Show your guilt—I want to see you Jews take responsibility for what you did to our Lord!" Father Martin said, livid with rage.

"Repeat it until it sinks into your evil hearts!" Father Martin shouted while making sure the orchestra backed up this dramatic moment.

Zishe could hear the hoarse voices crack under the strain. What little strength the inmates had was waning, after being forced to stand through this long performance. It was thirty minutes before Father Martin allowed them to stop.

Zishe choked back a cry as he watched the Nazis humiliate his people.

Father Martin waited until there was complete silence. He cleared his throat. With a voice full of sorrow, he said, "Then released he Barabbas onto them, and when he had scourged Jesus, he delivered him to be crucified."

The most heartrending part of the music followed, emphasizing the pain Jesus felt. They bound Zishe to a pillar at the center of the stage and stripped him of his cloak to expose his back. A large muscular Jew, dressed in Roman uniform, whipped Zishe with all the force at his command until Zishe's back was raw and blood was pouring out.

Zishe had never felt such pain. Each lash felt as if it cut right into his bones. He gritted his teeth trying not to scream. Each lash made it harder and harder to breathe. He could feel himself slowly suffocating to death. Finally the lashing stopped. Now the music changed its pace, and Father Martin continued.

"Then the soldiers of the governor took Jesus into the common hall. They stripped him, put on him a scarlet robe, and when they had woven a crowd of thorns, they put it upon his head, and a reed in his right hand, and they bowed before him, and mocked him." Father Martin paused.

Zishe was stripped and dressed. Blood ran from his head, as the sharp edges of the thorns pierced Zishe's skull. Jews dressed in metal vests and pointed helmets, chanted, "Hail, king of the Jews." Each spit in his face, striking him with their wooden staffs. Zishe could feel the crown penetrating deeper into his skull with each successive blow.

Father Martin continued. "And after that, they took the robe off of him, and put his own raiment on him, and led him away to crucify him. And as they came out, they found a man of Cyrene, Simon by name, this man they compelled to bear the cross."

Father Martin waited until the Jews dressed as Romans lifted the middle cross from the mound and laid it on the back of the Jew who played Simon. Zishe was marched, with the guards at his sides, on an imaginary road maneuvering along the stage. A Jew bore a cross behind him.

"When they were come into a place called Golgotha, they gave him vinegar mixed with gall to drink." He paused.

Zishe lifted the cup to his lips, tasted it, and pushed it away. "And when he tasted, he would not drink," Father Martin said.

Zishe watched Simon lay the cross down, where it had been planted before. A squad of ten Roman soldiers marched forward and took the other crosses down.

Zishe stood next to his cross. The soldiers took their positions at the side. The music was adding to the increased tension.

Two more Jews were brought on the stage. They were dressed in rags and flanked by Roman guards. Zishe could not turn his head around, but he could see them from the corner of his eyes.

Father Martin started the next verse. "And they crucified him and parted his garments."

Zishe did not hear the rest. This was the moment he'd dreaded, but he was no longer afraid. He'd withstood the whip and the blows. He knew he could withstand pain.

The Jews in Roman clothes had ropes, hammers, and nails in their hands. Zishe could feel their discomfort, he could see their shame.

Father Martin continued. "And sitting down, they watched him there. And they set over his head his accusation, saying, 'This is Jesus the king of the Jews.'"

Zishe watched Father Martin. He wondered what thoughts could run through a mind like that. What kind of religion could produce such a contradictory view, such a love for Jesus and a hate for his people?

"Then there were two thieves crucified with him," Father Martin said as Zishe turned his head to see the two thieves who would be sharing the spotlight with him.

"One on the right hand, and another on the left," Martin said.

"Oh my God, Yosi and Mark." Zishe recognized who they were, and they looked into each other's eyes. That monster Himmler was punishing them too. Zishe watched the smile of revenge on Himmler's face. Zishe averted his eyes and tried to collect his thoughts.

Suddenly the music stopped. Father Martin was silent. Two Romans tied Zishe's arms with ropes to the crossbar, driving nails through his palms. Two others nailed his heels to the wooden post. Yosi and Mark were also placed on their crosses. All three were strangely silent.

Zishe felt pain shoot through him as his cross was planted into the earth. He looked to his left and to his right to see his companions hanging at his sides.

The orchestra's tympanies had been dramatically pounding out an accompaniment to the hammering in of the nails, and now the orchestra joined in at the raising of the crosses. Father Martin's voice boomed. "Those passing by kept taunting him, wagging their heads, and saying, 'You who would destroy the temple and rebuild it in three days, save yourself. If you're God's son, come down from the cross.'

"Likewise the ranking priest tormented him along with the scholars and elders. They would say, 'He saved others but he can't even save himself.'" Martin's voice droned on while the costumed Jews walked by with exaggerated sneers. "In the same way those who were crucified with him abused him."

Zishe turned his head to the right and the left, whispering, "I love you" to both Yosi and Mark.

Father Martin said, "Beginning at noon, darkness blanketed the entire land until midafternoon. At three o'clock, Jesus cried with a loud voice, saying, 'My God, my God, why hast Thou forsaken me?'"

Zishe felt the meaning of those words.

"When some of those standing there heard, they would say, 'This fellow's calling Elijah.' And immediately one of them ran and took a sponge filled with sour wine and fixed it on a pole and offered him a drink."

Zishe spit out the rag shoved in his mouth. He felt nauseous. He'd never tasted anything so awful. He felt himself vomit. He'd barely stopped his retching when Father Martin pointed to a corner of the stage. Three women appeared.

"Many women were there, observing this from a distance—those who had followed from Galilee to assist Jesus. Among them were Mary Magdalene and Mary the mother of James and Joses and the mother of the sons of Zebedee."

Zishe was struggling to breathe. At first he hardly noticed Gretchen was one of the three women. Then he realized she was playing the part of Mary Magdalene. Zishe and Gretchen's eyes met momentarily, and he could see that she was suffering more than he was. That son of a bitch Himmler, he thought. That bastard.

Zishe closed his eyes and began to pray.

Father Martin's voice droned on. "But the rest would say, 'Wait, let's see if Elijah comes to rescue him.'"

Zishe hung limp and silent, filled with thirst and pain. He had to conserve his waning strength. He found he could breathe if he sucked in all the air he could while jerking quickly upward.

Gretchen was close enough to hear Zishe's struggle. "I love you so much," she whispered.

"I love you—with all my heart," Zishe replied in gasps before lunging upward again.

His pain was intense. Within it, Zishe could feel the pain of each Jew in the yard and on the stage. He even felt the pain of the guards, the soldiers, the Nazis. It was as if they were suffering with him, as if they too were hanging on the cross. He was taking the sorrow of the whole world on himself.

It was not so easy to die. Zishe looked over the yard and thought how good it would be to be free, without pain. The Jews would be released from this ordeal of waiting for him to die.

He hung, staring at the horizon. His mouth opened, exposing his dry, swollen tongue.

And it was as if God descended—as if He had stopped hiding His face.

Zishe saw lips moving, thousands of them, reciting prayers: the rosary, the *Shema*, the Kaddish.

The cross, the Jews forced to watch him die, and the guards walking idly by made Zishe realize he was in another time. He was simultaneously on the cross in the camp and in Palestine.

It was unseasonably hot for springtime, and all the crosses on the hills faded into the mirages. The ground was parched and dusty, and under the brilliant sun, dark ironclad men hid in the shadows of their withering victims on the crosses. A shower of fine sand blew into Zishe's face, making him squint his eyes and press his lips together.

This is Palestine, he thought, but it's two thousand years ago. Time had disappeared. He was being crucified as Jesus. He felt at one with him, suffering the same excruciating pain, seeing the world through Jesus's eyes.

Zishe now understood the words "a Just Man." He had taken on the world's suffering. Zishe was overwhelmed. I never realized how much Jesus suffers for every one of us, he thought.

He looked at the Jews on the crosses beside him twisting in the hot sun. The Roman guards stood silently, keeping an eye on the crowd.

"Crucify anyone who looks suspicious. Don't ask any questions. Teach them the power of Rome. This will squelch any ideas of revolt they might have."

The order was signed by Pontius Pilate himself.

It had all started so quickly, from arrest to crucifixion. The trial had been a foregone conclusion. Rome used the trial to show its justice. He'd been rounded up with hundreds merely on suspicion, dragged through the streets, then whipped, nailed to a cross, and left to die in the hot desert sun.

"I came to bear the brunt of evil at God's request, to give the world another chance, so the Creator, blessed be His name, may delay the Last Judgment for a little while." These thoughts ran through Zishe's head. "It hurts to see my people suffer so, to be forced to stand until I die. Dear God, for their sakes, let it end soon. Into your hands I entrust my spirit in death."

Zishe prayed as one with Jesus. He could feel God was ready to let him die. His gasping had become labored, his heart was barely pounding. Life was slipping out of him.

The voice of Father Martin brought Zishe back to the camp.

"Jesus again shouted in a loud voice and died," Father Martin said.

Zishe let go with a loud groan. Martin and Binder both stepped back, frightened. The Jews, the Nazis, and the guards were all crying.

Zishe and Jesus were now dead. Zishe was hovering overhead. He had left his body. Zishe could now see himself and Jesus hanging lifeless below. There was no gap between the camp and Palestine.

Zishe saw he was not alone. Jesus was there beside him surrounded by an indescribable light. Like the Just Man in Proskurov, the statue in the Mariakirsche. That same unfathomable figure so full of pain and compassion. Zishe now saw things with new eyes. Jesus was everywhere, giving his love to everyone. He was there suffering with every Jew, absorbing the most terrible abuse.

Zishe had never seen such love. *Whatever you did for the least of these brothers of mine you did for me.* Those words now had a real meaning.

Gretchen was crying. He wished he could come down and console her. Jesus's family, and his disciples were begging the Roman guards to let them get closer and take him down. Zishe wished he could reassure them and show them they were now more alive than before.

✡ CHAPTER NINETEEN

Pastor Binder continued, his voice trembling. "And suddenly the curtain of the Temple was torn in two from top to bottom, and the earth quaked, and rocks were split apart."

The orchestra's cymbals, drums, and tympanies crashed and clanged while the actors rushed about. The stage actually shook to give the scene a semblance of realism.

"The Roman officers and those keeping watch over Jesus witnessed the sign and were terrified, and said, 'This man really was God's son.'" Zishe could see Pastor Binder and Father Martin's fear. Then Father Martin regained his composure. He walked over to resume the recitation. Binder seemed relieved to be replaced.

Father Martin said, "The Jews asked Pilate to have the legs of the three broken and the bodies taken away."

Five Jews approached Pilate with exaggerated postures of pleading and begging. Pontius Pilate hesitated, placed his hand judiciously on his chin, then nodded.

Father Martin barked out the next scene. "The soldiers came and broke the legs of the first man, and then of the other who had been crucified with him. But when they came to see Jesus, they could see he was already dead, so they didn't break his legs."

Zishe heard the painful screams as he watched the legs of Yosi and Mark being broken with the large iron pikes. The orchestra played while Father Martin waited until Yosi and Mark had stopped screaming and moving.

"Instead, one of the soldiers jabbed him in the side with his spear, and blood and water came pouring out."

Zishe was joined by Mark and Yosi, who were confused to see the play continue and their bodies hanging lifeless below them. Zishe saw his own body mutilated by the actors.

Gretchen had stopped crying, but pain was evident on her face. The Jews in the yard were still standing, but they had a glazed look, as if they were watching their own deaths.

Father Martin hurried. "After all this, Joseph of Arimathea, a disciple of Jesus, but only secretly because he was afraid of the Jews, asked Pilate's permission to take Jesus's body down. Pilate agreed, so Joseph came and took his body down."

The Jews took out the nails, removed the bodies from the crosses, and carried them off the stage.

Before the bodies had been completely removed from the crosses, Father Martin said, "And taking the body, Joseph wrapped it in a clean linen shroud and put it in the opening of his new tomb, which had been cut in the rock. He rolled a huge stone to the opening of the tomb and went away. But Mary Magdalene and the other Mary stayed there, sitting opposite the tomb."

Gretchen moved close to the hole where they had placed Zishe's body. It was crudely made with cement and bricks. The stone now rolled in front of the hole, hiding Zishe's body.

Father Martin continued. "After the Sabbath day, in early morning on the first day of the week, Mary Magdalene and the other Mary came to inspect the tomb. And just then there was a strong earthquake."

Again the stage shook, and all the instruments of the orchestra imitated the sound of earth shaking.

Father Martin started speaking slowly. "A messenger of the Lord had come down from the sky to the tomb, rolled away the stone. He was sitting on it. The messenger gave off a dazzling light and wore clothes as white as snow."

A Jew dressed in a silver-sequined robe rolled away the stone and sat on it.

Father Martin grasped the podium. He cleared his throat, leaned back, and directed his attention to the Jews.

"Now those who kept watch were paralyzed with fear when they saw the messenger. The messenger said to the woman, 'Don't be frightened. I know you are looking for Jesus who was crucified. He is not here. He was raised, just as he said. Come, look at the spot where he was lying. And run, tell his disciples that he has risen from the dead. He is going ahead of you to Galilee. There you will see him.'

"And they hurried away from the tomb, filled with joy, and ran to tell his disciples."

The stage was full of Jews scurrying about, pretending they were happy and full of joy. Gretchen was center stage in the spotlight.

"And there Jesus met them," Father Martin said.

A long-haired, white-robed actor came from where he'd been waiting behind the stage.

"They came up and took hold of his feet and paid homage."

Gretchen dropped to her knees at the actor's feet and the other Jews followed.

The orchestra played, and the special choir that had been waiting patiently offstage began to sing.

"It's Zishe!"

At first the cry came from the Jews on stage, then from the yard, until hundreds of voices were screaming as if what they saw was meant just for them, to give them hope.

"It's you." Gretchen's eyes were full of tears, but she was smiling for joy.

Zishe came closer toward Gretchen and the Jewish actors. There were holes in his nail-pierced palms, a wound in his side where the spear had entered, and blood all over the white robe and his head.

"It's Zishe. He's been resurrected!"

The Jews were now shouting with joy.

"A Just Man—God has sent us a Just Man." These words were on every Jews' lips.

Gretchen came forward and put her arms around Zishe. "You kept your promise and came back to be with me." She kissed his cheeks, and he pressed her head against his chest.

217

"Only for a little while. I thank God for letting me come back at this time to show that life continues on, that the righteous shall indeed get their reward, and that there is a world to come."

Zishe spoke loud enough to be heard by Father Martin, the audience in the pavilion, and the Jews in the yard.

He could see the marked change in the guards. Many were crossing themselves, repeating the rosary, praying. Some were even kneeling.

Father Martin and Pastor Binder retreated from the podium and huddled together. Many were crying. Others were praying or paralyzed with fear.

Himmler's face was red, and he was perspiring. He suddenly rose and raced toward the podium where Martin and Binder stood frozen with fear. Zishe could see Himmler shouting at the pastors while pushing them toward the microphone. Pastor Binder seemed reluctant to return.

"Then Jesus said to them, 'Don't be afraid. Go tell my companions so they can leave for Galilee, where they will see me,'" Pastor Binder said, shaking.

His words were barely heard. Zishe was still the center of everyone's attention. He walked among the actors on the stage, then proceeded down the stairs, passing through the ranks of the inmates.

Zishe let the Jews, the guards, and the Nazis touch him as he passed through the crowd repeating the Shema.

"*Shema Yisrael Adonai elohenu Adonai eh'oth.*" The voices rose. The inmates no longer looked like slaves, but like magnificent angels.

Zishe returned to the stage. Gretchen was still standing where he'd last embraced her.

"I love you. Have faith. You'll see me again soon." Zishe touched her cheek as he spoke. Then he disappeared.

No one moved. Not a voice was heard.

Himmler broke the silence with a mighty roar. He grabbed the microphone. "Attention—all Jews back to the barracks immediately."

The inmates were slaves again. The guards shouted orders, and the Nazis descended from the pavilion, muttering.

"All operations will begin again. The holiday is over." Himmler said.

Zishe could see the inmates start the large diesel engines again. The trains arrived with more human cargo. The *toten Juden*, the death Jews, were getting ready to receive the first delivery of corpses.

Zishe watched the crowds fill the camps. Everyone looked so dejected. He could see himself in both worlds. The suffering was the same. The Jews were being crucified again.

Thousands of Jews were now being processed from the trains to the lines that led to the gas chamber. Zishe watched as Gretchen was placed in line. Himmler had ordered her execution as soon as the play ended. Zishe watched her as she was herded into the gas chambers with two hundred others.

She was praying. "Hear, O Israel, the Lord our God, the Lord is One. O Lord, by Your grace You nourish the living, and by Your great pity You resurrect the dead and You uphold the weak, cure the sick, break the chain of the slaves. And faithfully You keep Your promise to those who sleep in the dust. Who is like unto You, oh merciful Father, and who can be like unto You…"

Zishe heard every word. The gas only made her prayers stronger. They rose above the raspy breaths and the retching coughs as the victims struggled to keep living a little while longer.

Zishe had never seen people die so bravely. Gretchen was the last one to go. She hung onto life, her prayers guiding the other souls, showing them the light that was waiting for them in the world to come. Only then did she let go. Zishe watched her brave soul. The angels were there in the gas chamber with her.

Gretchen now rose, the angels escorting her toward the light.

"Gretchen. It's me," Zishe said.

"You kept your promise. I love you. Now I know who you are. We've known each other forever. We were meant to be together," Gretchen said, looking toward the light.

The light was growing brighter. Brighter than a million suns, yet my eyes can still see, Zishe thought.

"It's Jesus," Gretchen said, her face glowing with ecstasy.

Zishe saw the face of Jesus changing, yet the same, merging with the light from which he came. Zishe could feel the presence of God. He held Gretchen in his arms.

"Heaven," Gretchen said.

"Yes, heaven."

"We'll be here forever," Gretchen said, excitedly.

"For a while," a voice coming from the light said, reassuringly. "I can't put off the Last Judgment forever. This murder, this Holocaust of my people cannot last. The next time will be the last," the voice spoke with authority.

"When evil runs rampant, I will have no choice but to allow the consequences to follow. Then as in Noah's time there will be wars, horrors, and destruction." The voice became louder and the light grew brighter. "Then the Judgment begins. The Righteous will inherit the earth, and all suffering will cease." The light flickered and the voice grew softer.

Gretchen was excited. They could see far into the future.

"I see Israel," she said.

"Yes, Israel," Zishe repeated.

Give the Gift of
The Broken Cross
to Your Friends and Loved Ones

CHECK YOUR LEADING BOOKSTORE OR ORDER HERE

❏ **YES**, I want _____ copies of *The Broken Cross* at $24.95 each, plus $5 shipping per book ($1 each additional book). California residents please add $1.25 sales tax per book. Canadian orders must be accompanied by a postal money order in U.S. funds. Allow 15 days for delivery.

My check or money order for $_____ is enclosed.
Please charge my ❏ MasterCard ❏ VISA

Name _____

Organization _____

Address _____

City/State/Zip _____

Phone _____

Card No. _____

Exp. Date_____ Signature _____

Please make your check payable and return to:

Ad-Lib Publications
51 W. Adams • PO Box 1102
Fairfield, IA 52556-1102

Call your credit card order to:
Phone: 1-800-669-0773
Fax: 1-515-472-3186
e-mail: MarieK7734@aol.com